MISTER N

Mister N

NAJWA BARAKAT

translated by Luke Leafgren

SHEFFIELD – LONDON – NEW YORK

And Other Stories
Sheffield – London – New York
www.andotherstories.org

Originally published in Arabic in 2019
First edition in English, 2022, And Other Stories

1 3 5 7 9 8 6 4 2

ISBN: 9781913505325
eBook ISBN: 9781913505332

Editor: Jeremy M. Davies; Copy-editor: Jane Haxby; Proofreader:
Sarah Terry; Typesetter: Tetragon, London; Typefaces: Albertan Pro
and Linotype Syntax; Cover Design: Tom Etherington. Printed and
bound by the CPI Group (UK) Ltd, Croydon, CRO 4YY.

A catalogue record for this book is available from the British Library.

And Other Stories gratefully acknowledge that our work is
supported using public funding by Arts Council England.

CONTENTS

To Nay, the verdant green of my soul.

Writing has led me to silence.

SAMUEL BECKETT

"Our beloved Lazarus has gone to sleep, yet I will go and wake him . . . "

"Why, O Lord? Have I done something to displease you?" Lazarus whispered in his darkness. Apprehensive, the Messiah rolled away the stone, called to Lazarus, and waited. After only a few seconds, Lazarus emerged, blinded by the blaze of light that struck his eyes. When they started unwinding his white wrappings, he realized that the miracle had actually been performed. He had fallen sick, and the illness became so severe that death had come as a mercy, carrying him off to a place without any pain or suffering. He spent four days there in nonexistence. He had been sleeping, and then he had been awakened; secure, and then disturbed; floating in the beyond, and then the Messiah arrived and brought him out. "Why, O Lord? Have I done something to displease you?"

The whistle of the electric teakettle startled Mr. N. He left his papers on the table and got up to switch it off. He turned to face the window, where a black fly caught his attention, perched motionless on the wall above one of the panes of glass. He reached out to catch it, but it flew away and landed on the wall over the other windowpane. Mr. N stepped toward it, and the fly circled back again. Mr. N smiled. He drew the curtain back halfway and opened the window, sliding one pane behind the other. The fly cocked its head and gave him a wink out of the corner of its eye before swooping through, leaving no trace.

The sky spilled down an enormous quantity of light that struck Mr. N all at once. His eyelids dropped involuntarily as the light poured onto his face, his neck, his chest, his arms. The light stopped at his waist, which was as far as the window allowed it to reach. Looking down, Mr. N backed away two steps from the window and drew a long, deep breath—like someone about to jump. Even with his eyes averted, however, the white metal bars forming their squares over the window reminded him of their existence by casting shadows across the floor tiles.

A car horn blared, startling Mr. N. Other horns followed, proclaiming their own excellence. Then the flock of horns raced off, without any shepherd to guide them or any sheepdog to bring them back to the straight and narrow. Their hooves crushed everything in their path: passengers, pedestrians, children, residents of the neighboring buildings, sparrows, trees, shops.

Mr. N pressed his face against those white iron squares and looked down, annoyed. Why all these cars, and where could they be going? The clock showed 10:25. Employees were at their offices, children were at their schools and universities, mothers were in their kitchens, he was in his room. So who were all these people, and why were they all going for a drive together?

More than once over the years, it had occurred to him to abandon this apartment on account of its terrible location and the noise that poured through the window and into his ears at all hours. But Andrew—the tall building manager with the friendly face—had resisted the idea, had tried to dissuade him, suggesting that Mr. N move instead to a room on the opposite side of the complex. There, he would forget about the street and look down on the beautiful garden in the rear courtyard. Still, Mr. N had hesitated. He wasn't a person who liked change. He might be fed up by the noise, but his fear of giving up the window was greater. What if this window proved to be his last, and giving it up meant he was giving up the world as well? From here he could take the pulse of the outside world and look out upon God's creation. He saw time racing by, the departure of each day. He enjoyed the air and seeing the sky. If he ever missed the sight of nature, he went down to his hotel's garden at night when it was empty and at rest. He greeted the plants and their blossoms, he embraced the trees, and he touched the stone benches, inspecting what time had stolen from them. And if his tired body protested, he just went down to the end of the hallway outside his room. He would get a chair, open the window, and sit there absent-mindedly, looking out. He hated leaving his apartment. He only ever braved the streets to visit his mother. No, Mr. N found his lodgings quite sufficient; he walked from room to room, content with his home and his guests, feeling no need for the world beyond.

Mr. N closed his window and dropped its white curtain back into place. The insolent light retreated, the noise began to behave itself, and the traffic congestion melted away. Mr. N went over to his teakettle, produced a mug that had his name written on it in black ink, poured the tea, and drank. The flavor was strange. The tea was cold and the color of water. No matter. He pulled out the chair and sat back down to his papers.

Our beloved Lazarus awoke with the taste of fire in his mouth. He cleaned his teeth and his tongue and all around behind his lips. He gargled water repeatedly, and still he couldn't get rid of the taste of fire and decay. He realized his salvation lay in water alone. That is why he had always loved it so much . . .

The pencil lead snapped under Mr. N's hand. At once he snatched up the shard between his fingertips and placed it in a small plastic yogurt container. He had set aside two such containers, the first of which was completely full, the second nearly so. One day, thought Mr. N eagerly, he would set about counting them, one by one, so he would know how many pencils he'd gone through. He stopped short at the idea that the lead of each pencil sometimes broke more than once. No matter. He could estimate the average number of times that a single pencil broke, and then make a simple calculation to arrive at the approximate number of pencils.

And yet to yield to the approximate made him grimace. He liked precision and hated rough estimates. The approximate was arbitrary, the arbitrary was random, the random was chaotic, and chaos was a killer. Mr. N liked to cut away the imprecise, as he did with his pencils when he sharpened them, shaving their tips into points to make their lines clear and defined. Pens? Pens were unacceptable. Pens could leak, flooding pages with smothering ink. Ink behaved like a dictator: ordering, forbidding, controlling, brooking no dissent. Lead, meanwhile, was merciful, quick to forgive mistakes. Whatever your soul was brooding over, lead would let it speak. Ink soiled the white page; lead dissolved upon the surface, exactly as pain dissolved in the act of writing . . .

Mr. N let his pencil fall and read what he had written. *Why, Lord? Have I done something to displease you?* The meaning of his words escaped him, and he read them again. It didn't help. He took the page and calmly tore it into four pieces, trying to make them all the same size.

Then came an unexpected knock at the door. Mr. N looked up, but otherwise remained frozen in place, the better to encourage his caller to think he wasn't home and so go away, back to wherever they came from. But the knock came again, quick and soft, and Mr. N knew it was Miss Zahra come to examine him. Cracking open the door, Miss Zahra whispered with her wonted delicacy and even tenderness, "Mr. N, may I come in?"

Mr. N smiled and nodded. Miss Zahra eased herself inside and saw Mr. N sitting at his papers. She set what she was carrying on the table where he was working and then tapped his shoulder with a benevolent hand to invite him to stand. She looked over at his bed nearby, and Mr. N got up, following her eyes to sit on its edge, where she wanted him. He was smiling, and she was smiling too. She came in smiling and went out smiling, and in between she kept smiling no matter what he did. And after she left? Mr. N wondered. And after Lazarus awakened?

Miss Zahra lifted his arm. She tapped his elbow and passed her soft fingers along his bulging, blue veins. Then she bent over . . .

"Ouch!" cried Mr. N. "What sharp teeth you have! The better, I suppose, to nibble through these veins of mine that you seem to love so much."

She apologized and pressed the spot where she'd hurt him. The pain vanished. Miss Zahra then returned to the table and gathered up her things, casting a quick glance over the papers lying there.

"I'm so happy you've gone back to writing," she said. "I'm dying to read what you're working on."

"Where are you going?" Mr. N asked, hurrying after her. "Aren't you going to stay with me any longer?"

With a laugh, Miss Zahra raised her eyes to the ceiling in the customary gesture of refusal. Then she slipped out, closing the door behind her with the same gentleness she had shown upon entering. As she left, Mr. N glimpsed a small hole in her nylons. The run started underneath her foot and stopped at her anklebone. If only she put a drop of clear nail polish on it, he thought, it would stay where it was and not threaten to sneak farther up. That's what Mary would do, who was so unlucky with her nylons, as she put it; Mary with her rough hands, scraped raw by housework for Mrs. Thurayya and her family.

One Sunday morning, before anyone else was up, Mr. N had caught Mary sneaking her fingers into her mouth to moisten them before holding open her stockings to insert her feet. The stockings were a gift from Mrs. Thurayya after years of service, and Mary lived in dread of snagging them.

Two translucent, skin-toned silk stockings. Mary wore them proudly on Sundays and holidays, taking pride in them before her friends and relatives, who had to make do with thick, dark, opaque stockings of cotton or wool. Whenever her stockings were too tight at her knees, Mary would reach underneath the tight elastic bands and roll the edges down to ease the red bracelets they left on her white flesh after a day of wearing them. Each Sunday, Mary would put on her silk stockings and try to sneak off to the nearby church for mass—because if Mr. N woke up and started crying before she left, she would have to pick him up and rock him back to sleep in her arms. Sometimes, though, he would cling to her bosom and only pretend to fall back asleep because he relished being taken along—the warmth of the church, the faint illumination, the scent of incense, the hopeful imploring voices. But he would drift off for real the moment he heard the hymns and the prayers, and then come around only when Mary stood to receive the Eucharist and to present her little N at the altar for the priest to bless with a splash of holy water on his head.

Had Miss Zahra noticed the run in her stockings and worn them anyway? That would be a black mark against her, thought Mr. N. Until today her appearance had always been impeccable. Neat and well turned out, giving off a scent that was a mix of rubbing alcohol and soap. Just like Thurayya. As though she were a new doll, fresh out of the package. Thurayya wouldn't tolerate any scratch, any wrinkle, any speck of dust. She was all clipped fingernails, trimmed hair, elegant clothes, earrings, necklaces, and rings. Even when she slept. Even when she dreamed. Traces of her perfume—that penetrating French perfume, *Femme*—would permeate every corner of the apartment. In both summer and winter, the scent would emanate from her room in the morning when she opened her door after applying her hair spray, the final step in her lengthy daily beauty routine.

Thurayya had ruined Mr. N's taste in women. Despite the detachment and aversion he felt for her at the time, he couldn't help being influenced by her tastes. What he wanted in a woman was someone who could look as clean and orderly as Thurayya on the outside, yet contained all the abundance, plenty, and warmth that Mary had offered Mr. N. Miss Zahra did have some of Thurayya's coldness, it was true, balanced by some of Mary's kindness, but Mr. N would hardly have called her his ideal. Still, when she came back, he would point out the matter of her damaged stocking. It wasn't right for a woman like her to go around looking sloppy. And when he brought it up, he would also insist that she stay a while.

Not that Miss Zahra hadn't been right to hurry out. There really wasn't space for two people in Mr. N's room. Not that it was small, exactly, but neither was it especially inviting, particularly since it was longer than it was wide. Longitudinal spaces do not inspire a sense of harmony. Instead, they make you feel remote, as though they've decided to keep their distance out of some sense of aversion. Mr. N's wooden table was nothing more than a long slab of wood, and as one of the few items of furniture, it was put to many uses besides eating. The television, almost never turned on, was set into the wall like a dark window behind which who knew what sorts of phantoms lurked. As for the bed, it was neither small nor large. A "twin-plus," as Miss Zahra put it, meaning it was big enough for one and a half people. The half person being the whole person's shadow, perhaps. An absent lover, or the ghost of some other loss.

Back in the old apartment, his bed had been a mere "twin." He grew, but his bed did not. That building had been something of an antique; their apartment didn't much resemble the ones now being built, all stacked on top of one another like cardboard boxes. A beautiful apartment, large and comfortable, in a yellow building from a different era. There was no elevator, and its five floors never had vacancies for strangers. Mr. N loved the building's tiles: small brown triangles, purple and yellow squares. He loved its high ceilings and its tall, arched windows, decorated at the top with pieces of stained glass that reminded him of church windows. He was familiar with each and every one of its details: the old Arabic toilet that he preferred to European toilets because it didn't provide any perch to sit and ponder; the shower nozzle that used to wash the bathroom and everything in it about as much as it washed him; the dark, corroded mirror in whose glass his skin looked fairer than it actually was; the kitchen as spacious as a sitting room, with its old couch that no longer matched the actual sitting room; his bedroom; the bedroom of his older brother, Sa'id; his parents' room; the guest room, which had been converted to an office for his father; and Mary's room. All this he remembered, all this he loved; just as he loved other things, now forgotten from having lived in their company from the day he was born.

But the thing he'd loved most of all about that apartment was its broad, indulgent balcony, over which the building's roof extended, and which was ringed around by a railing supported by small white columns. The balustrade acted as a shield, protecting the apartment from whatever annoyances might reach up from their calm, narrow, dead-end road, which was accessed via a street less narrow and far busier, Abdel Wahab El Inglizi, in the neighborhood of Achrafieh.

Mr. N—though it's true he wasn't called Mr. N in those days—used to live on this fifth-floor balcony more than he lived inside the apartment. He'd found his natural place there. It was he who picked out a corner for himself among the crowded flowerpots. He put a small table there and two chairs, a chaise longue to lie on while reading, and a straight-backed chair for drinking his coffee, or when he sat with his papers to work. Later on, he added a large, sesame-colored umbrella to that corner of his, which gave an appealing intimacy to the place, such that the other members of the household were satisfied that that part of the balcony, adjacent to his bedroom, was Mr. N's own property.

Mr. N could no longer clearly recall what led him to leave his beloved balcony and check into this hotel. And were it not for the mutual affection he shared with the hotel manager, Mr. Andrew, and his prodigious attachment to Miss Zahra, who cared for him and served him with such self-sacrifice and devotion, he wouldn't have been able to overlook all the inconveniences of life here, chief among which was his neighbor's constant quarreling with his mute wife, and his other neighbor across the hall, an elegant and confused woman who never stopped inviting him to dinner. To say nothing of the noise from the floor below, where the guests took their meals—all except Mr. N, who insisted on having his food alone in his room.

In fact, Mr. N was feeling a pang in his stomach. He wished he could dive into a bowl of mushroom and saffron risotto, like the ones he used to order from Saleem, the maître d' in the Albergo Hotel Restaurant, preceded by a mozzarella salad with slices of sun-dried tomatoes, pickled cardamom, and olive oil. He turned to the clock: 10:25. He still had some time before Miss Zahra brought him lunch at noon on the dot. No matter. He would pour another cup of tea to suppress his hunger, or he would read his books and nap a while.

———

Mr. N jolted out of his nap like a madman, frightened and wet with perspiration. He had seen himself as a colt running across a broad plain, thick with tender grass, happy and free, caressed by the wind. He was racing his shadow, which ran across the ground beside him. But then the world went black, and he was thrown to the dirt. Legs bound, he struggled to rise. There was a crackling of fire and sizzling iron, and he let out a whinny in case someone might hear him and come to his aid. But all that came was a red-hot iron on a long metal pole, burning into his thigh. He, the colt, was pressed against the ground as the smell of seared flesh filled his nostrils. When he turned his head, he saw that a large letter N had been branded at the top of his leg.

He inched over to the window. He pulled back the curtain and let the breeze flow over his damp head. It stole through his shirt, traveling down the back of his neck to his spine. His shirt was wet too; he stripped it off and threw it onto the bathroom floor. Half-naked, he stood and spread his

23

arms wide. He laughed as the mischievous wind tickled his armpits. Then he turned his back to the breeze and went over to the table, where Miss Zahra had set out his clean laundry. He put on the plain white short-sleeved cotton T-shirt that happened to be on top of the pile and went back to close the window. The curtains he would leave open—the better to keep the full day present. Not that the white cloth blocked all the light even when closed, but it did get in the way, and Mr. N didn't want anything to interfere with the free entry of light that had yet to commit any sin against him.

What month was it? Mr. N wondered. Nothing in the street or the appearance of the people outside gave any clear indication. The small trees lined up at the end of the street—what he was able to see of them, anyway—had green leaves. The bitter oranges, which they called *naranj*, were growing old at their mother's breast, lost, as usual, in the ambiguous middle ground between a proper shape and a palatable flavor. The people passing by in the street below were wearing clothes appropriate for more than one season. Mr. N could still recall a time when regular seasons divided the year equally, three months each, and the climate had been perfectly in order, rotating right on schedule like soldiers on watch; the plants coming only in their proper time, each with its own fragrance; a time when even the city itself—whatever the poverty and nakedness of its buildings—stood in lovely, regular, meticulous rows. But now there was no clear identity to its structures, whose ugly outdoor awnings hid not only the balconies but also the characters of their inhabitants, revealing only that their tastes were chintzy and perverse. When had those abominable awnings rolled in to spoil the city? The eighties? Before that, the balconies had been uncovered and free, decorated with flowerpots, with people's faces, with the laughter and cries of children. But someone had come along and decided to hide all that away, bringing in the damned awnings to wrap the city in a thousand gaudy colors.

Mr. N contemplated the buildings across from his window. Towering beggars' bodies in threadbare, tattered clothes, he thought. No floor looking like another. No building in harmony with the one beside it, either. Each doing its own thing, with no regard for the others. Striped fabric, polka-dotted, smudged and stained, in every shade: orange, red, blue, green, brown . . . Side by side, without any regulation, harmony, or coordination. It hurt the eyes to look at them, especially the awnings that were neglected, torn, and abandoned to the wind, remnants of cloth that neither protected nor concealed but hung down, emaciated, together with random objects that dangled from the dying awning frames.

His own neighborhood had not yet been exposed to this butchery. It had resisted for years, for decades. And when Mr. N left for the hotel, it was still as it had always been. Were it not for the damned tower going up in front of his beloved building, with all the noise, dust, and darkness that it brought, his neighborhood would perhaps have been among the last of the blessed isles remaining in a country of abominable ugliness. Even wealth provided no protection. In neighborhoods of higher social status, the vulgar awnings were replaced by so-called "curtain walls" of glass. "*Kurton*," people repeated proudly, twisting their tongues to say the foreign word. Screw them and their *kurtons*! They were uglifying the city even more than their predecessors had, disfiguring its balconies—those aerial bridges, those connections to the warmth and the air, those shelters for the soul—and then boasting of those horrible glass enclosures, "They can be sealed shut in winter and then opened up again whenever you want!" If that wasn't a perversion of the city's very identity, then what was? Did they do it out of spite? wondered Mr. N. And then spite against what? The sun? The neighbors? In any case, it was certainly against him, even if no one else cared or suffered as he did.

Thousands of festering tongues hanging suspended in the air, an outrage to any sense of engineering or taste. That is what a stunned Mr. N discovered the day he wandered on foot through the alleys of the Bourj Hammoud district, as his neighbor Kevork—a friend of Mr. N's late father—had recommended. "Don't worry about trying to figure out which street you're on, or really anything else either! Just keep walking in any direction, and you'll come across whatever you're after." That's how the seventy-year-old man had put it, in the middle of one of his usual tirades about their local plumber, Hammouda, and his disgust at the plumber's habit of setting the price for any repairs at twice the going rate. He was basically robbing the apartment tenants, besides which the new parts he installed didn't even work. And each time someone called this thief to account or directed any blame his way, did he take any responsibility? No, he would pour out his overflowing cup of rage upon the Chinese, on everything Chinese, placing the blame on China and its people and its products.

"Hammouda, the fraud," Mr. N's neighbor Kevork whispered in his pleasant Armenian accent, casting a glance in each direction. "Hammouda, the cheat. He installs something

Chinese and charges you for a European part." Kevork went on to say that for his part, he'd learned to do without the man's services, going instead to Bourj Hammoud to buy whatever he needed. Sometimes he brought a Syrian worker with him, one of those who spent the day at Daoura Circle, waiting for someone to come and offer any kind of work in exchange for ten American dollars. Mr. N nodded and inquired about the parts needed to repair the water tank of a European-style toilet, and then the address of where he could buy them.

"You'll easily find the parts in Bourj Hammoud," replied Kevork. "Take the old bits with you and just ask around the alleys down there. You don't need an address."

In any case, given that Mr. N was more used to Arabic-style toilets, he always kept a bucket of water next to his European toilet regardless, like families used to do in the days of the war, when the water could be cut off at any time and they were forced to store water in whatever containers they had. So he didn't consider the repair essential. He could put it off.

———

"Miss Zahra, Miss Zahra, come quick! Someone has stolen my papers!"

Mr. N gave a terrified scream and nearly choked on his own tongue when he discovered the surface of his wooden table bare. He ran to his door and yelled at top volume, but Miss Zahra didn't appear at the end of the hallway as she usually did when he called. She would run to him, smiling, reassuring, bearing the antidote to all his panic attacks. He repeated her name in a plaintive tone and waited. Then he stepped into the corridor himself, trembling, afraid that the thief would be hiding in the shadows there, ready to swoop down and attack him.

The door across the hall was open, but beyond it was only silence. Mr. N cautiously approached and entered the room. He found a woman there, standing. Familiar. The same woman who invited him to dinner every time she saw him, despite knowing nothing about Mr. N. This was her apartment, he must have known that already, but he rarely saw her, afraid as he was to leave his own space. Or, if not afraid—he preferred not to. Miss Zahra brought him whatever he needed, and the manager, Andrew, visited often enough, chatting for hours, to keep loneliness at bay. Besides, he also had his papers to occupy him. They wore him out, and didn't leave much time for socializing.

Still, the woman didn't acknowledge Mr. N's presence. As though she were trying to remember something she'd been about to do but forgot, and which was now taking an exceptional degree of concentration to recall. Perhaps she was going out, thought Mr. N. The elegant clothes, lipstick, and hair pinned atop her head all seemed to indicate as much. Mr. N figured he would withdraw, and he turned to go, but that's when she finally noticed him and said, as usual, "Please, come in!" As she spoke, she took two steps back and invited him to advance further with a sweep of her right hand.

Mr. N found himself sitting in front of a slab of wood much like his own, but which, unlike his own, had found its true identity as a dining table, he felt, set with bowls and white plastic spoons wrapped in paper napkins. Well, after all, they did live in a hotel; there was nothing strange in all that. The lady parted her red-painted lips, and, holding one hand aloft with her fingers pressed to her thumb, said, "*Al dente!* That's how my children like it. And you, Mr. . . .?"

Mr. N nodded and said, "Of course. Spaghetti must be cooked until there is only a hint of softness, no more. That's how Thurayya insisted on making it, and it was the only dish she would make herself. She would grab a noodle and throw it against the side of the sink. If it stuck, she would say it was done and turn off the stove, pick up the saucepan, and pour it into a colander. Then she would pour cold water over it to get rid of all the starch."

The lady was smiling and showing her interest in what Mr. N had to say. But his well quickly ran dry. He bowed his head over his hands, folded in his lap, as he remembered Thurayya, who refused to cook anything except pasta on account of her preoccupation with her own strained nerves, her excessive sensitivity to the tragedy of her own life—a life that hadn't treated her fairly at all, marrying her to a decent and humble doctor when she deserved so much better, she who was a queen among commoners: the queen of beauty, the queen of good taste, the queen of high emotion, the queen of the salons—

"What are you two doing in there?" asked a rather distasteful voice.

Startled, Mr. N turned. It was his neighbor; that is, the resident of the room alongside his own, whom he could not stand to see on account of the torments Mr. N suffered from hearing his voice through the wall. The never-ending quarrels the man had with his poor wife, whom Mr. N never once heard defend herself or object, for the husband talked nonstop, filled Mr. N's ears to bursting every single day. One moment the neighbor would tell his wife that she was to blame for every misfortune; the next, he would flirt with her and tell her she was the only thing that made his life bearable. Sometimes he would cry and beg her pardon, only to become angry with her again.

Early on, Mr. N used to pound on the wall they shared to let him know he was there, listening, in case that would make the man feel embarrassed. Then he did it to inform the man of his annoyance at all the noise. Later on, he knocked to appeal to the neighbor's modesty, since it isn't appropriate for people to shame their loved ones publicly. In the end, when the neighbor took no notice of any of these knockings, Mr. N complained about the man to Andrew and to Miss Zahra, and they promised to move him to a different room. That never happened. But Miss Zahra had started coming around whenever the neighbor raised his voice. She would go into his room for a few minutes, and when she came back out she left only silence behind.

Once, when Mr. N was complaining about his situation to Miss Zahra, he asked her about his neighbor's wife, asked her how any woman could bear all that cruelty without uttering a sound. Miss Zahra replied, "It's better that we don't get involved in the affairs of others, don't you think?" Mr. N agreed, concluding that the man's wife had to be mute, for, as he saw it, there was no other explanation for her behavior.

Without asking permission, that mute woman's husband, who had been standing over the two of them in his striped pants and blue short-sleeved shirt, sat down at the table too. He pushed away the bowl in front of him, scratched the back of his head, crossed his legs, and said, laughing, "You're absolutely correct, my dear lady. But it's not just pasta that needs to be *al dente*, but emotions too! Especially love. It should always be left just a touch underdone, don't you think? That's the secret: right on the cusp, as it were, neither more nor less. For if love cooks longer than it should, it gets mushy and tastes burned. That's what I'm always telling my wife . . . But alas, Daoud, to whom do you sing your psalms?"

"Is his name Daoud?" wondered Mr. N. He thought to invite the man's wife to have dinner with them too, but then he remembered the words of Miss Zahra, and checked himself in time. Was he really going to enter the life of this man he despised? In any case, he had begun to feel an aversion for everyone and everything that possessed a voice and, more-over, used it to speak. And yet . . . there were signs of a deep, weathered sadness in his neighbor's eye as the man spoke that final sentence.

"Dante," said the woman with the stained lips, as though she had arrived just that moment, "was my favorite poet before I died." Then, like someone on stage, she recited:

> *We set off across the water, leaving the shore behind.*
> *Sluggish, that ancient boat embarked,*
> *Weighted on its passage as never before.*
> *As we crossed that lifeless slough*
> *The mud rose up before us—sorry—before me,*
>   *and from within came a voice:*
> *"Who are you, you who have come here before your time?"*
> *"Even if I have come here," I replied, "I will not remain.*

31

But you, who are you, O fallen, unclean man?"
"I am one who weeps," he replied. And I said,
"May you weep and wail forevermore . . . "

"That's Dante's *Inferno*," whispered Mr. N, stunned and fascinated by what the woman was reciting from memory.

Daoud, indifferent to it all, asked, "By the way, why were you yelling like that? Calling for Miss Zahra?"

Of course! Mr. N struck his forehead. He shot to his feet and stammered, "Someone stole all my papers, everything I've been writing for weeks."

"You're a writer? I'm very pleased to meet you! I've never come across a writer before. You'll have to tell us more sometime about what you're writing. As for your papers, it has to be Miss Zahra, no? There's no one else, believe me. Take it from me: she often goes into our room when we're sleeping to steal our things."

Mr. N didn't care to hear Daoud accuse Miss Zahra of petty theft. Besides which, he was upset with himself for forgetting such an important matter as the loss of his work. He excused himself, muttering, explaining his hasty withdrawal by saying he had important things to attend to.

He hurried to his room and closed the door behind him, chest heaving. His hatred for Daoud, the mute woman's husband, was now complete. He knew his name! "To whom do you sing your psalms?" How dare he! Mr. N sat down on the edge of his bed before his knees could betray him. Why couldn't Andrew be the thief, after all, seeing as he was always butting into things that didn't concern him and peppering his guests with questions about things that weren't his business?

Surely he was the one who'd slipped in and stolen his papers. Mr. N would go find him and raise the issue. Yet, no matter how he tried, he couldn't quite get the idea out of his head that Miss Zahra might be the thief. But why? Wasn't she constantly encouraging him to get back to writing? Hadn't she made clear her pleasure at seeing him write, watching his stacks of paper multiply?

Because she knew, because he had confessed to her, that he'd given up writing long ago. Snipped it off like a thread, without having made a conscious decision, without prior intent. He'd thrown away his pencil and stepped away from its lines. Unable to swallow a single letter more, he'd turned away from his meal like a dyspeptic, instead taking up a diet of *not writing*, a period of light relaxation, during which he felt neither hunger nor indigestion. This new regimen was soothing at first, and he thought it would be temporary, like any diet. But months passed, followed by years, and he luxuriated in his withdrawal and isolation. Soon, whenever someone spoke a sentence in his hearing, he found himself picking apart their words as they rose and fell, turned and spun, examining them until the continuity of their thought was severed, and whatever remained quickly evaporated. Then, on the rare occasion that he picked up something to read, he discovered that the letters would separate from each other to make space for squirming, ugly little intruders that robbed the words of their meaning. He found it more and more difficult to get his eyes to travel from the first letter to the last in words that seemed to distend as he read, like pale, flabby bodies whose heads can't be told from their asses.

In the end, he was certain that speech itself had lost its shape. It had deteriorated, worn out, to melt over his hands like candle wax, where it began to burn and caused a near-physical pain. There was nothing in the world so infuriating as the words a man couldn't help but read, hear, stammer, and repeat. It became his sole object of complaint. Mr. N decided that he hated writing. Maybe the time would come when he was ready to pick up his pencil again, but that time was slow in coming. He would give up all thought of being a writer, at least for a while.

Then that tyrannical high-rise, that tower sprouted up. It kept rising until he felt as though its bulk was somehow crushing his chest. He left his balcony and his apartment and checked into the hotel. This was years ago now, but Miss Zahra never grew weary of reminding him about his writing, insisting that he get back to work. "Writing will relax you," she once told him. Then, taking hold of his hand, she added, "Your gifts are a blessing!"

Mr. N just laughed. "If it were up to me, I'd share out this 'gift,' as you call it, with everyone," he said. "Why shouldn't anyone who likes the idea enjoy this coveted little hell?" It was clear that she didn't understand, and how could he explain to her that his body, separated from writing for so long, had become a smooth, orderly landscape after having been a mountain pocked with rocky slopes and caves?

"If you don't want to write anymore, at least go back to reading?" suggested Miss Zahra.

"Phooey on the whole damn thing," Mr. N had whispered, disapprovingly, as the old nausea rose inside. Nevertheless, Miss Zahra didn't get weary or discouraged. For months, she kept trying to get him to write, while Mr. N doted upon her smile as though it were a pitcher of water he could pour over his desiccated heart. He wanted to win her affection. He wanted to please her, to beguile her. So he decided to give it a try. He would give in and write—write anything at all, just so she would come in and see him leaning over his papers, or else see the papers themselves, blackened with letters, piling up in a stack. And so, one morning, when she heard Mr. N suggest that she buy him a box of pencils of a specific kind, writing its precise brand name on a small slip of paper, as well as some white, 80 mm-thick paper, a pencil sharpener, and an eraser, Miss Zahra could barely restrain her joy and asked, nearly hopping in place, whether that was everything he needed. "Yes," he replied. "That's the whole set."

It took days for him to relearn how to eke out a few letters. These were followed by syllables and sounds that he put together any which way to see whether some meaning might arise from various combinations. Then he began writing complete sentences, which he would sometimes copy out dozens of times, until they resounded in his head like a drumbeat. He began following a schedule, like a robot programmed to the task—until his language dyspepsia struck again, in any case. He would sit at his table every morning, arrange his pencils and erasers, and write—like a disabled man training an injured limb to resume its function—until he could do so without any anxiety or discomfort.

Miss Zahra didn't ask him what he was writing about. She did her best to show no curiosity, in case that might disturb him. It was enough for them both that she concluded each of her visits with a quick glance at his papers and a proud smile, considering herself to be the source of his inspiration. And perhaps it didn't matter to her what he wrote. The important thing was that he was doing it, and that she saw him doing it. No doubt the idea that he was a writer pleased her, thought Mr. N—or maybe it was more that she liked the idea of herself pleasing a writer? Women love writers, yes? Well, not counting Thurayya and Neda. So, Miss Zahra wanted him to be a writer? Okay, he would go back to being a writer. For her sake. And if it was all for her sake, then why should he be angry if she was the one who stole his papers—or borrowed them, rather, in order to read them? Didn't that only confirm she was interested and wanted to know at last what her favorite writer was working on?

Mr. N felt joy at the notion. It settled over his skin like a cold nightgown, then like a bath of warm water, and finally like a comfortable blanket. He felt the sap coursing through him again to nourish his arteries and veins. He looked at his watch. It was 10:25. Fantastic! He still had plenty of time. He took out a sheet of paper, a new pencil, and an eraser from the table's drawer. From now on, he would try to keep his handwriting as legible as possible, and he would erase rather than cross out. Without mentioning a word about it, he would write what he wanted Miss Zahra to know, pleading to God that she would want to read more.

———

For days after I emerged from the grave, I kept feeling phlegm gather relentlessly in my lungs and work its way up my throat, yet without a single cough. Was it brought on by my long period of silence? Or all the dirt that got through the wrappings of my grave clothes and lodged in my mouth and lungs? For a time, I was afraid to open my lips. Then it became clear to me that what was gathering inside me and clogging my chest so cruelly wasn't phlegm but rather congealed words. They rose until they started hurting my throat and interfering with my breathing. The words had gotten stuck, and evolved into little slugs, their spinal columns metamorphosing into sticky, clinging pseudopods that left viscous trails behind. One day, the nausea rose within me like a tidal wave, and bile came gushing out of my mouth. I vomited up everything in my guts, followed by everything in my soul, and then everything in my memory. I disgorged ink, paper, murderers, the corrupt, liars, hangmen, and . . . To be brief, I vomited up my spirit, and I sat there looking at it, writhing in its juices on the pavement, gasping like a fish out of water. It implored me to take it back inside. All the while, I kept looking at it like someone rejoicing over an enemy's pain.

Back when I was still a writer, I liked the way words filled my imagination. They made no claims, played no tricks. They didn't lie the way they do now. All they did was come out, one after the other, each leading the next, as though holding hands, trooping out of the dark, a train of words. Unless it was one of those days when they jumped and danced, unbound by gravity. But today, or yesterday, or tomorrow, now that I've given up writing because I can no longer bear it—despite my incredible power to endure everything—they are no longer so innocent; I feel their putrid souls rushing in, choking me with their yellow rot. I resist. I wake every dawn and flush from my holes whatever might have pushed its way in overnight to operate inside me without my permission. I dump it all into the toilet and flush it away. Nevertheless, the intruders keep coming, more and more every night. I'm no good at judging between them, at taking the measure of things. Just like everybody else, I suspect—unless, my God, I'm the only one?

Miss Zahra reassures me, saying that this putrescence in me is my truth, and that its source is not some flaw in me, but in the outside world. Meanwhile, she talks about the garbage crisis—about huge piles of trash that have nowhere to go and will eventually bury the country and all of us with it. She talks and talks and I don't pay any attention because I'm too busy trying to keep the proper distance from life, trying to keep the equanimity that everyone is always recommending. I don't know where I'm supposed to have acquired this sangfroid, let alone how I'm supposed to keep hold of it like everyone else claims to do. Yes, they carry it wherever they go and set it up as a barrier between themselves and the things of this world. I think it must be made of some very tough stuff, this distance, otherwise how could it offer any refuge, how could it be used for protection? And it must be pretty big, too, otherwise how would anyone hide under it? Or is it that nobody has really achieved that distance, that it's entirely hypothetical, something people talk about in the hope that it will finally be granted to them, an invisible, impervious glass wall around their persons, or maybe some kind of freestanding force field off which heartbreak and sorrow would simply bounce, harmlessly, and disappear . . .

In any case, I have no such protection. It's like I'm completely naked. No, it's like I'm naked and missing my skin too, with my nerves exposed to the light. Yes, that's me: an invisible, hypothetical creature that the wind blows right through. Protect yourself! they scream to me. Break free, man. Get away! And don't look back . . .

Mr. N placed his palm upon the page, fingers stretching toward the corners. He closed his hand and slowly squeezed, concentrating on the quiet protests made by the crumpling paper. When the sheet, filled with lines of gray insects, now squashed, was balled up in the palm of his hand, he went to the bathroom and threw it in the wastebasket. He worried that if Miss Zahra happened to read what had just come out of him, it might make her afraid. Mr. N hadn't realized how free he'd been before the woman developed an interest in what he was writing. Now he was weighed down, fettered by the image she had of him in her mind. He turned on the water in the sink and washed the pencil marks from his hands. He splashed cold water over his face as he resisted the appalling nausea still gathering in the pit of his stomach, fighting to keep it from blasting like a rocket out through his esophagus, his throat, his teeth. No, no, it's alright now. He took the crumpled page out of the wastebasket and tore it into tiny pieces that he threw into the toilet bowl. It wasn't long before felt his stomach muscles relax again. He could picture Miss Zahra coming back to him, smiling and reassuring. Mr. N looked into the mirror, meeting his own eyes without hesitation, without anxiety. He felt a new vigor, a desire to try again. He counted—one, two, three—and then raced back to where the stack of white pages was waiting.

What's better, a book or a tree? A tree, of course. Books mostly die, and those that live on are very few, even if they do tend to accumulate over the course of a few centuries. God, why am I not a tree? Why am I not a tree? Why am I not a tree? I'm waiting for an answer, God. Sentences float in my head like filth in a clogged sink; they spill through my fingers and my hands . . . That's actually a sentence I've written before, and though I have died, it is still alive, lodged underneath my tongue.

The calendar says it's Wednesday. Yes, the calendar speaks, even if it's asked to be quiet. I don't like Wednesdays; Lazarus rose on a Saturday. Lazarus, who was from Bayt Aniya, which means "the house of misery and tribulation" in Aramaic. The whole world is Bayt Aniya. I feel sweat running down my scalp, even though it isn't hot and the sun isn't burning. At least I've kept my spirits up for a little while by washing my face and hands. I wiped them on the white towel that has some small rust spots in the right corner; spots that move, when I turn the towel over, to the left side. I look at both sides every time I use this towel, then I hang it back up next to the bathroom sink. It's my favorite of the towels here because I can tell it apart from the others, which are identical to it in every other respect. It comes and goes, though, this towel; it vanishes out of circulation once in a while, hiding who knows where, only to reappear suddenly, as though nothing had happened, as though it hadn't been eluding me for weeks. The most disgusting things in the world are similarity and repetition, I think. Towels are like faces, which you also can't tell apart: circles with five holes—or seven, if we count the ears. The Arabic word for towel comes from the verb "to dry." There's nothing better than bringing language back to its roots. Language everywhere is starting to drift away from where it began.

I get up from my bed every day like someone picking himself off the field of battle, rising from the slaughter and destruction. The first thing I do is draw my net out of the water of sleep and gather the images, the bodies, and the ideas that are caught within it, that sloughed off of me in slumber and which I've left behind. Having caught them, I throw them down on paper, and then I throw the paper into the bathroom wastebasket before returning once more to set up my net and wait until night—as it does with such terrible consistency—falls at last. This night that comes to visit me every night . . . and the night is salt.

The night is salt . . . Whose line is that, I wonder? I'm pretty sure it's not mine—I'm not a writer anymore—but where did it come from? There's a cloud in my head. And wind. And cotton. How I loved words in the old days! All the clean, clear, light, graceful words. I loved being able to line up the three consonants like backgammon pieces: milh, hulm, lahm, hamal, lamah, lahh, hall, mall, hamm, muhh. I loved whatever was short and sweet, or short and not sweet, or sweet and not short. How I wish I could bring speech back to its origins! If only I could raise it from its grave, like Lazarus, and bring it back to the light. O Lord, asked Lazarus, is all that talking on my account? Why did you bring me back to the night to face what I have done?

Whenever I'm not paying attention, my room fills up with the words I've spent my day shooing away from my face like flies. If I doze off for a few moments, they begin seeping from my ears, my eyes, and my nostrils, like I've hemorrhaged inside, quietly and without warning... Out they come, little devils dragging along all their little sins, their pointy teeth, their tongues that are themselves the heads of snakes ... They scream, scratch, and hiss before being driven off by the good light shining through my window. At first, like everyone else, I didn't know what I was doing. I went out of my way to place my own head among the snakeheads of language, never once realizing that words were my enemy, wanting only to sneak into my mouth and leave poison under my tongue. And there's no remedy, no antidote, no vaccine. Words are everywhere, they're the atoms in the air, vibrations rising from the ground; they fall from the sky. An epidemic. You write a word: it rises from nothingness, puts on clothes, acquires a body and a face. Then people come up and greet it and act like it's the one in charge! Oh, and sometimes that well-dressed word forms a gang, and that gang starts roving around and knocking people to the ground, sometimes beating them to death ...

That's what happened to me. I wrote a name. Then the name rose off the paper and became a man ...

———

Mr. N was standing on his beloved apartment balcony, using a feather duster to clean the dirt piling up in the corners. Going over to the gardenia and the carnation in their pots near his writing table, he raised his head to look up at the looming tower overhead, with all its many levels, rising higher each day and casting a shadow not only over his building but upon Mr. N himself, making him feel like a dwarf contending with a giant. He and his spacious balcony had dwindled to the size of a fly beneath the tower's gaze. Even during the war, Mr. N hadn't felt that anything really threatened his neighborhood. Not because it was spared the bombings that all neighborhoods were exposed to then, share and share alike, but because N—though he wasn't called N back then—was certain that his building was too solidly built, too low to the ground, too hidden on its side street, to make for a worthy target. And so it was—with the exception of the building's glass, which got broken and needed replacing all the time.

"It won't be long before this damn tower drives me from my balcony and my home!" Mr. N said aloud, feeling his chest tighten. He went inside. Maybe emigration was the solution. He could shut his front door, head for the airport, and buy a ticket on the first available flight. Just like in the movies. Without any suitcases, visas, or complications. He would trot around the globe to his heart's content, and if he got tired, he could just rest wherever he happened to find himself. That's how his earliest ancestors did it after they rose up onto their hind legs and learned how to look off into the distance. They would just get going. They would have a bite and then get going. Have sex, stand up, and get going. They would give birth to their children and nurse them as they walked. They traversed all of Africa on foot. Then they moved on to the rest of the continents, occupying the globe, barefoot and naked. I too want to travel like that, thought Mr. N. I will walk in a straight line, and when I run into the sea, I will wind my way along the coast, step by step, until I've circled the Mediterranean and . . . and returned to where I started.

One day, Mr. N decided to go out. But where to? It was a long time since N had departed his little circle of light. The number of his friends was already zero. Relationships with other human beings were nonexistent. His basic, daily social interactions amounted to nothing. "Why not go down to Bourj Hammoud?" he heard himself saying. He could take along whatever he needed and make a day of it. He could stay away until the construction noise went quiet for the day. The idea was persuasive. More, the idea was intriguing. It would allow Mr. N to take stock of an area of the city he'd rarely visited. His life tended to take him toward the city's center rather than its outskirts. He went into his bathroom to confront its nonfunctional, European-style toilet. Taking the bit that needed replacing from where he'd left it on top of the tank, he dropped it into a white cotton tote bag, slung the bag over his shoulder, and exited his sanctuary, hurrying down the steep staircase.

Outside, he looked up at what remained of the blue sky above his neighborhood. Then, eyes on the ground, he walked on, trying to avoid any glimpse of that monstrosity up there ruining his life. He left his familiar precincts and ambled through the streets leading down to Mar Mikhael. When he reached Armenia Street, he turned right and followed its gradual descent. He was used to walking in the opposite direction, toward Gemmayzeh Street, Martyr's Square, and downtown. From there, he would continue on to where there was still a sea, a boardwalk, and seaside cafés.

Mr. N reached the corniche along the Beirut River, where he was forced to a stop at an intersection, waiting for the light. He could see the small bridge spanning the river. Sometimes the riverbed filled with streams of rainwater that had lost their way, but more often it was empty, a slick of mud waiting to be dried in the sun into a solid mass with all the filth that tended to accumulate there. The light turned green, but the line of cars did not move. Drivers began leaning on their horns to rebuke the dawdling cars at the head of the line. As they came to life and shot off down the road, Mr. N smiled at their idiocy and pressed his palms over his ears to protect them from the blaring horns. After he made his escape to the narrow, rising sidewalk on the far side, he slowed to a walk as the muscles of his legs reined him in, struggling with this modest ascent after so long with almost no exertion. He stopped, wiped away the sweat, and put his hands on his hips until he caught his breath. The district houses, most of them grouped on the left-hand side of the river as you looked downstream, came into view with a thousand colors and shapes. The first was a square apartment building, some of its seven floors decorated with green curtains, looking as though it had somehow escaped a thousand and one wars. At the next turn, Mr. N saw the outskirts of the Karantina district and the overpass to the highway to Daoura.

A picture sprang to mind of his father putting on his sunglasses as he drove his white Chevrolet with its red leather interior alongside the river. Mr. N sat in the back, not yet ten years old, while his brother, older by seven years and seven months, got to sit in front. They were listening to their father talk about the river, which in decades past had actually been a river, one to which the families of the surrounding neighborhoods would make their way to bathe or else to clean and dry their sheep's wool before using it to

45

stuff mattresses and blankets. Mr. N's father also spoke about the train that crossed the river nearby on its way to Mount Lebanon or the north.

These days, Mr. N could barely remember the city of corrugated metal structures they used to pass on their way to Achrafieh. Lying low and dense in the distance, its tin roofs blazed under unobstructed sun. Once, when Mr. N asked his father what it was and who lived there, his father replied, "That's Karantina, the quarantine, a name it received for being a lazaretto set up by Muhammad Ali when he came from Egypt to conquer this region in the 1800s. It burned in 1933, and the Armenian residents who survived moved to Bourj Hammoud, only for their place to be taken by the Palestinians. Today, twenty-seven thousand souls live in Karantina, a majority of them sick. They're the ones who come in to the clinic every Saturday."

Indeed, Mr. N preferred not to remember. He put his father out of his mind, along with the white Chevrolet. He banished the thought of his older brother and of Karantina, which had burned with all its poor more than once. Everything from Mr. N's past seemed to bite him like a snake. Everything he kept inside was poison in his heart.

By the time he reached the middle of the bridge, he felt a burning in his throat as the tears came. It was as though he'd crashed into some invisible wall, felt but not seen, bringing him to a halt, nauseating him, hemming him in. Mr. N gagged; he had to clench his teeth to keep his stomach from spilling out of his mouth. The odor descended like the Last Judgment, solid and forceful, a mix of vomit, burning, rot, excrement, mold, and rust, all collected and concentrated and perfectly balanced, rising and falling with every breeze, advancing and retreating like a wave. Mr. N tried to pinch his nose shut, but he could still feel the loathsome smell as it breached his defenses and slithered inside. Pulling up the collar of his shirt to cover his face, he hurried forward to cross the border.

Yes, a border, for the line he crossed with only two steps might as well have separated two alien countries: Mar Mikhael and environs on the one side, Bourj Hammoud on the other. In the former were old houses of two or three stories, some with front gardens smelling of life. In the latter, Mr. N navigated high, dilapidated buildings, haphazardly placed, pushing against one another, tottering together, like man-made cumulus clouds locked in combat as they floated along with scents of decay from the slaughterhouses and the mountains of trash. These neighborhoods had begun as refugee camps—for survivors of the Armenian massacres and the first Karantina fire. First came the tents, then the tents transformed into tin shacks, and then the tin became concrete. There were buildings that became houses that became markets for various crafts. Armenia, Arax, Agabus, Cilicia; Camp Tarad, Camp Amanous, and Camp Mar'as; the jewelry market, the clothes market, the shoe and leather goods market, the food market, the vegetable market, and still others could now be found in the narrow lanes that branched off until they wound their ways to the homes of the poor who'd left their mountain villages for the outskirts of the capital, striving for their daily bread. The little streets boiled like a beehive with workers of a thousand races and colors alongside refugees from all the wars in all the regional nations: Nepalese, Ethiopians, Sri Lankans, Filipinos, Egyptians, Sudanese, Syrians, Iraqis,

Kurds, Armenians, Syriacs, Assyrians, Chaldeans, Buddhists, Christians, Muslims, and . . .

"My God!" Mr. N heard himself say, unable to control his eyes, which darted here and there like frenzied dogs. He wanted to touch everything he passed. He kept on walking, turning in circles as he went, until he reached the bridge connecting Achrafieh to the Dekwaneh neighborhood. This one was a cement bridge as wide as the entire street, running between houses forever choked on dust and car exhaust. Actually, it didn't so much run between them as squeeze itself in, abutting the balconies, touching them even, such that someone taking the air could easily shake hands with a passing driver—or the driver, if he so desired, could easily jump from his car to a balcony. Mr. N enjoyed a momentary fantasy in which his own home was relocated to one of those buildings, his own balcony, his own gardenia and carnation, his own chair and table and all the papers on it. And then he imagined himself as a sniper, looking down at the road, holding a rifle and sighting his prey . . .

"Outskirters," Thurayya would say, in a tone of superiority tinged with disgust, when she noticed one of those people to whom Mr. N's father dedicated his Saturdays at the clinic. You couldn't just say "that riffraff," for example, or even "the poor," though the people who came to see Mr. N's father, a doctor renowned for providing his services free of charge on Saturdays, were indeed the poorest of the poor. The doctor did this in honor of his own father, Nadeem, Mr. N's grandfather, a farmer who came from his village to one of these same suburbs of Beirut to study in the city after his family sold all their land in order to educate their only son.

Mr. N's father also did it to spite his mother, Eugénie, Mr. N's grandmother, who came from the Jaffa bourgeoisie, from a family that used to send steamships full of oranges around the world and then escaped to Lebanon from Palestine in 1948. After the Nakba, they abandoned oranges and began importing cars. Eugénie wanted her son, who hated business, to become a doctor in order to preserve the honor and status of the family. Mr. N hardly remembered his grandmother Eugénie. She had white skin, he knew, with freckles covering her face and hands. Unfailingly elegant, she would always wear her full set of jewelry no matter the occasion: a small pearl necklace, pearl earrings, gold bracelets, and her wedding band with a diamond ring alongside. She didn't like Thurayya, though she preserved the rudiments of a relationship with her daughter-in-law and tried to treat her with respect. Still, she never missed an opportunity to remind this interloper that she, Thurayya, could never catch up to Mrs. Eugénie with respect to her lineage, no matter how much she boasted, how much she exalted herself, how much she looked down on others. This was one of the old woman's few qualities of which Mr. N's father, the doctor, was—secretly—pleased.

Worried he was getting lost, Mr. N left the El Sekkeh district and went back toward Arax, and from there to Armenia Street. He followed it and saw gold on both sides of the road, with women stopping in front of the glittering windows, their greed drooling down their chins. There was a shop selling sandwiches, and people were eating even though it was too late for breakfast and too early for lunch. He saw boys selling facial tissues, gum, and lottery tickets. He saw beggars sprawled on the ground with infants in their laps, flies massing on their faces. There were gift shops with curious items for sale under brand names from around the world, but actually all Chinese counterfeits. Criminals were the same everywhere, the poor preying on the poor—one side producing and the other consuming. Shop windows abounded in wallets, jewelry, shoes, clothes, glasses, and accessories. Moving on, there were shops for odds and ends, various tools, electronics, buttons, fabrics, juices, mobile phones, games, beauty supplies, and so on. Mr. N met wives, mothers, and migrant workers carrying plastic bags full of vegetables in one hand, while in the other they held imitation handbags claiming to be Gucci, Burberry, Louis Vuitton, Chanel, Michael Kors, and Dior.

Mr. N raised his face to the sky. He was shocked to see the intersecting lines, hanging any which way, so many that they nearly obscured the blue of the sky. Ropes, copper wires, insulated lines for electricity and the internet. He also saw much laundry stretching over the streets, as well as over the narrow, branching alleys where pieces of furniture too seemed to be spreading, down below, across the asphalt, as though abandoned at the entrances to these dark, narrow houses no more than two stories tall. Big desks of wood or metal, an ancient sofa, and sometimes a table, a fan, or a television. These would be surrounded by metal flowerpots bearing seed-lings or shrubbery or flowers in order to form a border around these external "rooms" or else trying to hide them from view. Here the street was open and free to all: people passing by, residents of sunless ground-level apartments, cars, stray cats and dogs. Yet that furniture, just like the people who sat on and among it morning and night, remained in place and was never brought inside, where there was no longer any room for it. Mr. N raised his eyes to the small balconies common here, sometimes no larger than a few square feet. He noticed how each window greeted its counterpart in the building directly across the way. Likewise, each door faced a door, and each balcony a balcony. There could be no sense of privacy here, where each structure sat cheek-by-jowl with its neighbor. The word could have no meaning in these cramped corners.

Yes, the poor do not possess the luxury of having their own spaces; they don't even fit in the margins of life; their own bodies close them in . . . Too literary a sentence, thought Mr. N. A bookish sentence, feeble and out of place, the sort of thing he would have to renounce, and cold turkey; just as someone who has given up cigarettes, alcohol, or drugs learns to fear even the presence of his old addiction, lest he succumb anew. Mr. N changed direction and, with it, the course of his thoughts.

He passed by a number of shrines and religious statues set in niches on the corners of those narrow streets. At their feet or between their arms had been laid the pictures of some "martyr," some "bridegroom of heaven," as they were called, unless they'd been dubbed "the nation's lost": those who had been killed in one of the big wars or else one of the many small ones, or maybe during a parking dispute, or because of an obscene word touching on the honor of someone's mother or sister, or in a car crash, or on account of having the bad luck to turn up in the wrong place at the wrong time, or simply without any reason at all. Most of the shrines were to Saint Charbel, whose features were different from one shrine to the next, even if his beard and his long black robe were always the same. The ones that weren't to Charbel were to the Holy

Virgin, who kept watch at the entrances to houses, the corners of side alleys, and even on balconies. Her shrines came in various sizes, from the enormous to the minute, and in various colors, some a perfect shining white, and others showing the crimson of her lips and her blue cloak, the color of the sky. People always painted her as a young woman kneeling in front of Jesus on the cross, even though her son breathed his last at the age of thirty-three, and if she became pregnant with him when she was fifteen, she would have been pushing fifty when he died. Fifty in those days bore no resemblance to fifty today. Yet any wrinkles the artists had given Mary—and likewise painted onto the skin and hair of the Messiah, whom they had made a blond with blue eyes—were due to the rending pain of seeing her son first nailed to the cross and then giving up the ghost.

Mr. N thought it strange at first that it wasn't Jesus himself who was found everywhere in those neighborhoods. It was true that the shrines there weren't totally lacking in some bare crosses, absent the body of the Messiah, and that a single large crucifix could be found at the intersection of one main street. There was also a gigantic cross hanging by rope over a more modern street that appeared to have been built in the sixties, when the population was still expanding and the use of concrete likewise. That street led to a huge marble statue, and when Mr. N asked about it, he was told it commemorated the Armenian genocide. On top of this was the incense that burned in front of so many shops and establishments, lit by those seeking to earn their daily bread or to ward off the putrid odors that ruined the calm of the morning. Perhaps the people of those districts just wanted a certain consolation.

They needed a shoulder to cry upon, a hand to take theirs, someone promising signs and wonders that gave them hope for a kinder tomorrow. And who better to turn to than a local saint who spoke their own language, or else a compassionate mother who stood ready to comfort them?

Mr. N came to feel, with some embarrassment, that he might as well be a tourist here. He was a stranger visiting a country in which he hadn't set foot for a long time, though it was the country where he was born, along with his father, his father's father, and his grandfather's grandfather. It was as though, for the first time in his life, he were going down to the cellar, down where the servants lived, raised their children, grew old, and died in silence, unseen by their masters. For here was where the laborers lived, our farmers, our trash collectors, our servants, our craftsmen, our oppressed; our drivers, cooks, shoemakers, tinsmiths, tailors . . . Here, and in places like it, lived the Lord's flock, like cattle yoked to millstones, grinding away their days, their dreams, and every ounce of energy. They go around in circles like pack animals so that we might eat flour made into a paste by their sweat—we, the masters, whom the Lord has chosen and made into his officers, his helpers, the nobles of his retinue, his chosen few.

The awful smell that Mr. N believed he had left behind was coming now from ahead, so Mr. N changed direction again to seek relief from the rancid air, heading down small side streets that more often than not were dead ends. A woman deeply camouflaged under several veils appeared alongside several fake blondes. Some of the blondes tended toward a neon yellow, while others were in a state of ruin after their roots had reclaimed their original color and advanced like an army under a black flag. On some corners, Mr. N even saw the reddish tinge of an orange dye struggling through thick, curly hair gathered in tight braids, twisted like snakes, or flowing free over the dark skin of exposed breasts, bellies, and thighs as the women wandered, nowhere in particular, hoping to strike the catch of the day.

"Twenty thousand!"

Broken Arabic was barked from a dark open doorway. Mr. N tried to see the woman who'd called, unsure of what he'd heard. She winked at him and smiled, revealing gleaming white teeth between narrow lips. She took a step forward and stood on the threshold, which raised her a few centimeters higher as she thrust her breasts nearly into Mr. N's face and pushed out her butt. The scent of cheap perfume filled Mr. N's nostrils, mixed with the smell of sweat and spices. He pulled his head back a little, taking the liberty of looking past her shoulder: a dark hallway rumbling with the motors from water tanks of various sizes, lined up haphazardly. At the end of the hall was a decrepit tile staircase missing some steps.

The young woman raised her arm and waved her hand as though to dispel any concerns. "Do you have a car?" she said. "We'll do it in your car. Or, if you want, we'll go to a hotel. Or to your place, okay? I'll spend the entire day with you for one hundred thousand lira. Well? What do you say?"

She grabbed Mr. N, wanting him to check out her goods, trying to stick his hand between her legs, but the way he stepped back without the least word dashed her hopes. His subsequent retreat down the alley angered her, and suddenly she was raising her middle finger at him and uttering expressions in Ethiopian accompanied by curses in Arabic. Mr. N avoided her eye but then turned to look back from a distance. He saw her with two workmen who stood haggling over the price of a quick orgasm. She called a greeting to another woman who passed by at a run, her breasts bouncing in front of her and her slippers nearly falling off her feet.

———

For a long time, Thurayya refused to employ foreign house-keepers. But when the work became too much for Mary, and she decided to return to her village in order to grow old there and be buried close to her people, Thurayya was forced to accept a Sri Lankan woman—better her than a Filipina who wasn't good with any language besides English. Thurayya preferred French, considering it an aristocratic language, while she saw English as the language of the rabble. And if someone ever tried to contradict her, saying that English after all was the language of Shakespeare and other great poets, Thurayya would have objected that anyone using that mongrel tongue today was only speaking the language of the riffraff, not the language of poets.

Suwarna put up with Thurayya for nine years. She was made to suffer every single day, but offered no complaint beyond a smile that only incensed Thurayya further. So she would send Suwarna away, only to change her mind and call her back a little later as though nothing had happened. Thurayya would rarely apologize for her harsh behavior with that angel of a servant, who loved her and showed her compassion through her advancing years. Thurayya did, however, insist on calling Suwarna's successors by that sainted Sri

Lankan's name, even though she knew the new girls' names perfectly well.

This continued until Aryagash came, the crazy Ethiopian, with hair that she would spend days in front of the mirror trying to tame into some semblance of shape. After arriving from her country with long braids and blond highlights, she showed up at work only a few days later with short hair combed down around the delicate features of her small face. The tips had been colored a burnt orange, using the last of an old tube of dye. Her hair was short, and her mood was foul. She cried that her mistress had rebuked her, and asked Mr. N to bring her back to the agency because she didn't want to stay. But then she changed her mind and asked him for money to go to a hair salon. She left and then returned with long hair, dyed and braided, as well as a cheerful mood and smiling, black-lined eyes. Thus, back and forth, with hair that was long and then short, tame and then running riot, and with many hours spent in front of the bathroom mirror or looking at the screen of her cell phone, Aryagash fell in love with her hairdresser's neighbor, an Assyrian Iraqi who owned a smartphone repair shop. She ran off with him without looking back—without a thought for her passport, nor for her husband and her three-year-old child, whom she had left behind in Addis Ababa.

When Mr. N called the office of the housekeeping agency, he was told it was necessary to make a report about her abscondence so that the responsibility for her would no longer be his. He went to the police station and did what was asked of him. One of the officers tried to persuade him to accuse her of theft because that would increase their chances of catching and arresting her, but Mr. N couldn't bring himself to do it. After some days, he headed to the General Security office, having been summoned there for an investigation into the reasons behind the foreigner's flight. Afterward, he had nowhere to go but home, where the worm of dotage was already boring into Thurayya's head. She no longer spoke in complete sentences, but would stop in the middle of a thought like someone losing their footing or driving into a roadblock. It began subtly, with her repeating words, sometimes asking the same question multiple times. She would ask, and Mr. N would reply, and after a while, she would put the question to him again. He would again give the answer, then she would forget and start from scratch. When Aryagash first warned Mr. N about this behavior, he'd lost his temper, for reasons he didn't care to explore. Yet he suppressed his anger, since, for so long, anger had been the sole province of Thurayya. It was as though the emotion was her private possession. She had registered a patent on the invention and posted it on the gates of her kingdom, so that no one else dared even to touch it.

When Mr. N got close to Armenia Street, which led to Daoura Circle, he started reading the signs of the shops that were crowding in around him. He liked that they were written in Arabic, Armenian, English, and French, and sometimes in Sinhalese, which was Suwarna's language, and Amharic and Oromo—which is what Aryagash and those before her spoke—and Hindi, Nepalese, Filipino, and so on, down to the languages whose identity he could only guess from the faces of the people in the shop, or from the types of commodities on display in their refrigerators or in the boxes spread across the pavement.

At Daoura Circle, which got its name from a large round-about, Mr. N craned his neck to take in the full panorama. The bustle around him had reached a climax; he was harried on every side. There were wooden carts, their goods on display; buses headed for all corners of Lebanon, hunting for passengers and filling the seats, one by one; gigantic semitrucks; private cars as well as taxis. To say nothing of the vendors, pedestrians, and day laborers; sandwich shops, fresh fruit-juice shops, and narghile shops, exhaling their smoke since morning; coffee machines; shoe-shiners; gas stations; money changers, Western Union, and Cash Express; and shops for making inexpensive internet calls. There were buildings with enormous signs reaching high overhead and also discount clothing stores, where each item cost five thousand lira, two went for ten thousand, and the third was free . . .

Mr. N's head was spinning. He was coming to understand that traversing this place on foot was not at all like passing through by car. He made a sudden dash across the street, pursued by car horns as well the curses of blotch-faced drivers, and ducked into a narrow side street with no sidewalks. Noticing a group of noisy young men crowding together ahead of him, he hesitated briefly before pressing forward. He took courage when it became clear to him that they were only looking at the goods of an African street vendor they had crowded around as he showed them the contents of a leather bag filled with lighters, watches, and leather belts.

"How much for this Rolex?" asked one of the men.

"Twenty-five thousand," said the vendor. "Or two for forty. Did you see the Lanvin belt? It's genuine leather and only costs ten thousand."

"Where are you from?"

"I'm Muhammad. From Sudan."

"Listen, Muhammad. If I take a Rolex watch, this S. T. Dupont lighter, and a Lanvin belt, how much would that be?"

"Fifty-five thousand."

"What! I'll pay you thirty, not one lira more."

"No, no way," said the vendor, who made ready to leave. The others got involved in the haggling, then, and after a little give-and-take, they made a deal for forty thousand.

The buyer was a young man in his twenties with a splendid build, whose features Mr. N didn't get a good look at. "What's all this stuff for?" one of his companions asked.

"My gigolo life!" replied the young man before jumping down two steps into the store he had come out of. Mr. N approached the door and saw the same man sitting in front of a computer with a race car on its screen. There were others just like him glued to their own computers, driving. One car froze on its screen, and an annoyed voice called, "Luqman!" A man got up from behind his desk and eased his way toward the complaining customer. Mr. N's heart leapt in terror at the sight of him. Was it really him? He studied the man's face. Once this so-called Luqman finished whatever he needed to do, he looked around his domain and caught Mr. N staring at him, standing frozen in the internet café's doorway.

Mr. N drew back and headed back the way he had come as quickly as he could manage. Behind him, Luqman climbed the two steps separating the store from the pavement. When Mr. N had made good his escape, sure he could no longer be seen from the shop, he took a moment to catch his breath. Poking his head around the corner to make sure that no one was following him, he glimpsed the man called Luqman standing in front of his shop. Luqman turned to look in both directions and then lit a cigarette. "Impossible!" Mr. N whispered, trembling, as the man tilted back his head and blew a stream of smoke straight up. "It's him!" The same body, even if it had grown a belly: the same wide shoulders, the broad chest, the head thrown back.

Luqman didn't finish his cigarette. He dropped it and ground it out under the toe of his shoe. Before entering his shop, he looked back toward the mouth of the alley, where Mr. N was hiding. "He saw me," thought Mr. N in terror. "I'm sure he saw me. But after all these years, did he recognize me?"

———

"*Good morning, Mister N*," Miss Zahra gushed in English. "Guess who's coming to visit us today!"

Miss Zahra generally spoke to Mr. N using the first-person plural. Andrew did it too. Or, rather, Andrew did it, and Miss Zahra followed suit, seeing as he was her boss. Perhaps they addressed Mr. N with that *we* because deep down they thought he was impaired, inadequate, and needed someone else to complete him. Or because they saw him as their social inferior, and were feigning a kind of equality between them out of politeness. "Did we sleep well last night? Are we hungry? Do we need new pencils? Did we write enough for one day?" One question after another, with every visit or service. Sometimes Mr. N laughed at this habit of theirs; he didn't know whether he should consider it insolence, exaggeration, or merely a faux pas. Bit by bit, it had become common for people to address each other without showing any respect for their different positions in life, and without using the proper titles, be it young people to adults, employees to supervisors, or students to professors. For this was the age of communication, equality, access, brotherhood, neoliberalism, the global village, everyone a citizen of the world, sharing the same conditions . . .

Miss Zahra closed the door. The smell of her perfume preceded her and flew straight up Mr. N's nostrils. Indeed, it tousled his hair, cracked open his skull, and penetrated his very pores with a shudder that crackled in his belly like lightning. *Femme*, thought Mr. N with irritation, realizing that the visitor was certainly his brother, Sa'id. Who else could it be? He came to see Mr. N once or twice each year, whenever his work and his many travels permitted, though they rarely did. No doubt Sa'id had given Miss Zahra this perfume on some previous visit, and she'd decided to put it on that day for his sake after he'd called to say he was coming.

Sa'id never came without giving notice of his arrival. He always liked people to be ready for him, never leaving them any room for pretext or excuse, which gave him all the more license to reproach them if they failed to roll out the red carpet for him. As for the perfume, he gave the same brand— his mother's—to every woman he knew, because, as far as he was concerned, every woman was a project, someone to mold. It would start with the perfume, and then they would invariably fall for Sa'id's good looks and dazzling charm. In Sa'id's heart, all women were variations upon the theme of Thurayya, attempts to return to the model she'd presented, transcriptions of various portions of her melody, at least, if not, indeed, full and comparable copies. This was why he'd married Asiya, daughter of the owner of the largest and most important marketing company in the Middle East. She embodied the beauty and elegance of a woman on a billboard, so Sa'id had nothing to add apart from Thurayya's perfume, which Thurayya always boasted was created especially for her. She never used any other, and she would go on at length about it until the person listening to her really did begin to believe it had been blended for her sake and according to her own specifications. "*Femme*! That's a real woman's perfume. It first hit the market the same year I was born! A telling coincidence, no?"

Then Thurayya would lean over little Sa'id, inviting him to smell her wrist, followed by her neck, adding, "I put it where you can feel my pulse—that's so the heat helps diffuse all its notes . . . Close your eyes, and savor the first scents: apricot, peach, and cinnamon. Inhale the Brazilian rosewood and lemon! Then enjoy the underlying hints: clove, lily, rosemary, jasmine, and rose. Finally, swim in its depths, where you'll find leather, ambergris, patchouli, benzoin, vanilla, and musk . . ."

Sa'id listened, smiling, enrapt, while N circled about, furtively listening from his hiding place between two couches. He saw Thurayya as a sorceress, gathering flowers, grasses, and spices to mix them in copper pots before breathing upon the mixture to finish her special perfume. Then she distilled the potion into bottles of translucent crystal that she distributed to the girls of the neighborhood, who would queue up in endless lines, waiting and waiting for their own bottle.

That was why Sa'id began giving his women Thurayya's perfume when he was still a young man. And if he did sometimes try out a new brand in those early years, thinking that *Femme* was perhaps losing its impact, that there were plenty of other perfumes on the market that might speak to a woman, he always came back to it in the end, having discovered that *Femme* communicated different and better things to women that the other perfumes could not—or so he imagined. By simply repeating Thurayya's words when she introduced him to the perfume for the first time, he would give the stuff a romantic dimension in women's eyes that made all his other captivating qualities burn hotter and brighter.

Now Miss Zahra was posing questions without waiting for the answers, and Mr. N saw that she was talking to his brother, Sa'id, even though Sa'id was nowhere to be seen, even though she was looking at Mr. N. Strange. How could a simple detail like a new perfume turn a woman's mood so completely upside down? Rather, how could it transform her identity and make her behave as though she were someone else? Miss Zahra, wearing her *Femme*, was not the same Miss Zahra as she was without. Her gait was embellished, as was the tone of her voice, and the shiny lip gloss that she used looked even shinier. Here she was, addressing through Mr. N someone who wasn't there, behaving in front of Mr. N like a woman ready for anything, her senses alive and her skin tingling. Mr. N had read that sexual attraction and even romantic love were nothing more than chemical reactions to certain sets of invisible stimuli. Pheromones set off hormonal reactions and, voilà, you're in love. It was clear Sa'id had killer pheromones; they seduced pretty much every woman he ran into, as opposed to Mr. N's, which enticed only a few, and even then not too well, seeing as they never stuck around for long.

The record was Neda's seven years. After that, it was "I can no longer bear you," as she'd put it before bursting into tears one day. Not "I can't endure you" or "put up with you," but *bear*, as though Mr. N were some piece of luggage, some heavy burden that she'd been carrying for the length of their relationship until, exhausted and overwhelmed, she had to surrender and set her burden down. She said she still loved him, but they had to part regardless—she just couldn't take him anymore. She set a paper bag in front of him that contained the letters and little gifts he'd given her, none of which she wanted to keep. Mr. N looked at the bag: pink and white stripes, a black satin handle, and "Victoria's Secret" written out in black letters. No doubt she'd chosen it at random from the bags she was always collecting, knowing that she would reuse them.

Neda never did like waste. Throwing things away was hard for her, even when an object's useful life was clearly at an end. At the beginning of their relationship, when she allowed Mr. N to visit her room, he was shocked to see all the junk she had in her closets. She was one of those people who developed an emotional attachment to things, who clung even to those possessions that were completely worn out. This comforted Mr. N somewhat, since he felt that, in light of her other hoarding, there was a good chance her affection toward him would last a lifetime—that she would preserve him just as she did shopping bags and magazines and trinkets. But then she threw him away. She, who never threw things away, threw away Mr. N.

When they were first getting to know each other, Neda told him she didn't like men with bulging muscles. Mr. N was neither alarmed nor comforted by this. She also mentioned that she found something strangely attractive about men who were medium height, especially when they had big feet. Mr. N stole a glance at his own feet and wished he had simply confessed they were not size 43, as he had claimed at first, but 42. He had continued to wear shoes larger than his actual size for her sake, trying to match her ideal.

On the day she broke it off with him, their waiter appeared right after she'd delivered the blow. Mr. N contented himself with ordering a cup of coffee, but Neda didn't order anything at all. Really! Was she really in such a hurry? Oh well. Her phone rang. She excused herself and stood up, moving a little distance away. After a quick conversation, she came back to sit across from Mr. N. She would keep their meeting brief, try to let him down easy, then head off to another appointment. That's what Mr. N saw her thinking. Saw her doing. And why shouldn't she already be in a relationship with someone else? Probably that was who'd just called her, the better to hurry her along in ending things with Mr. N, or to reassure himself that she'd already done so. Perhaps the other man was outside at that very moment, watching them, to make sure. How long had she been going behind his back and stringing him along until she was sure she wanted to leave?

Mr. N's coffee arrived. He took a sip, then asked for the bill and paid. He would go. There wasn't anything else to say. Anyway, he had gotten lost in his own head, and whenever that happened, there was no chance of any connection with the outside world. He stood up to say goodbye, careful to avoid looking at Neda. Seven years melted away in an instant, just like that. A lump of salt, nothing more! "Finished already?" she asked him in a low voice. When he didn't reply, she held out the Victoria's Secret bag. He took it and left after another moment of contemplation. Now he had to figure out how to wipe away the last seven years of his life. How? Well, just as he'd previously wiped away his entire childhood.

Outside the café, Mr. N had felt a kind of satisfaction. This kind of suffering was something he was used to. And each time he was put through it, he learned more about how to handle it. He projected himself forward, toward the moment he knew was coming, that moment in the future when he would wake up having forgotten his pain. There was only one problem with this strategy: he couldn't be quite sure how much time separated him from that day. Oh well. He'd left Neda choking on an overflowing pile of words, useless sentences. What she had already said was enough for him. He could have sat and given her time to explain, clarify, elaborate. But reasons never justified anything. They couldn't make him into someone else, and they couldn't soften his fall. Reasons were like guns: when someone pointed one at you, you had to assume it was going to go off. Growing up, he never asked about Thurayya's reasons; he certainly wasn't going to ask Neda about hers. Not trying to understand had always been his way. In the end, understanding was no different from its absence: neither changed his pain in the least. A lack of dependence upon objects and people was the only thing that did any good, because when abandonment came, it came, and there wasn't anything he could do about it. Even writing made no difference. The most it could do was erase the self from the self when the days became heavy as boulders . . .

Miss Zahra touched Mr. N's forearm, and he stood up with a shiver. "Excuse me," he said, turning his face away. "I find strong perfumes nauseating in the morning."

She gave a small gasp and put a hand over her mouth. "I'm sorry. Why didn't you tell me before?"

"Because you don't usually put on perfume. Miss Zahra, where are all my papers hiding?"

Posing that question to her, he hid his consternation behind rapidly blinking eyes. Miss Zahra didn't answer him but got up and straightened her white dress. Sensing he was in a bad mood, she headed for the door.

"If you wanted to read them," said Mr. N, "I wouldn't have objected. You only had to ask permission first . . . But I want them now, if you don't mind."

Miss Zahra nodded and then slipped out. Mr. N nearly leapt for joy. For once in his life he had been stern and decisive. He had rebuked her for her perfume, accused her of hiding his papers, and ordered her to return them to him. The way she held her silence and accepted it all meant that she was responsible, just as Daoud had suggested.

Mr. N grunted in disgust. He opened the window to encourage the perfume to leave with her. A fresh breeze entered, followed by a new and disgusting odor, as though of decaying bodies. God, what was it? The older Mr. N got, the stronger his sense of smell became, as though he were turning into a dog. Odors entered his mind and remained there, tickling his brain and toying with his nerves before taking up permanent residence. He remembered the scent of his father's shaving soap in the morning, and the scent of his medicine and alcohol in the evening. From Mary, the scents of flour, grass, and cinnamon. From Sa'id, the overpowering odor of his sweat. And from Thurayya . . . No, Thurayya didn't have a scent of her own. Or else Mr. N never got close enough to smell it. Perfume aside, he couldn't remember her having any flavor or fragrance at all.

Mr. N suddenly felt a great weariness settle upon his arms and the base of his neck. He wished he could stop the flow of his thoughts so he could lie down and sleep. He had gotten so wrapped up in the story of the papers and the scents that he forgot his intention to go into the bathroom to get ready for his brother's arrival. But had Miss Zahra really said that Sa'id was coming to visit him? Had she really put on Thurayya's perfume? Or had Mr. N just wished it to be so?

———

Mr. N remained baffled for days by his visit to Bourj Hammoud. He felt as though he'd visited some distant land and left himself behind even after he came back. At night, he dreamed of the neighborhood's streets and alleys, and of the multitude of shops and people he had seen. In the mornings, he would sit on his balcony with his papers, yet his thoughts took him right back to that teeming bazaar until he forgot himself, forgot the tower and its noise, the scars of its construction. It would have been a mild curiosity, maybe even a blessing, except for that face—the face that began invading his dreams and his waking reveries both, a face so terrifying that it brought Mr. N plummeting back to earth. Mr. N was sure he knew that face. It had been purged from his memory for years, it's true, and even now it wavered and retreated when he tried to fix it in place. Indeed, Mr. N only had to apply a little logic in order to doubt himself and conclude, given the gap of more than a decade and a half, that he was merely the victim of a cruel coincidence. Why shouldn't there be two men with the same name as well as a certain similarity in their build and facial features . . .?

When he was a child, and he cried out in his sleep, it was Mary who would run to little N and scold him gently before reciting prayers in her village dialect, so dear to his heart. Then, when his nightmares started coming every night, she sprinkled his bed and all the floor around it with newly blessed holy water. Later, she beseeched the help of Mar Matanyous—the local name for Saint Anthony, patron saint of the mentally ill—as she tucked the blanket under his chin. Like N himself, Mary refused to inform Thurayya about what the boy was seeing in his dreams—nor would she tell his father, the doctor. This was natural enough, since she knew in advance it would do no good, and even knew what N's parents would say: "Please, Mary, don't worry me like this," or "I beg you, Mary, don't put such ideas in the boy's head." No, Mary wouldn't say anything to anyone except N himself, reassuring the child that Mar Matanyous—"bless his name"—would drive away N's "companion," and afterward, he would sleep in peace, undisturbed by any fears or jinn. When the boy asked her what this "companion" was, she informed him that each of us has a counterpart in the world of the jinn, and that it's best for us not to fear them, or else they will gain mastery over us.

Despite everything that Mary did, the boy continued to suffer from his dreams. He saw strange figures and heard terrible noises that frightened him so much that he would run, agonized and soaked in sweat, to Mary's room. She would make room for him in her bed without bothering to open her eyes. "Come up then," she'd say, throwing her blanket over him. He would get in and drift off. If only she had been the one who gave birth to him, he thought. If only she could adopt him and take him away with her! N liked to imagine that Mary was his real mother, and that, one day, she would reveal the truth. He would cry, she would cry, and they would fall into each other's arms for a long embrace, just like in the Bollywood films she used to watch when she didn't have any pressing tasks or when Thurayya went out. The two of them would say goodbye to everyone and set off on a journey, never to return.

Mr. N subsequently returned to Bourj Hammoud. Not a week passed before he made the trip, following the same route and carrying in his hand the same broken bit of plumbing that needed replacing. The previous time, he had abandoned his errand when his mind started racing after running into a certain person he thought he had recognized. He now ambled along, following the same route, putting his feet precisely in the tracks left by his previous journey. He crossed the bridge, choked on the fetid smell, and turned off toward Arax. Again, he took Armenia Street. He lost his way, however, in the narrow, branching alleys, soon feeling as though he'd entered a labyrinth and was doomed to wander until he couldn't remember how he'd gotten in, let alone how he might get out again. At last he followed the advice his neighbor had given him and started asking the people he saw about where to buy plumbing supplies. Mr. N got several apologies in foreign accents until he found a teenage boy who gave him directions to a shop run by an Armenian that sold all sorts of sundries: "That way. Take a left, and then it's the third alley on the right. Ask for Muallem Fahih. He'll have what you're looking for."

Mr. N hesitated, then asked, "Is there also an internet café nearby?"

"Of course," replied the youth eagerly. "I'm on my way there now. Follow me!"

Mr. N's color changed, his lips trembled, his legs were weak. The young man stepped forward to keep him from falling. He asked earnestly whether the stranger wasn't feeling well. Did Mr. N need anything?

"I'm fine," Mr. N said, trying to force a smile onto his face. Could the youth really be headed to the very same internet café? What were the odds? Mr. N had returned to the area on the pretext of replacing a toilet part, but deep down, he realized that his real motive was that face, that face that answered to such an uncommon name. "Don't worry," he said. "I think it's the heat."

The boy suggested he accompany Mr. N to Fahih's shop, and from there to the internet café. But Mr. N objected, saying, "It's best that I rest first in the café. I'll go to Fahih's afterward."

When he had descended the two steps that separated the street from the level of the internet café—having first confirmed the absence of the man on whose account he'd come—Mr. N felt as though he had cast himself into a pit. His eyes, used to the riot of lights outside, had to acclimate to this room where the only illumination was that cast by the computer screens filled with the violent images of video games. He found himself lost among these strange shades, hunched over on their chairs, exhausted, wearing headsets to cut them off from the world around them. It would be fine to sit in the corner near the door, Mr. N figured. If he sensed any danger, he could slip out and flee.

"Kareem, at your service," said the youth, introducing himself and shaking Mr. N's hand. "And you?"

"Call me N."

"N?" The kid was amused. With a laugh and a shrug, he said, "Fine! It's nice to meet you, Mr. N!"

Kareem made room for him nearby, at the computer next to the one where he stationed himself. Mr. N began looking the place over as his eyes adjusted to the gloom. He saw that most of those present were young enough to be his children. They sat with faces glued to screens, their fingers dancing with amazing rapidity over their keyboards, in another world. Sometimes they smiled; at other times they got angry. Sometimes they would get up to light a cigarette, going outside to smoke; when they came back in, they would call for the Egyptian working behind the desk to bring them a bottle of soda or water.

"Want anything to drink?" Kareem asked Mr. N. "There's no alcohol here, unfortunately. Luqman forbids it."

"Forbids alcohol?" Mr. N echoed.

"One day, the guys got drunk, started fighting, and broke a bunch of stuff. From that day on, he forbade any selling or drinking of alcohol here."

"And everyone obeys?" said Mr. N, feigning disinterest.

Kareem's eyes opened wide in surprise. "It's clear you don't know Luqman. You'd have to come by in the afternoon to see him, but as soon as you do, you'll understand. He was a big man during the war: very powerful, and with a special squad that carried out his orders. They called him 'the hero' in those days. Everyone around here knew him and dreaded him. I think he's roughly your age. Excuse me," Kareem said, abruptly ending his story as a Skype call came in. "This is Joyce calling, my English fiancée."

On his own screen, Mr. N perused some foreign-language newspapers, passing the time cautiously, reassured by the absence of Luqman. Kareem turned back to him when the connection went bad and his call was interrupted. He explained his relationship with Joyce, whom he had met on the internet eight months earlier, and whom he intended to marry so that she could get a visa to bring him to Ireland, where she lived with her teenage daughter.

"And from there," said Kareem, breaking into English, "*Bye, bye, Lebanon—hello, world! Aside from gaming, of course, a lot of people come in here hoping to make connections online with foreign girls. When you set the hook, that's a good way to get out of the country. My friend Mario got lucky with an Australian girl whose family owns a supermarket chain all over the country. They got married, she gave him her citizenship, and today he lives like a king. It's true that Joyce is many years older than me, but so what? I won't be tied to her my whole life. She works in a rest home for the elderly, which means we can chat even when she's on duty. She says she's lonely and needs a man in her life. When I told her I want to go to university and complete my studies, she proposed sending me to university if I agreed to marry her. So I agreed!"

Mr. N listened gratefully to Kareem. Without him, he wouldn't have known that Luqman came in only on afternoons, which inspired a deep curiosity and a desire to stick around. This kid was just like Luqman, that handsome young rogue, in the days when he launched himself upon Shireen, greedy for her citizenship. But Luqman, unlike the youth of today, was actually a war criminal, one of the war's great killers, a true lord of war, and the world was too much for him when peace came. He lost his way until he found his former companions, killers like himself. Together, they founded a company for exterminating rats. That's how he met Shireen, a French archaeology scholar of Lebanese descent, who came to Beirut to take part in the reconstruction. Ha! Reconstruction of what? Shireen fell in love with Luqman, and he, for his part, considered her a prize catch, a means of expunging his record and starting life again, with a new identity in a distant country. He strove desperately to make her fall in love with him, and he achieved his aim. She went ahead to Paris in order to arrange his paperwork and then send for him.

Two days before Luqman left to meet her, Mr. N was going mad. How could he let him go? How could he let him get away? "Everyone like Luqman is getting off scot-free," people consoled Mr. N. "Just look around. This one, at least, looks like he might be able to turn over a new leaf . . . " But no, Mr. N lost it. Did they really believe a murderer could change? When did the ones he murdered get a chance to start over? When did they get new lives? And people wanted to give him a free pass after everything he's done? All the things he's blown up or stolen, all the human beings he put in the ground? "A general amnesty," they told Mr. N, and: "Let's turn the page on the war and begin a new chapter." A new chapter? Really?

A new chapter starring the same vile criminals, thieves, and butchers? Did they think even God could forgive what was past? Well, maybe so—but not I! I've never forgiven, and I never will.

Mr. N couldn't believe how strange other people considered it that he refused to reconcile, that he insisted on a reckoning and an interrogation of the past, insisted on seeing that everyone who had committed deliberate, premeditated murder and who had turned the survivors' lives into a living hell should pay for it. He spent forty-eight hours turning things over in his head, pacing back and forth across his room, finally climbing the walls and bouncing off the ceiling, trying to think. He came up with a plan, but just as quickly replaced it with another. Meanwhile, time rushed on, the war receded, and Luqman was getting ready to travel. He was packing his things, saying goodbye to his friends, and answering phone calls from Shireen, who followed along—long-distance—with each and every step he took. As the sun set, Mr. N was at the railing of his beloved balcony, still thinking. The other buildings were all asleep, the defiant tower was quiet, the street was empty. If only Mr. N could take the only logical step. If only he could end the murderer's life ...

At the internet café, Mr. N flinched when the tiny trickle of natural light coming through the front door was suddenly blocked. The shadow fell upon the back of the Egyptian employee, making him jump up from his desk. All the young men present ceased their typing and chatting to call out a greeting. Then a smothering stillness settled over the room as the new presence made itself felt. Mr. N could hear nothing now but the sound of the ceiling fans, their metal blades turning upon their axles, trying to encourage the café's air to become a breeze.

Luqman had arrived early that day.

———

When Sa'id came in and greeted him, Mr. N's hair was still wet, and he was still wearing his white, short-sleeved undershirt. Miss Zahra let Sa'id in after knocking lightly on the door and leading the way. Once inside, she hung a large plastic garment bag in Mr. N's wardrobe. She was still wearing Thurayya's scent, thought Mr. N, and for the first time, he felt a kind of hatred for her, a violent desire to kick her and push her out of the room. But she quickly withdrew without such encouragement, which was a good thing.

Sa'id was as tall as ever. He kissed his brother's head from above and remained standing over Mr. N, frowning. His face was wan and stubbly, which was unusual for him. He looked around at the room and put his hands into his pockets. "I hope being here is making you happy," he said. "Do they treat you well? You know your stay is costing me a considerable sum."

Mr. N nodded and was about to reply, "Which you're paying out of our father's estate!" But he checked himself. Oh well. Let Sa'id flex his muscles to show how important and influential he was.

"You'll have to get dressed," Sa'id went on. "I brought your suit from the apartment. I hope it still fits."

What did he mean? Get dressed for what? Didn't he know that Mr. N refused to leave the hotel these days? And that he hadn't done so for a long time now? Whenever Sa'id came by, he offered to take Mr. N out to lunch or dinner, and Mr. N refused the invitation just as consistently as it was offered. Sa'id didn't insist, and Mr. N didn't need to repeat his refusal. It happened once a year at most. Whenever Sa'id came to visit, he would never stay longer than an hour. The two of them spent half their time together watching television; the other half Mr. N spent listening to Sa'id talk about himself.

Mr. N blinked his eyes at his brother a few times before saying, "You know I don't go out. Why do you insist on inviting me somewhere every time you're here?"

Sa'id said, "Thurayya... She died the day before yesterday, and I've come to bury her."

Mr. N leapt from his chair, knocking it back, then tripped over it and nearly fell on top of it. He felt as though his spinal cord had been cut. He wanted to ask how and why and whether she had been alone. But Mr. N's mouth was dry, his tongue stiff as stone, and he was unable to move his lips, not even to utter a single syllable.

Sa'id went to the wardrobe and swung open its double doors. He took out the garment bag that Miss Zahra had brought in and threw it on Mr. N's bed. Silently, efficiently, like an automaton, he opened the zipper and removed a jacket, followed by some pants, a white dress shirt, a black tie, and finally a leather belt. Setting everything to one side, he returned the hanger and the bag to the wardrobe. Then he took a pair of socks out of a drawer, and pulled a pair of black shoes with laces from underneath the bed. That done, he took off his own jacket and slung it over a chair. He reached over and opened the window because sweat had started running down his temples and his armpits. A sour odor filled the room, the kind that would invade the apartment whenever Sa'id came back dripping from one of his workouts, muscles gleaming with perspiration. Thurayya would hurry to dry him off with a towel, calling for Mary to drop whatever she was doing and draw a bath for him. Yes, Thurayya, Sa'id's mother: she was the one who had died the day before yesterday, alone in the old folks' home, without any friends or family around her.

Sa'id took in the sight of Mr. N frozen in the middle of the room, staring at the floor. Then Sa'id checked his watch. If he allowed his little brother to move at his own pace, they'd be late for the burial. He took charge and began dressing him, just as he used to do when N was a child—and Mr. N let him do it, just as he'd done when he was that child. Sa'id threaded one of Mr. N's arms through a shirtsleeve, then he crossed behind his brother to do the other. Satisfied, he started on the buttons, moving from the top down.

When their father left them, so to speak, this was precisely how Sa'id had positioned himself to do up N's necktie. N was nine, Sa'id sixteen. Thurayya had been too preoccupied with the ideal forms her own grief might take—what to wear, how to do her hair, and whether to put a black scarf over her head or not—to pay much attention to her boys. Her stylist, Isa, hurried to find her, as did her tailor, Angel, and many of her friends—those she felt she could trust with the news of her widowhood, and who she thought would behave well under the circumstances. N sat alone in his room, not wanting to see anyone. Mary kept looking in on him from time to time, afraid for him. She brought him water to drink and used some to wipe his face. "God protect you, my dear," she said, concerned. "How could he not think about you . . . " And then, with tears, she added, "What have you done, poor Doctor!"

N—though he was not called N at that time—had been sitting in the office with his father when it happened. It was a Sunday, one of those depressing Sundays that neither adults nor children know how to use. His father was behind his desk, his eyes glued to a book lying open in front of him, and N's eyes were glued to his father.

At first, he thought his father was playing a game. He sometimes pretended to be a statue, then moved as soon as N came near, making N jump in fright and run away, squealing. N had snuck through the door and was sitting on the leather sofa in the corner, holding in his laughter with both hands and pressing his back into the cushions. The leather was smooth, soft, and cool on his bare legs below his shorts. It took some time before N decided that his father wasn't playing with him but was entirely absorbed in whatever he was reading. The waiting made N sleepy, and he dozed off for some seconds or minutes—he didn't know how long—until he was woken by the noise his father made by standing up and scraping his heavy chair over the tiles. N looked at the clock on the wall; the hands pointed to 10:25.

His father said nothing. Didn't sigh or hold his breath. He wasn't panting and his chest didn't heave. All he did was get up on a chair, open the window, and go through it. He stepped forward confidently, as though the air itself would hold his weight and let him walk through the void. He stepped and fell, just like that, fast and easy. N heard him hit the ground, and he went over to the window to look. His father was lying on the sidewalk, his face pointed up, eyes half-open, a thread of blood running from his nose and mouth. His right leg was folded inward; the left was straight but twisted at the ankle, broken. His arms too looked both straight and twisted. How had he managed to step out as he had and land on his back rather than his stomach? Had he twisted around in midair because he was afraid to meet the ground head-on? Or because he wanted to be found with his eyes open? Or because he wanted to give a farewell glance to where Thurayya was sleeping in the next room? In any case, with his exit through the window, N's father had left his life. He'd left Thurayya, Sa'id, and N. He had left his pain, his disappointment, his failures, and his sickness of heart. He had treated the ill and taken away their pain until his own blood went bad.

When the doorbell rang, and he heard movement and muffled shouts, N knew that someone had come to inform them. He ran to his room and locked the door. He didn't want to receive the news confirming that what he had witnessed wasn't a dream. His father hadn't hesitated for a second. He hadn't spent a single moment thinking about N, caring about the presence of a child on the sofa in the corner of the room. It was as though he had departed some time earlier, and all that remained was for his body to catch up. The doctor had been depressed for years, it was true. Thurayya went on shining brilliantly while her husband hesitated and faded. She felt compassion for him and treated him well, but she had begun living where he was not.

The people came in waves to offer their respects to the deceased. Thurayya extended her hand to those she knew and recoiled from shaking hands with those she had always shunned—which is to say, the ones who used to come to see her late husband, doctor to the poor. They came in wearing their cheap clothes and their worn-out shoes and offering generous prayers for the soul of the departed. Men in red, black, and white kaffiyehs; women, veiled and unveiled, carrying their children, some suckling their babes in full view of the other visitors. Porters, villagers, day laborers, refugees, and foreigners: they came timidly and left with eyes streaming.

Thurayya's cheeks reddened and her blood pressure rose. She gave a signal for Mary to get on with bringing out the coffee so that the masses might "get off my imported carpets and my velvet couches" as soon as possible. Then she made up her mind that, for the funeral on the following day, she would put out chairs on the landing, which was large enough to hold any number of people. The mourners would be many, and the apartment wasn't big enough for all of them. In the early morning, wooden and wicker chairs arrived in a truck that stopped at the entrance to the narrow street. They were carried up just four flights of stairs and arranged in rows, side by side, in front of small, low tables bearing ashtrays and boxes of white facial tissues. Thurayya directed Mary to greet new arrivals in front of the apartment at the top of the stairs, and to seat "those people" outside, on the landings, while respectable people of any standing would be brought into the salon. She summoned two waiters to take over Mary's normal role of preparing and serving coffee.

N went out to the landing, and no one in the salon called him back. He sat beside Mary, not talking and not telling anyone that he had witnessed his father's suicide. He hid the matter for a long time; he was still hiding it now. For his father to have killed himself in N's presence was too much to endure.

For his father to have let go of N's little hand forever and jumped; for his father to have left N sitting in the corner, just like that, and jumped; for his father to know that N had no real family but him and yet still to jump; for his father to know that he was forever abdicating the role of N's father, ensuring that N would never again be a son to anyone for the rest of his life.

It wasn't that Thurayya treated his father badly, though it was very likely that she had a lover. After the doctor's death, however, Thurayya refused to marry her other man in order to spite the one who had dared to leave her, her and the two children—and also so it could not be said that the doctor had done himself in because of her, and so that no one could possibly find fault in her performance as a widow. She cried for days and looked good in mourning. She chose a black dress that left her neck exposed, revealing its slender profile. She was splendid in her sadness, like some actress from the golden age of Hollywood. That's how she saw herself, and that's how others saw her. She kept her head held high. You could see the two tendons on the sides of her neck, long and taut, looking as though they alone were keeping her head from rolling off in sorrow.

Thurayya would always say that the war was what killed her husband. She would tell how he had escaped a terrible massacre, and how he made it home and told her he had seen the face of the killer, knew his name, and that even so, the man had not opened fire upon him. No! cried Mr. N in his heart: you are the one who killed him with your neglect and your betrayal. You are the one who sparked a war inside him.

———

Children come according to their mothers' stories about them. A mother loads her child down with fairy tales, nothing more, and then sends him out to the world—either full and self-sufficient or else lacking and deficient forever. My brother, Sa'id, was born already bearing a story that told him he was unique and destined to shine, that he was the smartest and most beautiful. I, however, barged my way into life, uninvited, unwanted, the supernumerary son; which perhaps is why I clung so tight to the womb. Just the opposite of my three sisters, whom Thurayya claimed miscarried in their second and third months. And whenever anyone worked up the courage to ask her how she was so sure they were female, Thurayya would shiver with anger and swear that she was certain of it because of maternal intuition, the same intuition that made her realize even before she saw my face that I wouldn't look like my brother or have any of his virtues. Sometimes, when life feels too much for me, I find myself replaying that moment when the midwife dropped me in Thurayya's hands and she discovered that I was a boy. She, who said she wanted it to be a girl after Sa'id; I, who think she didn't want anything at all after Sa'id. I picture her look of disappointment, irritation, and grief when she saw me, unplanned, unwanted, and unloved. A moment that I can't remember, of course, but the scene is nonetheless as vivid as if seared into my flesh. I can even see the moment she first looked at me like a thing, some object she had no need for and for which she could think of no specific use. A tumor working its way into her system and threatening her existence. Yes. Thurayya treated me as though I were an intruder in her life. And I treated myself as though I were an intruder upon life itself . . .

Mr. N opened the drawer where he kept his pencils. He didn't like the one in his hand. It was some cheap model that required him to press down harder than he liked in order to make the words clear—not to mention the fact that the thing slowed him down and hurt his fingers. He had explained to Miss Zahra exactly what type of pencil he wanted, Faber-Castell 2B, and she had brought him a box of this Chinese junk that barely wrote. He took out the box, replaced the one he was holding, and threw the whole package in the wastebasket. But no, he thought, she might not see it there. She ought to realize what she's done wrong. So he took the box back out and dumped out the six pencils inside. He broke them, one after another. Then he set them beside the box on the table so she would notice them as soon as she entered. Miss Zahra had clearly forgotten who he was, had forgotten that she was there to carry out his requests. She needed to be cut down to size. He was the customer there, she was the employee, and the customer is always right. He had explained to her exactly how pencils were classified. He had taken out a piece of paper and written:

9H . . . 4H 3H 2H H F HB B B1 2B 3B 4B 5B 6B . . . 9B
(*Lighter*)   (*Darker*)

And she had folded the piece of paper and put it in her pocket so as not to forget. Nevertheless, she had forgotten or ignored it. It's true that Mr. N had taken a liking to her; that she was good and kind to him; that he sometimes surprised himself by dreaming the kind of dreams about her that made him wake up embarrassed and damp. But the episode of her taking his papers without permission was sufficient to make

Mr. N reevaluate their relationship. As did her perfume and her other recent lapses.

With his last remaining Faber-Castell 2B pencil, which he had sharpened so many times that it was no longer than his pinky, Mr. N scratched out his frustration with Miss Zahra and resumed writing:

Sa'id dressed me in the black suit. It was a little too tight for me around the middle. I sucked in my stomach and told him, "Button it! Button the pants!" Then I put on the belt so the button wouldn't pop off and get lost on the floor. He knotted the tie around my neck. Then he moved me back a little to get a good look at me before brushing off some specks of dust he saw on my shoulders. "Ready?" he asked, tears in his eyes. I frowned at him. I felt that my feet were starting to sink into the tiles. "What's wrong with you?" Sa'id asked. "Answer me. Are you ready?" I shook my head and retreated. I was having trouble breathing. Chest heaving, I felt I was working too hard just to take in tiny quantities of air. "It's alright," Sa'id said, closing the distance between us. "Just loosen the belt. You've made it too tight." He undid my belt, unbuttoned the pants, and sat me down on the chair. "Don't worry," he said. "We'll go right down to the market and buy you a suit that fits better. It won't take us more than half an hour, trust me." I nodded. Then I shook my head. I felt liquid running down my face, and I didn't know if it was sweat or what. Sa'id was losing patience. "What's wrong with you?" he asked again. "This is no time for tears. We have to bury Thurayya. Come on. Get up and wash your face. We're going to be late."

I went into the bathroom and locked the door. Sa'id was still telling me to hurry, but I took off my clothes and refused to come out. Naked, I stood in front of the mirror and whispered, "Please make Sa'id leave now!" Sa'id gave me a moment and then he began pounding on the door. "Come on, N! Let's go! What did I do to deserve a brother like you?"

I couldn't bear that from him, couldn't bear for him always to be complaining about me—he, whom life had never shortchanged, a prince unaccountably born into a family of neurotics. "And what do you think I did to deserve Thurayya?" I shouted at him. "And to deserve you and our father? Just go! I don't want to hear about any of you ever again!"

Sa'id made no reply. I could hear him breathing on the other side of the door, just opposite where I stood. Then I heard his footsteps as he walked away. I heard him put on his jacket, leave the hotel room, and close the door behind him. I didn't emerge from the bathroom in case it was a trap. But why would he bother trying to trick me? Sa'id knew better than anyone that Thurayya was never a mother to anyone besides him. He came to pick me up so it wouldn't be said he hadn't informed his younger brother of her passing. Now, I told myself, he would say that I had refused to attend, and no one would blame him. I alone would be the one to blame, same as always. Sa'id was the social one. He was good with people. Pleasant to have around and easy to talk to. Witty. Smart. N, on the other hand? Naïve, silent, sulky, cautious, shy. When someone was bullying me, yelling at me, mistreating me, Sa'id would listen in silence, never breathing a word of protest. Instead, he calculated what he stood to lose by interfering: things you'd think were of trifling value compared to brotherhood. Yes, people were mean to me, and he never got upset or defended me. Indeed, he would hide a satisfied smile, for his ego inflated and swelled in direct proportion to the degree that I shrank. I couldn't understand why Sa'id was jealous of me. He was the favorite. He was the pampered son, whose least request was never refused. In everything he did, Thurayya supported him, indulged him, cheered him on, while she hardly ever noticed me or praised me—I who was smarter and more studious than Sa'id, I who had been head of my class for years. There wasn't a single day that Sa'id declined to play the role Thurayya had written for him. Not only did he perform it to her exact requirements, he relished it and began chewing the scenery. He never once told Thurayya to stop, and he never once defended me, his little brother. He enjoyed his authority, and he didn't want to lose even a scintilla of his distinction, even if it meant trampling me on his path to success. To this day, I don't understand his attitude. How was he able to stomach such favoritism? To not only stomach it but swallow it whole, to really see himself as royalty both by nature and by birth? If I had been in his place, I would have choked on the injustice of it, the flagrant unfairness. I would have put a stop to it . . .

As for me, I didn't dare stand up to Thurayya—not as a boy, not as a teenager, and not as an adult. It was her lack of love that crippled me and made me weak before her . . . and toward everyone else too, come to think of it. In abandoning us, my father deprived me of my final stronghold. I was afraid of Thurayya and her fits of anger that came so unexpectedly. I didn't know what caused them or how to weather them, apart from hiding in corners and behind doors until she calmed down. Which meant living my entire childhood in corners. That's where my character was truly formed, and it's where I remain. My brother, Sa'id, was the opposite, of course. He did everything he could to occupy the center. Thurayya loved that about him, and made room for him wherever she went. She pushed me to the corner and him to the center, erasing me from her sight. She would praise Sa'id for resembling her and wonder aloud how I could possibly be related to her. She'd say he was born to lead, to be in charge, and how, from the very first, he was white and perfect as the full moon, with a high brow, a full head of shiny black hair, and eyes that were blue and wide as though the sky itself had taken root in them. She said that drums had been pounded, desserts distributed, and guns fired to proclaim that a son had been born unto the family. She worked herself into a tizzy telling the story of how the Virgin had come to her during the pregnancy, informing her that she would receive a gift to delight her heart and paint the name of Thurayya in gold.

I found that last claim of hers very odd when I was a child, pondering over it for years. What did it mean for a mother to have her name painted in gold? Children tend to bear their fathers' names, not their mothers'. Later, though, I understood: Thurayya loved winning, but she also loved winners. Neither I nor my father had ever won anything, but Thurayya saw from the start that my older brother suited her to a tee, more than compensating for her disappointment in the two of us. And she was right. Today, Sa'id is a first-class winner. He owns a giant company that has branches in some of the most important world capitals. His picture occupies the front pages of papers that carry the news of the rich and famous. He married a woman from a family of noble descent, quite worthy of Thurayya, who became grandmother to two lovely granddaughters and a magnificent grandson, given the name Sa'id Junior by his father.

Yes. Children come according to their mothers' stories about them. A mother loads her child down with fairy tales, nothing more, and then sends him out to the world—either full and self-sufficient or else lacking and deficient forever. My own story began with Thurayya's disappointment that I wasn't a girl, then her frustration that my skin was so dark, my eyes black, that I came out with hair on my face, and that my birth weight was so paltry. All this frustration compelled Thurayya to refuse me her breast when I was born, because, as she said, I most certainly couldn't have sprung from her loins but was someone else's baby, swapped for her own. The proof? That I didn't look like my brother. And Thurayya said all of this in front of me, without batting an eye. Half-smiling, she'd then relate how the nun in charge had rebuked her and compelled her to feed me after I was washed and dressed and my hair was combed. I took in the story of my birth without feeling much of anything, since it was forbidden for me to be sad, reproachful, or angry, in case Thurayya might get annoyed and so become sick.

And when Thurayya did get sick, even though he knew we could hardly have been the cause of her illness—an illness of some mysterious variety we could never quite identify—my father, who never lost his temper with us, would lose his temper. His anger would be diluted with a deep sadness when Thurayya informed him, so improbably, that we were behind her fatigue and the decline in her health. Because we wouldn't comply with her wishes, she said; we didn't obey her, and we showed so little respect. As for this "we," which included me, it should have been directed only at my brother, seeing as I was far more a child of the corners, the shadows, the silent, shameful hiding places of the apartment, than I was her son. Nevertheless, my father would scold and threaten to punish me, with hardly a glance at Sa'id, who ignored my father right back. Then he would order the two of us off where he wouldn't have to look at us anymore, but my mother, in the meantime having been overcome by regret and compassion, would order my father to go after us and bring Sa'id back, at least, because he hadn't had his dinner yet. She was worried, she said, because Sa'id was looking a little too pale lately. And my father would do it, and Sa'id would return to our mother triumphantly, as always, while I remained a prisoner in my room, where the doctor of the poor would eventually take pity on me, take me on his lap and hug me, and offer me fruit or candy, which I would refuse, not being hungry. Then he would pick me up and put me to bed, since he knew he shouldn't keep Thurayya waiting too long.

Despite all the gaps in my memory, I remember—and always will remember—how hard I tried to rise to even the lowest verge of the image Thurayya clearly would have preferred to see in me, thinking that maybe she would be satisfied and love me a little if I could manage it. After I had my own little nervous breakdown as a child, and after

Mary arrived, I realized that Thurayya couldn't bear the idea of having a sick child, even if the sick one was me, so I became a healthy boy, obedient, kind, and content. I lost my appetite, and the desire to disappear overwhelmed me, a disgust with both speaking and eating, though I pretended quite the opposite in Thurayya's presence. Then I started doing so well in school that I was first in my class, year after year. I brought home awards and certificates of distinction, but Thurayya would turn away, saying only that she knew already that I was smart, that there was no need to elaborate. Meanwhile, I read in her eyes the regret that Sa'id wasn't the one who could achieve such excellence and bring home those grades.

Whenever she had company over, she went on and on, praising Sa'id in my presence, giving elaborate descriptions of his small triumphs, while I would listen contentedly, happy about my older brother, waiting for my turn to come, convinced that this time she surely wouldn't ignore whatever I'd just accomplished, sitting as I was directly opposite her. Except my turn didn't come, and it never came a single day as far as she was concerned. Even when she grew gentler and weaker, when my father left us for his grave, and then my brother left us to make his fortune, and I alone remained with her, happy that I now finally had the opportunity to get close to her and win her heart . . . even then I couldn't win. Almost at once, she started forgetting my name and calling me by his. She would kiss my hands as they fed her, and take hold of my arms as they supported her. And if I asked, in her moments of clarity, "Who am I?" she would smile and say, "You are my father." I would tell her, "No, I'm your son," and she would reply, joyfully, "Of course! You are Sa'id." And when I corrected her, when I said, "No, not Sa'id," she would begin sobbing, "You don't love me anymore."

We all have a spot on our backs that is vulnerable to loss, where love and security can leak out. They're square, these areas, the size of a hand, cut into the middle of that smooth, flat surface of our body, where all our nerves, all our feelings, all our longings are exposed. A secret panel that grants entrance to the heart for reassurance, or its absence, to spread within. When we are born, and our first sob makes us realize that we have entered this vale of tears, the doctor lays us on our mother's breast for her to press the palm of her hand onto that spot. That's how the heart is unsealed, how the lungs begin working. Oxygen comes in, our organs throb with life. But when a mother doesn't put her hand on that secret spot in her child's back to rub and massage and caress, the baby isn't let off the hook, no: life itself steps in to keep its pulse moving, like those machines we plug our hopeless cases into so as to prevent them from leaving this world too soon . . . and the child becomes just another digit in life's tally, without an identity or family of its own.

Me? You've probably guessed that no mother pressed her hand onto that special spot on my back. She neither kissed nor nursed me. She suffered me to live in her vicinity, that's all. Perhaps my father took an interest in me, inasmuch as fatherhood allows, but a father's hand is not the lifeline that can save the little creature who's been floating inside his mother's belly for nine months . . .

II

I am Mr. N.

Son of a distraught doctor and of Thurayya, cruel and unfeeling as a rock. Brother of Sa'id, the shining one. And master of Mary . . . the true virgin. On this day, at 10:25, writing my story, my second birth is taking place. My pencil spins around in a game of truth or dare. It comes to a halt, pointing at me. My turn. So I've decided not to swallow all those pills that Miss Zahra brings me. I'll hold them in my mouth and then secretly spit them out. In their place, I'll blacken a number of white pages.

Thurayya—and I'll keep calling her Thurayya, even if she's the one who gave me birth—kept me at a distance from the time I was born. The spot on my back remained closed and clandestine; it didn't respond no matter how often loving hands tried to trick it later on. And the truth is, I never once called her Mother, because I was no son to her and she no mother to me. Nevertheless, her name is present on my ID card because she is my biological mother. What it all boils down to is that she squeezed me out of her body like a turd, only to pinch her nose and turn away.

Meanwhile, Thurayya fed skinny Sa'id from her own hand, making up funny games to get him to eat more, urging and cajoling him to drink his juice. When he was finished, she would look at me, annoyed, as though only then and unwillingly did she remember I was there. She would spoon out a bit more food beside whatever Sa'id hadn't eaten and drop the plate in front of me. "Eat," she'd say as she left the room, and it didn't matter to her one bit whether I did or didn't, what I ate or how much, even though she knew quite well that I suffered from a poor appetite and would sometimes refuse to eat for days. It was Mary who got me fed. I would go to the kitchen, carrying my plate, and Mary would sit me down at the table, taking a seat close by. She would begin talking to me, saying anything at all to extract the lump that was caught in my throat and prevented my food from going down. She'd pour me a cup of water and invite me to drink a little, placing her hand on my back, right on that spot that might loosen what was tied up and locked away inside me. I would forget, and I would eat, listening to her stories about the friends she'd seen at mass, about the presents her family in the village had sent her because her little N liked them, and all the strange tales she'd heard as a child about the jinn and the ifrit. Mary would pull me toward her, and I'd feel myself pressed against her heart, sitting still on my chair. She'd raise the spoon to my mouth, and I'd give in. Everything turned into airy cotton candy and melted away, leaving sticky traces on my lips. I'd eat absentmindedly and become full before even tasting my food. I would feel heat stealing into my limbs like someone sitting beside a blazing hearth after being cold for so long, when warm drowsiness gradually thaws their body. Mary would pick me up when she saw my eyelids droop and my head start to lean. She'd hold me against her and gently rock me in a rhythm that sent me into a deep, undisturbed slumber. And if I did wake after a while, I would find myself in my own bed as the orange of the sunset slipped through the blinds.

Mary wasn't aware of the story of my secret spot, but all the same, her rough hand would move automatically to my back. A numbness would steal through my entire body, and I'd forget the pain that Thurayya had caused. Mary would take me onto her lap; into her world; into her smell, redolent of exotic grasses, wild thyme, and olive oil soap; into her hoarse voice; into her bed, lined with cotton and wool and pictures of the saints. I would almost forget that I—the child she served, for whom she worked so hard and on whose behalf she feared—wasn't her child. I played tricks on her when she was busy with housework, going up to her and pretending that something had stung me on the back. She'd quickly drop whatever she was doing to raise my shirt and make sure nothing was there. Then she would stretch out her fingers and begin rubbing my back with her coarse palm, not with her nails, which were cut short, as Madame Thurayya had instructed. When Mary saw that this treatment relaxed me, made me sleepy, that it gave me back my appetite, that it alleviated my depression somewhat, she began using it for my anxiety and insomnia whenever I woke up crying or refused to eat or when sleep eluded me entirely, on days when Thurayya's persecutions became even worse.

I never opened up or expressed myself, but instead swallowed all my words and choked on them. That's why I refused to eat, refused to speak, refused to obey. My father, the doctor, took me to pediatricians who diagnosed me with various

me? But no, to see a second boy come out of her made me meaningless in her eyes, a repetition, a defective copy, with no connection to its point of origin.

I told Neda about all this one time when I was drunk. I started crying and became delirious, talking about that secret spot on my back! She pulled me toward her, peeled off my shirt and stood behind me. With her finger, she traced the square between my shoulder blades and pressed her lips to its center. I felt a hole opening there and imagined a strange feather floating out. Which is to say that I felt as though my heart was being torn out from behind. Neda was a colleague at the college where I gave lectures on creative writing to children who dreamed they might become writers one day, even though they didn't have the talent, resolve, or stubbornness required to assure anything of the sort. I taught them and strove desperately to convey something of the meaning of literature until I began to feel for them what Thurayya must have felt for me. When I told this to Neda, she advised me to resign. Easily persuaded, I resigned, justifying my decision as a desire to devote myself entirely to my writing. Neda was the only person to whom I disclosed my secrets: this one, that one, and all the rest. Even so, when she dumped me, she selected the bag closest to hand—Victoria's Secret—as the receptacle into which she would toss my secrets in order to return them to me. And then she was gone, after telling me that I was weighing her down, that she could no longer carry me along with her.

Thurayya, Neda, Miss Zahra . . . That's the story of my luck with women. No, there's Mary too. My own Virgin Mary, whom no man's hand had touched, and who carried me in her heart and filled my need for a mother. Yes, and Shaygha, the little woman who loved me, and whose memory still makes my heart bleed after all these years. And then there was that blessed angel who fell from the sky and screamed at the mob thronging around me to go away when I would have choked on the tears forming in my eyes. She screamed and shook with emotion, as though I were hers, had come from her, as though she knew me and had only stumbled across me on her way as I lay prostrate on the ground. She only had to push them away and bend over me for her dark hair to pour down like cooling water upon my head and face, which were boiling with violence and the burning sun. "What are *you* doing here?" I would have asked, had I known her, but she was a stranger. She put her hand on my mouth to wipe away the dirt. "Don't be afraid!" she said. "I'm here with you, and I won't let anyone else get close to you." I nearly laughed as I listened to her reassuring me in her soft voice. "Are you an angel?" I asked, struggling to get the words out through the intensity of the pain. Then I grabbed her hand and squeezed. It was soft and warm as a sparrow. She called an ambulance and waited with me until it arrived. Her presence protected me and kept away the bullies. They hadn't actually scattered out of fear, but in confusion and surprise at the sight of that woman who appeared out of nowhere. They were uncertain about her exact connection to me, and they could only assume that the woman—who didn't resemble that place or its residents or its smell—was there with me. They forgot the trouble they had so recently stirred up and became spectators, watching the elegant, beautiful lady, who looked like the ones they saw in advertisements and on TV—pure and misty, as though someone had erected a filter to separate her from the land of reality where the rest of us existed.

When the EMTs picked me up to take me to the hospital, I tried to lift my head, which was strapped down on the stretcher. I caught just a glimpse of her. She looked like a lost child searching for her parents in a crowd, and I thought then that she was the one who needed help, not I. But the harsh, metallic sound of the siren overwhelmed me, and I lost consciousness.

———

The first blow landed right on my face. It seemed to have been aimed at my ear, since it left behind a ringing that quickly became a rock skipping over the surface of the water, making ripples that expanded out into infinity. The blow didn't actually fall on my ear itself but rather just in front of it. From there, its force had resounded through my eardrum, then my brain, and then my spinal column.

At first, I couldn't really process all that, nor whether the punch sent my way had something to do with my knowing Luqman, or his knowing me, as I can only now assume. I just heard a wave of sound rising around me, rising and then falling. I didn't turn toward the source, but instead contracted within myself and made myself small, to avoid doing anything that might further aggravate the crowd. But as soon as I recovered from the impact, panic set in, and I hurried blindly in the very direction from which the blow had originated. I was caught by another, though, that knocked me backward and got my skull acquainted with the stone curb. My eyes crossed and blood gushed hot from the back of my head. The locus of the pain stayed sharp and confined—it condensed rather than spread.

I tried to raise my arm to feel around the wound and to offer it whatever protection I still could, but I didn't have the strength. A dizziness came over me like a puddle of oil and I felt mired in it. It was only seconds before a foot smashed into my flank. My body curled back up. "God!" I screamed. It felt as though a small cluster bomb had passed through my ribs and exploded in my side. I gasped, trying to suck in some atoms of oxygen from the air that had been knocked out of me, but my chest contracted, my windpipe was blocked, and I lost consciousness.

In theory, anyway, that's what happened, though I couldn't take it all in at the time. It was only when I regained consciousness that I knew I had fainted, and I heard the trembling voice of my angel repeating, "Don't be afraid! I'm here with you." My angel, whose unsteady hand grasped my own, had white, manicured fingernails, with rings of pearls and diamonds on her delicate fingers. She had honey eyes, rich chestnut hair with golden strands of various hues, and a voice like water that glittered as it bubbled from the spring. Her scent was a mixture of wet grass and lemon and apple blossoms. I closed my eyes and breathed deep. When I opened them again, I saw Luqman, solid and dark, standing with his back against a wall, smoking a cigarette and watching us. I remembered how they had chased me out of his shop and sent me flying, as though the many hands and feet of the crowd were the limbs of one single, impossible creature

103

conjured for just that purpose. Then the angel appeared, and they scattered.

Luqman watched her. His mouth was watering, same as it always did when it came to women. And he spared a glance for me as well, stretched out on the pavement, right down where he wanted me to be. And that's when he decided to peel his back off the wall and call to his Egyptian employee to bring him two glasses of water. After bending over to wash my face and let me drink, Luqman offered the second glass to the angel. She accepted it gratefully and drank to calm her fright while the ambulance siren got louder and louder.

In the ambulance, while the EMTs were busy taking my blood pressure, examining my wounds, and wiping off the blood, I remembered that Luqman hadn't laid a hand on me. Never got close to me during the scrum. Hadn't thrown so much as a flower petal at me. All he did to me directly was shock me, deprive me of oxygen, as though the ceiling fans had ceased spinning when he first stepped through the door. His big body blocked the light coming from outside; the shop dimmed. The Egyptian employee jumped up from behind his desk to stand as straight as a spear; the young men sitting behind the computers stared at their screens as though they wanted to pass right through them in order to show they weren't wasting time but were busy playing the games that brought in the best profits for the owner of the shop.

Luqman had sat at his desk and appeared to be absorbed in many things, all of them taking place on or through his mobile phone. There were text messages received and answered, voice messages that he replied to with recordings of his own. It seemed like a suitable time for me to observe him, to follow his actions and his movements, and to hear his voice in case I might be able to dispel my suspicion that this was my very own Luqman, the person I invented one day to be the anti-hero of a grim novel—*Oh, Salaam!*—the events of which took place after the end of Lebanon's civil war. Even though my Luqman died at the end of the novel, perhaps that charlatan had played a trick on me and escaped my book to live free and forgotten for years. There was no other logical explanation for such a degree of similarity between the two individuals.

Looking him over, I saw he'd gotten thicker. The passage of each year had added a thin layer all over, but the bulk of that time had congealed in his belly. Other features had grown lean: the hair on his head, his eyebrows, the muscles in his forearms. I stared, scrutinizing him. Those two hands with their thick hair had acquired an unmistakable roughness, as well as a gold watch and a ring engraved with the cedar of Lebanon. Those same wide shoulders, which now stooped slightly. The broad chest with a gold chain hanging down. His head, but with white hair that was thinning at the top. Those were his wide, black eyes, though the lids had begun drooping a little, and they were framed with deep lines. That was the furrow between his eyebrows, now deeper and even more rugged. Yes, it was Luqman, if with the usual minor differences that the years tend to inflict upon someone's fading good looks.

And what about that inseparable "partner" of his? How was it hanging, Oh Luqman? I suppressed with difficulty a smile at how my Luqman had been so crazy about his penis that he'd begun addressing it as "partner," after previously calling it "comrade," a title he'd had to change in order to distinguish it from his other comrades, the ones he acquired in the war. He trusted that organ of his like he trusted no one else, and he would ask its advice about all his comings and goings, and of course particularly about any prospective adventures with women. Without it, he would never have been able to seduce a woman as hard to get as Shireen. And if I hadn't killed him, he would have gotten to Paris with her, as planned . . .

"How is it that I killed you," I wondered, "and yet here you are sitting in front of me, swiping your screen like a maniac?"

As for you, when you notice me staring and think you might know me, when you look closer to confirm whether you actually do, what details could you possibly rely on to make up your mind one way or the other? Not only have I gained weight too, I've lost my hair, and my features have swelled thanks to the side effects of all my medication. Sometimes, naked, I stand in front of the mirror and think about how Thurayya would vomit at the sight of me now, how the disgust would stay with her for weeks. I have the legs of an elephant, crisscrossed with protruding blue veins that knot together in places like small bunches of grapes. At the top of my thighs, there are two balls hanging down, supported by a fold where the skin doubles back on itself. (And I'm not talking about my testicles, which have disappeared completely between the flaps of flesh below my belly and above my thighs. Oh no. They're something else entirely.)

There's a kind of obesity that doesn't come from overeating but is the result, let us say, of indigestion of the heart. It swells like a sponge in your chest. Just when you think the sponge has drunk its fill of pain, it finds space for more. Your torso stores it up, your limbs store it up, and your features bloat and go soft, padded with fluids puddling inside and rippling in the wind. I have become an enormous sponge with two huge breasts, a big belly, and two misplaced testicles. Yes, I resemble a pachyderm, tormented by children and falling to its knees, its flesh torn and shredded.

Kareem, who was sitting near me, and whom I'd been using as a shield against Luqman's glances as I made my initial examination, pushed back his chair. Scratching his belly, he said, "I'm hungry. There's a sandwich shop nearby. They've got grilled meat, meatballs, grilled sausages, fried sausages, pretty much every kind of delicacy you could wish, all for thirty-five hundred lira a pop. I'm paying. What do you say?" I raised my eyebrows to show my surprise at such cheap sandwiches, nearly asking, "Do you know for sure that what you're eating is actually meat?" But I didn't dare speak given how nauseated the situation, and his offer, was making me feel. As though sensing my apprehension, Kareem went on to say, "The owner of the shop is a butcher who raises livestock and does his own butchering and selling. He still keeps that up, but he's converted the butcher shop into a cheap grilled snack shop, that's all."

I thanked Kareem for his invitation and made some quick excuse. I felt exposed when he stood up and left, just as I used to feel whenever I had to move away from the sandbags that protected the neighborhood families from the snipers positioned on nearby rooftops, and walk down the street "naked," out in the open and exposed to their bullets. But despite my shrinking, my contraction, and how I glued myself to the computer screen so that Luqman wouldn't notice my presence, the bullets of his eyes struck me full in the face when

I stole another glance. Our eyes met, and the color drained out of me as the terror flowed in. My throat went dry, and I trembled all over.

Luqman abandoned whatever he was doing and leaned against the leather back of his chair, reclining it all the way. He closed his hands over his belly and then cocked his head to one side as he openly examined my face, betraying no emotion. Then he nodded, squinted one eye, and smiled out of the corner of his mouth in a way that said, without speaking a word, "Well? What do you want?"

Feeling as though I'd been caught red-handed in some crime, I stood up and backed toward the door. Luqman didn't budge, but his small smile turned into a frown, and he inclined his head in a clear order to his crew: don't let this guy get away. The Egyptian ran at me and grabbed my shoulder, tugged on my arm, shaking me violently as though I were a tree whose fruit he wanted to knock to the ground. It was only seconds before I found myself surrounded by every other denizen of that café, and by other, faceless people who had popped up out of nowhere. Their proliferating hands seized me and squeezed tight, propelling me outside with shoves and fists, and then feet and knees, until one particularly sharp blow landed on my head and I lost consciousness.

———

Three noble trees, the beating heart at the center of the garden, reach their hands up to the perfectly full moon, making us feel as though we aren't strangers in this hotel, all alone.

There are some who would scorn my choice of words, and correct my sentence to treat the trees like inanimate objects, not like sisters. Yet whoever, like me, sees trees as living beings, beings possessed of some mysterious wisdom, will undoubtedly support my choice.

Through the window at the end of the long corridor, I see my three beautiful sisters clothed in green leaves, then yellow leaves, and then naked, with no leaves at all. Later, they come to life again in the midst of a garden filled with shrubs that create narrow pathways leading to open spaces adorned with stone benches and a few tables. The tree dearest to my heart is the smallest of the three, who, obeying the law of gravity, bends over and spreads her branches with sympathy, affection, and a desire to touch and connect. Whenever I can go down to the garden, under the secret cover of darkness after everyone has gone to sleep, when all sounds disappear and nothing is heard apart from the creeping of the shadows, I head straight to that tree and take her in my arms, embracing her trunk. I remain like that for hours, rubbing my face and body into the furrowed bark, and nothing can pull me away and send me back to my room except the breaking of dawn.

No one knows, and no one ever will, what trees mean to me. Someday, I will adopt a tree on a plain and spend the rest of my life in its shadow until I die, loyal to it for better and for worse. And one day, when I was still a tender bud of a boy, I asked my father, "Dad, why aren't I a tree?" He looked at me, surprised, and then avoided the question, giving my hand a yank to keep me moving. I came back to my question, insistent. I repeated my words, and then I shouted them, until my father slapped me and I burst into tears. It felt as though his slap had crumbled some part of a dam, and my tears were the floodwaters bursting out. But I wasn't crying because of the slap—I was crying because I knew that no one in the world had an answer for this question of mine. The next day, my father brought me a book and told me it was a beautiful story about a teenager named Cosimo di Rondò who decided to live his whole life in a tree. "Why?" I asked, and Sa'id growled, "Because he was crazy, like you." My father handed me the book and said, "To find out why, you just have to read it." So I read about a young baron who rebelled against his feudal father and decided to live far from his lands and his authority. Where? In the treetops. But the whole time I read it, I kept praying that Cosimo, who grew old without his foot once touching the ground, would himself be transformed into a tree.

Sleepiness was seeping into my legs, and I realized I must have been standing in front of the window for some time. Just as I was about to turn and go back to my room, two spectral figures came into view below me and began winding their way through the garden paths until they reached the three sisters. I was startled and stepped away from the window. Who could they be? Not only was it late, but the garden was off-limits to strangers. I took a careful look. A man and woman. No doubt homeless lovers, looking for a safe spot to spend the night. There they were, spread out on the ground under my small tree. They began taking from a tote bag various objects that I couldn't identify from that distance.

With the exception of my two neighbors from the next rooms, and of course Miss Zahra and Andrew, I had not seen many people in the garden. I had even expressed my surprise at the matter to Miss Zahra, who hastened to reply, "The garden is reserved for residents on the top floor." I personally went down only at night so as not to meet those two strange people: Daoud, whose frequent noisy quarrels with his mute wife had recently diminished; and Madame "*Al Dente*," or, better, "Al-*Dante*," as I might call her, who recited poetry and never despaired about her dinner invitations.

The man bent over and took something out of the bag. He began tossing whatever it was at the branches above his head. When he kept missing, he got up on the stone bench under the middle tree and repeated his attempt. The object in his hands gleamed. It looked like rope with a metal knot, and whenever it caught a fleeting glimmer, it flashed in the night. In the end, the man succeeded in looping his rope over one of the branches. He took both ends and made them even before pulling one end a meter and a half longer than the other. It was Daoud! I was able to make out his features when he turned and raised his face to make sure the rope was secure. Undoubtedly, the woman beside him was Al-Dante. Yes, her slender figure confirmed it. What are you doing, Daoud, in the pitch black, and how did you two get outside, from right under my nose? How did I not see you, even though I've been stationed here in the hallway this whole time? What is it you're doing behind my back in the shade of my three sisters?

A picture came back to me, from several weeks earlier, of Daoud slipping stealthily into the room opposite mine and then locking it eagerly behind him. I was annoyed because I had been about to go out to the garden when I saw him. At first, the whole situation appalled me. The man berates his mute wife and then crosses the hallway in order to betray her right under her nose? But then I was delighted. Mrs. Al-Dante was hanging her hopes on Daoud now, and I would be free from her dinner invitations! I thought they might be lovers, who would exhaust their last bits of desire on each other, just as my own desire had left me years ago, before its time, to the point that I could hardly remember what it was like before its desertion.

We men have our own age of despair, though having said that, I realize that my despair was never tied to any particular age. I was told repeatedly that the medication I've taken since I was young was a beta-blocker, which is to say detrimental to sexual desire. Desire would come along, and this medication would block it, preventing it from reaching me. Desire travels through our bodies without knowing what's waiting around the next corner—and then a roadblock brings it up short: "Out of the car, desire! Move! Hands behind your head! Face against the wall!" And all that happens in the ordinary course of events, in broad daylight. Desire collapses in terror, expecting to be shot in the back. And even if it isn't killed, desire loses its will to live. Over time, it shrinks and fades away like any unused muscle or organ. Daoud and Al-Dante, though, as I saw them in that moment—their desire was still alive and well. Good for them, I suppose. But, even still— why leave the building under the cover of night? They were consenting adults, with two apartments between them . . . What were they up to?

It occurred to me to go and wake up Andrew and set him loose on them. Then I imagined Andrew's severe expression, his no doubt violent reaction. His face always turned bright red when he was suppressing his anger or hiding some emotion, even if he managed to remain calm and mild on the whole. Then I thought about opening the window and surprising them, calling down so they would know I saw them and knew what they were planning, so they wouldn't go through with it out there in the open like that. But then there was the oddness of their showing up in the garden at this late hour of the night when they could easily have met in a private room . . . so I held my tongue.

Al-Dante sat on the stone bench. Her back was bent and her movements slow, like an old lady's. Daoud sat too and she took his hand, holding it in her lap before she stood right up again. He stood up with her. They shook hands. Then he pulled her into a violent embrace and kissed her hand before taking several steps back. The lady, who'd been as still as a painting or a shop-window mannequin when he clutched at her, turned. She lifted her dress and raised one leg in order to step up onto the stone bench, but her strength proved insufficient to the task. Her white skin looked like marble under the light of the moon. Daoud hurried forward to help her, jumping onto the bench himself and then wrapping an arm around her to lift her to his side. He whispered something to her then, insinuating it into her ear, a soft and sinewy serpent. She stood as though nailed in place, meek and motionless, while Daoud waited for a reply. Yet, in that moment, as far as I was concerned, both parties seemed to have finished performing their roles.

A fat mosquito landed on my forearm and planted its needle in my skin. I gave it as firm a smack as I could without making any sound that might give me away. The mosquito was crushed, and our blood was smeared across my hand and forearm. I grabbed one of its legs and raised it to the level of my eyes. "Do you see?" I asked it. "Don't look on this as misfortune. This is the right and proper punishment for all unrestrained greed." After all, it was an industrious mosquito that had already launched a number of raids and feasted all night. But instead of being satisfied and taking itself off to sleep, it had decided to mount one final attack, and so it fell to me to send it off to its eternal rest.

Our mosquitoes and other local insects have developed quite the work ethic in recent years. They toil now not only to feed themselves, but from the pleasure of causing pain, which, having tasted once, they find impossible to relinquish. Rats, mosquitoes, flies, cockroaches, feral cats, pariah dogs: all of them are vicious now and liable to get drunk on the simple taste of killing, much as humans do. Their transformation began during the civil war, when they first grew strong on the bodies of the slain, which were of course lying in the streets wherever they fell. Even when the calm years came, these creatures, having acquired this addiction to our flesh, wouldn't relent, and soon reached unprecedented levels of savagery. I could sit on my balcony and see rats scamper through streets and neighborhoods and onto balconies, where once such incursions would have been unthinkable. No longer bound within the poor, forgotten districts and the wretched suburbs, they spread their squalor even to the precincts of the wealthy. Then came the mosquito attacks. Legions of mosquitoes, against which pesticide sprays, mists, and tablets were useless. I tried every brand: Raid, B-Gone, Katol, Mosquito Killers, Fab . . . Next I turned to natural pesticides: white vinegar mixed with water and lemon juice, coffee beans burned on coals . . . I began putting essential oils on my skin, or letting them evaporate throughout the apartment. Nothing worked. In the end, I was forced to admit the futility of exterminating them all when I realized that the female mosquito lays eggs every ten days, and between one and two hundred each time. And if safe, warm conditions are available, the eggs hatch almost immediately. I lowered my expectations. I bought those glowing electric traps. The mosquitoes swarmed toward them, and the traps burned them up, giving off a short hiss with each killing. I hung one in my corner of the balcony, another in the salon, and a third in the kitchen. In the bedrooms, though, I ended up using fine-mesh mosquito nets, since the sound of the electric death machine drove the sleep out of my eyes.

Here in the hotel, I just use those little electric fumigators, nothing else, and someone comes every week to spray an insecticide that leaves behind the smell of diesel. Formerly, I used to be sure to close the windows when evening fell, to keep the mosquitoes from getting in. But after the town filled with garbage, piling up everywhere, it turned out the mountain wasn't a mountain after all, the Devil not a devil, and mosquitoes hardly the worst reason to suffocate all night with your windows shut. I became almost nostalgic for the days I kept my windows shut only on account of some bugs, and not those horrible smells.

Returning my attention to the garden, I found I hadn't missed a thing. There was Al-Dante still motionless, eyes still cast down. As though stirred back to life by my attention, Daoud now placed his hand on her shoulder. She nodded as though agreeing to something that had been discussed dozens of times and so needed no further words. At that, Daoud raised his arms and grabbed the rope. He formed a loop, which he placed around her head. It hung down to the top of her chest. He undid the knot and placed the end in what looked like a metal ring, which he closed. This time it was the right length, snug to her neck.

Pleased with himself, Daoud moved away to the edge of the bench. Then he changed his mind, took a step back, and grasped the upper loop of the rope, which he began inching higher on the branch so that it was beyond the edge of the bench beneath. It took me a minute to figure out what he was up to, but then I realized that the idea was for her to swing over the ground, not over the bench. Daoud raised his hand, this time in a salute, and then stepped back again to his former position. I watched intently. There was no threat in Daoud's look, nor any fear in Al-Dante's. What was this foolish game they were playing? Could they really be acting out such a disgusting pantomime at their age?

I felt bored and tired and hungry, and my stomach was growling. I considered what I should eat, since I had in my room only unappetizing leftovers from the hotel meals. No, there were some cookies I hadn't eaten, which Miss Zahra had left for me in the bread basket she kept in my room. Nice. I'd make a little tea to drink with them, with plenty of sugar. It would warm my stomach, and I'd go to bed satisfied.

I left the window, heading back to my room. But when I heard a cracking sound, I ran back to my spot to see Al-Dante swinging, twitching like a fish on a hook, thrashing her arms and legs as her eyes bulged up at the sky. At the sight of her distress, her gasping for breath, Daoud stepped up to grab her feet. But instead of lifting them to relieve the pressure on her neck, he took a deep breath and lifted his own feet off the ground, pulling her down with his full weight. Her neck gave a pop and she went still.

I held my breath, sweat spouting from my pores. My body tingled as though touched by an electric current. I crouched down out of sight. Then I raised my eyes to the level of the window and saw Daoud moving back, eyes fixed on the hanging woman, like someone sighting a better angle for a picture. After smoothing back his hair and straightening his shirt, he took a deep breath. Then I saw him bend over to pick something up. It was one of Al-Dante's shoes. He put it back on her foot as she dangled from the tree branch like the strange fruit of that famous song. He went on to smooth the pleats of her dress.

When he was sure that everything was in order, Daoud picked up the tote bag and slung it over his shoulder. Alone, he returned to the darkness whence he came. I watched his back as he moved away. From the rear, it was a dispiriting surprise—indeed, a terrifying one—to notice he was the same build as Luqman.

———

I woke up: limbs splayed, joints aching, eyes unfocused, and neck twisted at an odd angle. Rising with a groan, I made my way to the bathroom. I dropped my pants, and the great stream of urine had a foul, acrid odor and seemed never to end. That cleared my mind as well as my eyes, as if all that liquid had caused the problem by flooding my skull and eye

117

sockets. Back in my room, I stretched and rolled my neck to get my head back into place. I gathered up the papers that were scattered over the table, where I'd sat for what remained of the previous night, blackening so many with my scribbles. Successive dreams had come and gone after I collapsed into bed. I saw the ghost of my father, tearing hunks of flesh from Thurayya's face as worms dropped from the pieces. I saw Mary hovering in the air, robed in blue. I saw myself in Luqman's shop, being sucked through a computer screen as he held my feet and tried to hold me back. Then I saw Miss Zahra, naked, one hand over her breasts and another modestly held between her legs. She ran off, laughing, and I saw she had a long tail coiling and twisting behind her. I woke up during the night, damp with perspiration, and scribbled down what I had seen in my hazy stupor. I could not drink enough water to cool the burning those images produced in my throat.

Hearing a knock at the door, I gave permission to enter, and Miss Zahra appeared with a breakfast tray. Contrary to her usual practice, she was frowning, her nose and eyes were red, and her voice was subdued. "Mr. N," she said, wearily, "Andrew would like to see you in his office at exactly eleven o'clock." She turned to the clock, which read 10:25. "Eat your breakfast and get ready. I'll come back soon," she added, before closing the door behind her.

Miss Zahra wasn't wearing any perfume this time, and my scrambled eggs were delicious with the heat of coarse, freshly ground black pepper. The bread was soft and tasty too, just baked and still warm on the inside. My tea was sweet and satisfying. I sank into that delicious moment, without any question, idea, or concern pulling me away. Yes. With practice,

I had finally mastered the game of detaching myself, creating a safe little space for myself, where I felt distant, remote. When my father committed suicide, I told no one that I had been present, watching, an eyewitness to his final steps, which transformed his body into a phantom sketched forever upon the pavement. Now here I was again with Al-Dante's suicide—certainly she had killed herself, even though I hadn't seen her jump off the bench, and all the evidence pointed to Daoud as the one who hanged her, even if she offered no resistance. I would tell no one, not Miss Zahra, Andrew, or anyone else, that I had been at the window and observed all the details under the bright full moon. All the details, that is, except that brief moment when I got bored and hungry and started going back to my room.

After breakfast, I washed my hands, brushed my teeth, put on my clothes, and slicked back my hair with water and comb. I even put on a little cologne to keep away all suspicions. Then it occurred to me to have some gum because chewing keeps the saliva flowing, whereas a dry mouth is taken as evidence of lies and facts misrepresented. When Miss Zahra knocked again, I didn't give her time to open the door but came out without a second's delay. Indeed, I walked ahead of her to the director's office, and she needed to hurry to keep up.

Andrew stood to welcome me. As usual, he was wearing his white jacket and had his Montblanc pen in the small outer pocket. As he ushered me forward to the leather chair facing his own, one hand placed at the level of my kidneys, he stole a glance at his watch, both to indicate how generous he was with his time for us, the residents, and also to highlight the value of his Rolex.

119

We sat facing one another. He inclined his head with a smile in my direction. "Well, how are we doing?" he asked.

"We're fine," I replied.

"Excellent," he said, nodding. Then he added, "Has your neighbor been bothering you recently?"

"No," I said, perhaps too quickly. "It's been weeks since I've heard him berating his wife."

"His wife?" asked the director.

"Yes, that woman he's constantly rebuking, but who always remains silent, without making the slightest peep."

Andrew leaned back in his chair and stretched his legs before crossing the right over the left. "How long ago did we stop taking our medicine, Mr. N?" he asked. He turned to Miss Zahra.

"When he stopped," Miss Zahra said quickly, "or when you approved the change?"

Yes, I had informed Miss Zahra of my secret decision to trick her and stop taking my medicine, and how I would keep the pills under my tongue and ostentatiously swallow the water, but then, after she left, run to the bathroom and spit them out. The reality is that ever since I'd resumed writing, I could no longer stand the side effects, which made me heavy, listless, and slow-witted. That went on until I finally gathered my courage and informed Miss Zahra of what I was doing. Eyes lowered, I had whispered, "How do you expect me to write under the influence of all that medication?" She sat down next to me on the bed, took my hand, and said she would come back after asking Andrew's advice. When she was gone, I stood up and tried to steel myself for the coming argument, promising myself an unprecedented resolve. It was my body, and I could do with it as I chose. Andrew was just an employee of the hotel where I was staying, and they had no authority over me, not even if they were following the instructions of Sa'id, who covered the cost of my stay. But Miss Zahra returned only a short time later with a smile on her face. She promised they'd reduce the medications gradually, as well as stop some of it immediately, for I actually appeared to be doing better, as both she and Director Andrew recognized. Of course, she was right, and Andrew too. I felt myself being reborn as I gradually recovered my energy and the clarity of my thoughts. The whole situation improved. "Our beloved N has gone to sleep, yet I will go and wake him . . . "

"Thirteen weeks without your medication?" said Andrew, smiling and shaking his head. Then he extended a hand to Miss Zahra, who went around behind me, opened a cabinet, and took out a file.

"Here you are, doctor."

If I'd been stung by a scorpion, I doubt I'd have jumped any higher. "My papers!" I cried.

"Yes," said Andrew, as he tossed the file on the low marble table between our two chairs. "All safe and sound. We're very happy that you've taken up writing again after this long interruption. Fifteen years is a very long time, don't you agree?"

I saw red. This was unacceptable. And, what's worse, he was totally unconcerned with my reaction to this nonchalant confession of his impudence, of his meddling in my personal affairs!

"I simply must share your brother's response to the news, too," Andrew said. "'Unbelievable! Unbelievable!' he kept shouting over the phone. He wanted me to fax him your papers, but I didn't do that, of course. He relented when he heard how many pages there were, and he was satisfied with just a few of them, if only to put his mind at ease. By the way, have you ever considered writing on a computer?"

I looked away. That's your excuse, then, just like every other time. Sa'id this, and Sa'id that, and I have to keep my mouth shut because he's my big brother, the son of Thurayya, who controlled our wealth and bequeathed it entirely to him. He is master of my affairs and my overseer; he has advised you, and you're helpless to act save with his permission and according to his recommendations. I turned to Miss Zahra, wearing my disgust openly, so she would understand that I despised her lies, her duplicity; so she would know that I would no longer consent to see her or even perceive her scent from a thousand miles away.

I felt the hatred growing inside me like a giant tree, its untended roots and branches reaching in every direction to coil around the necks of Andrew, his assistant Miss Zahra, the residents on my floor, and even the residents I haven't seen, whose voices sometimes reach me from the lower floors—yes, and the dead among them as well as those who still enjoy the breath of life. Its branches stretch to each of the hotel rooms, to its different floors, and the entrance, which I never cross; across the street and up to the balconies where people deposit all manner of garbage, piling them up with glass, plastic, and shabby, threadbare cloth, useless and discarded objects, empty boxes, rusty propane tanks, popped tires, dolls missing arms and legs, dead plants, empty bags ... Branches from the tree of my hatred encircle it all. The roots extend to the foundations of this accursed city and split the asphalt. They upend sidewalks and cars. They go deep to crack utility pipes and wells. Lofty buildings and apartments come toppling down. Then, from the ground, rise violent black waters, higher and higher. Water surges from the basement of the city—the dirty, stained, squalid, polluted, foul, deluded, and murderous city. Roiling toward the sea, the waves sweep away everything in their path.

But I came down from the tree of my hatred when I heard Andrew's voice rising higher than its usual pitch. He was looking at me expectantly. I inclined my head and looked at him askance, having no idea what he was getting at.

"What's the matter with you?" he snapped. "I asked if you'd heard anything out of the ordinary last night."

I tightened my lips to indicate I had not. That's when I noticed Miss Zahra was no longer in the office.

"Mr. N, a terrible thing has happened. Maryam, your neighbor in the room across the hall, has passed away. She died and was found hanging in the garden from a rope made of leather belts and straps. She had suffered from a severe case of depression over the years, and unfortunately, no treatment proved effective."

"Yes," I said, absently. "Depression does lead to suicide."

Andrew kept silent, examining me for any reaction. Then he asked, "Did she ever talk about suicide in your presence?"

I hurried to say that, despite being her neighbor for years, I didn't have any real acquaintance with her, and we rarely exchanged anything beyond the usual greetings in the morning and evening. In order not to appear excessive in my unconcern, I added, "Poor woman. No doubt whatever caused her long depression is what drove her to it."

Andrew agreed with me, pleased that I was engaging him in conversation. Then he added, "The police will be coming shortly. Maryam was a respected lady and a university professor. I don't know how a person can endure the loss of their entire family and still go on living. They all died from the barrel bombings that rained down over Aleppo: her husband, two teenaged sons, and a seven-year-old daughter. She alone survived, miraculously. It happened just a few days before they were scheduled to leave and follow her brother, who had married a Lebanese woman from the mountain near Beirut. By the way, have you seen your other neighbor today? Miss Zahra looked for him, but he wasn't in his room."

Andrew went on talking, but I drifted off and was no longer listening. I was able to endure only a limited amount of blather, and Andrew had more than exceeded that amount. My mind kept wandering to the image of Al-Dante, sitting down for dinner every night with her ghosts. The dinner hour when the family gathered around the table—that was all she had to hold onto. No doubt that was the essence of happiness for her: that they were all present, all of them well fed, all about to head off to bed, full and happy, the entire day having passed in peace and without any accidents.

Each night at her table, Maryam had counted herself among the lucky ones, those who escaped along with their loved ones. There was nothing more she wanted than to finish her day in peace, with no one from her family injured, missing, jailed, or killed. Let the war rage endlessly, for all eternity. What mattered was that her family gathered every evening in that magical moment that confirmed they had all escaped the car bombs, the kidnappings, the snipers, the explosions, and the barrel bombs. We Lebanese had been just the same—and still were. That feeling would never go away! Maryam thought she had escaped, but she hadn't. She carried that dearest of moments in her heart, and every evening she unwrapped it. She stretched it and pulled it, until she ripped a hole in the middle. And when it became worn out and torn, she killed herself. Yes, Maryam had committed suicide, even if Daoud was the one who finished her off.

I had been watching for Andrew to stand up and move to open the window on account of the sweat dripping down his neck from all that ranting and raving. When he did, I put the stack of my papers under my arm, took my leave, and quickly went out before he could say anything to stop me. When I reached my room, my eyes got caught on Al-Dante's door. Grim. I hurried past into my own room, only to be startled by a person standing in front of my window, still and silent as Al-Dante on the stone bench.

———

Kareem surprised me by saying the angel had returned to the internet café to ask about me. Me! Short, potbellied, featureless, but with beautiful eyes . . . Yes, beautiful eyes, the proof being that Thurayya—who melted with pleasure at the matchless perfection of her beautiful son Sa'id—thought my eyes were too good for me and wished there were some way to transfer them to him. My eyes are the color of green olives after they've been brined and soaked in water, and they shared some of that same bitterness. (I don't know why I say "are." It feels as though all of me "was." I "was." That's the tense that expresses the truth about me. I was. Even from the very moment of my birth, I was in the simple past.)

I ran into Kareem as I wandered through Bourj Hammoud, searching out the alleys adjacent and parallel to Luqman's. An invisible force had drawn me back to that neighborhood. Kareem was standing with a group of friends in front of a sandwich shop. He called to me from a distance and came up running. "Where've you been? Why'd you disappear like that? The guys told me they taught you a lesson when Luqman got the idea you were there to keep an eye on him, yeah? So what about it—are you working for someone? And did you actually come to spy on him?"

Kareem spoke with his mouth full, chewing on onions, tomatoes, and grilled meat. Between the rapid questions, he swigged mouthfuls from the juice bottle in his hand. I invited him for a cup of coffee. He hesitated a little before accepting my invitation. We sat inside so nobody would see us and bring the news back to Luqman.

Kareem got up to wash his hands. Then he came back, drying his hands on paper towels and saying, "I heard that the lady came back to the neighborhood to reassure herself about you. Did she get in touch with you?"

I asked if she had left a number or if he knew anything about her.

"I didn't see her," Kareem went on, "but the guys told me about the smackdown you received, about her arrival out of nowhere, and how she came back a few days later to ask about you. Luqman received her warmly, I heard, gave her water and juice, and hovered around her like a child. He must have fallen for her, they said! But seriously, don't tell anyone what

I've said. In any case, you won't be going back to the shop again, will you? If you're really so crazy as to return, you won't mention I've seen you, right?"

Kareem raised his eyebrows with the question, and a line appeared, small and long, bisecting his forehead. After a few decades, that line would be etched so deep upon his brow that it would only be necessary to carve it just a little deeper with the tip of a knife in order to split the skull and peek inside. It was all hidden there, in that bony ball protecting a white, gooey mass. At that moment, a large refrigerator with a glass front on my right startled me when it gave two coughs and died out. It was time to switch the electrical current and turn on the generators, just as it was time for me to return to Kareem's face, with his two foreheads, split across the middle, and his mouth still chewing a last bite as he ordered a cup of tea.

"Two spinal cords and two brains!" shouted someone from outside. There were containers of them in the refrigerator, next to other meats and not far from the hummus, cauliflower, and fried eggplant. When my father was still alive, brain and sweetbreads were his favorites, but Thurayya didn't allow anything of the sort inside her home; she couldn't even stomach hearing the words mentioned. So my father brought me to a sandwich shop and pointed out a container at the back of the refrigerator that held sliced brains, boiled in salt water and soaked in vinegar and oil. "Nothing comes close to the brain," he told me. "Up till now, we haven't grasped all its capabilities. But on top of all that—it has a flavor to die for." When his order came, he took his first bite with eyes closed in order to savor its deliciousness. He offered me a taste, but I declined, preferring to finish the grilled cheese sandwich I'd ordered. My father laughed. "Don't be afraid! It's just a sheep's brain. The things in the refrigerator that look like white worms are spinal cords, while the red pieces are cheeks. Your grandfather Nadeem used to order such things in advance from the butcher, along with raw esophagus, just as his father, the farmer, did before him. Then he would gather us around him as he enjoyed his feast with a glass of arak... Your grandmother Eugénie, a girl from a fancy family in Jaffa, always declined, declaring that she wasn't hungry, or that she had never eaten 'that' in the house of her father, the great merchant. Your grandfather would quarrel with her, saying that next time he would treat her right and offer her a meal of trotters... Here, have a taste and see how it melts in your mouth, just like Turkish delight."

Kareem answered a phone call from one of his friends. Then he excused himself and went off with a final reminder that he hadn't seen me, nor I him. He seemed annoyed by how distracted I was anyway, and how I kept staring at his forehead. I looked at my watch. It was 10:25. I decided to walk around a little until I could gather my thoughts and reach a decision.

I reached Armenia Street and walked in the direction of Baladiya Square, away from the big roundabout that formed the border of Luqman's neighborhood. I didn't want to run into him then, not when I was still uncertain what was going on with me and with the angel who had returned to ask about me. Was it possible that she had come only to reassure herself? Or had she been impressed by Luqman, that stud, and come back for him, using me as an excuse? I didn't know of any woman who noticed him without falling under his spell, despite his coarseness and his criminality. But a woman like her? So light and soft, she almost floated above the ground— how could she be attracted to a vulgar hulk like him? I recalled melting at the scent of her perfume, the velvet touch of her hands, and the way her voice trembled with compassion as she repeated, "Don't be afraid! I'm here with you." Who could have sent me such an angel? My father? No, he had not actually been a believer. To his final hour, he never spoke about what comes in the hereafter, about faith, or about the fear of death. Mary? Had one angel sent another to help a fallen angel get back up? My grandmother Eugénie? But if she could send angels, wouldn't she have sent one to stop her mad son from going out the window?

I suddenly realized I was lost. I had wandered too far and entered a different neighborhood. Al-Nab'a, according to the words of a blue metal sign hanging at an intersection. I stopped and turned in a circle. I found myself in unknown parts, tattered streets where severed limbs still hung from the power lines, while others wormed through the mud, still alive. Countless kids swarmed the streets at that unexpected hour, looking no different than they had the day they entered this life: barefoot, dirty, hair disheveled, skin splotchy, and desperately malnourished.

I moved forward as through a jungle. Rotten vegetables were smeared across the ground. There were fruit peels, plastic bags, bottles and cans, cardboard boxes, torn banners, and tattered clothes, knotted together and pissed upon by the sky. Bodies of large rats crushed by car tires, dried-up cockroaches, and flies buzzing in place as though glued to the air; crippled cats missing an eye or a leg and crouching under cars to escape the tormenting children. Beggars, refugees, the poor, the wretched, ragmen, hawkers, daytime drunks, scowling workers, tottering old men with teeth missing from their gaping mouths, the remains of women in tattered clothing, dyed hair, and makeup. These were the Lord's flock, crowded in together, fallen from on high into this accursed valley, without any savior, with neither hope nor helper.

The lacerated scene was too much for me. My deficient life was too much for me. I felt a tide of nausea rising inside, and I bent over as I emptied everything in my belly onto the road and myself. Whenever I thought I had at last finished, a new wave of vomit exploded like a fountain. This continued until I thought I was squeezing my organs out through my mouth. Then it was over, and the dirt began soaking up the last of my spit. Some of the people there, passersby and children, ran up and gathered around to watch, but without showing any disgust that I had just expelled my guts. Instead, they looked at my feet intently, as though I was bringing something for them. Their gaze moved back and forth from the bulging eyes and distended veins of my flushed face to the sticky vomit that puddled beneath me. As the successive waves of vomit came, they scrutinized me, engrossed and astonished, as if I were an alien who had just arrived from another planet, peculiar to look at yet vaguely resembling them.

A hand from behind me extended a blue plastic bottle that was dripping cold water. Immediately I realized how thirsty I was. My soul, to its very depths, had become a barren desert. The hand shook the bottle, and a hoarse voice said, "Here. Drink." I, meanwhile, was nailed in place, head bowed. My gaze moved between the cold water, the dirty fingers, thick and cracked, the sunburned forearm with its matted hair caked in dust, and the small, sticky, snot-covered faces that raised grave, expectant eyes to me.

I thought I could avoid the bottle directly below my chin by vomiting more, but nothing would come out. I was truly empty, and there was no easy escape from the situation. I turned toward the hand and found myself looking into a frowning, sweaty face that appeared over a large belly covered in a sleeveless T-shirt that had once been white. The face was cruel, its lips tight. Its sidelong glance was openly accusatory. For some reason, such accusations never come straight at you, but are always launched at exactly a forty-five-degree angle, with the face sloping away a little to fix the direction of the sidelong stare.

I smiled in spite of myself. Before me were two options, without any possible third. Either I take the water gratefully and down it all at once, quenching my thirst and poisoning myself, or I . . . It didn't take long for me to turn my face away. My body followed, with the goal of getting out of there. The man's rough hand grabbed my shoulder and forced me to stop as he poured the water over me. Then he spat in my face and squeezed the base of my neck until my soul was gasping out.

The pain was excruciating. I knelt, stained in my own vomit that mixed with the refuse of the street where I fell. With perfect clarity, he could sense my disgust at his merely looking at me, as well as my disgust for his water, his fingers, him, his street, and his entire world without exception. It was a sharp disgust, hard and impudent. The man looked directly into the eyes of that disgust and spat on it. It was only my disgust with myself that he failed to see.

―――

That spot on my back is itching again. I feel it getting hot and then burning, but I can't get at it. I turn in a circle, trying to reach it. Then I press myself against the door, but the cool touch of the wood only makes me feel more despair, and it itches worse. God! After the passage of all these years, the pain still comes back to me. I wish I were able to rip off the spot and replace it with a metal plate. Yet that would only replace the pain with an even bigger one.

I began to go down regularly to the place where the Lord's flock settled. Street by street, corner by corner, I discovered most of the places they lived. I wandered by day and got lost by night. I sometimes discovered passageways and alleys where time was lost and became meaningless. I would cast about, seeking my quarry, yearning for a beating, to present my body as a blood offering to people ground down by coercion and humiliation. This is my body: take it, trample it, pierce it, eat it . . . I did not succeed in giving everyone my "offering," for there were some who scorned and rejected me, thinking I was drunk, or a vagabond, or mentally ill. But by the end of the day, I always succeeded in provoking someone's rage.

I would throw my universal disgust in someone's face, and he would respond by beating me. In me and through me, he would beat the thing that we both hated: that we were the Lord's flock, even though our Master never turned toward us but left us standing alone at the edge of the abyss, fearing at every moment that the ground would fall from beneath our feet. We were promised a death that didn't come, even as we feared His punishment if we made so bold as to leap. I was

132

addicted to the beatings I received as I wandered through the labyrinths of the marginalized, the accursed, and the poor. One day, I'd go down to them in this neighborhood, and the next day in that. I'd get myself turned around, completely lost, and all I had to do was poison someone's mood with a glance to get him to respond with some provocative word or gesture. I'd respond in kind, and then he would explode with all the coercion and humiliation that had been injected into him. Rock by rock, boulder by boulder, he would collect all the hatred that had calcified within him and smash the stone into my insufferably offensive face.

Was I atoning for some sin? What connection did I have to their misery and wretchedness that made me feel this guilt? What about my own misery and wretchedness? Who was atoning for that? However strange the whole thing seemed, the beatings helped by loosening the painful knots inside. It was as though they healed me by making the pain tangible, visible, like the colors and shapes seen in a photographic negative. After years of treatment and deception, I was now finding my medicine where I least expected, out in the street among ghostly strangers of various dialects and hues.

I began going down to the neighborhoods of my salvation once a week—sometimes twice, according to the damage I could sustain. All things considered, the bruises were no more than spots that changed color with the passage of days, from red to blue and purple, and finally yellow. Then they would fade and disappear. In the yellow stage, it's possible to camouflage them with a strong skin-colored foundation, which I bought where the Sudanese sex workers bought their makeup supplies. Wounds were more complicated.

133

They were harder to hide, since the skin acquired a thick black crust as it reknit itself, followed by scars that were difficult to hide, especially on my face. So I learned to protect my face as much as possible. Skin needs twenty-one days to renew itself. That's a long wait, but in the beginning, I tried to respect it. Yet as time went on I gave that up, especially after I noticed that a violated body provokes greater violations, just as submission invites even further assaults. This discovery was a great relief, solving the problems posed by my lack of patience. I started going out for a beating whenever I felt the need, paying no attention to the pain, the damage it did me.

Mary once told me how a neighbor at her old house would lock his wife and children out of his room at night, when he would transform into a violent savage. Everyone heard him screaming and pleading to be left alone and for the torment to stop. I saw the fear in Mary's eyes as her voice lowered to a whisper: "Poor man! The jinn would come and play with his mind. So he locked himself up, fearing what he might do to his family." Later, she told me that the king of the jinn had a daughter who fell in love with the man, and she would beat him every night until he divorced his wife, left his family, and married her. Mary's naïveté was a kind of brilliant intelligence, but I never understood it until the jinn came and began telling their own stories inside my head.

It seems that the same jinn had come and whispered to my father before he walked to the window and stepped through, completely calm. He remained seated at his desk for hours, writing the same few sentences over and over on dozens of pieces of paper:

In my head are the voices of the dead. Whenever I hear someone has been killed, the voices rise, a wind howls, and black clouds unfurl. My head is a graveyard where the earth is dug up, and the dead live again.

Those screaming in my father's head were the victims whom the Albino kidnapped and tortured to death. This Albino was the friend of Luqman, my protagonist, and the most barbaric torturer in their gang. *The Albino stood up and began torturing the man in his bathtub. He washed him in the waters and read the Gospel over his head.* That's how I wrote it years ago. The Albino visited me that night, and I woke up to see him sitting on the edge of the bed. He just sat there, looking at me. Trembling, I told myself: He's only a character from the novel about Luqman, and in the novel, he's dead. Dead or not, I saw him alive before me, and then his lips started to move. "You wrote about me," he says. A delicate thread of blood began flowing from one nostril. A moment later it burst the dam and flooded my bed . . .

Out on the street, a young, thirtysomething man with the long beard and broad shoulders grabbed me after I pushed through a circle of people and overturned everything they had placed on a low chair. He rapped the top of my head with his knuckles like someone knocking on a door, saying, "Knock, knock . . . What're you doing? You blind?"

"Not at all," I replied, forcing a brash insolence. "The sidewalk belongs to everyone."

"I'll plant you here, then, right in the sidewalk. What do you say to that?"

He said it calmly. His companions laughed. I laughed too. He wasn't expecting that. It must have seemed a deliberate measure of scorn when he was expecting me to become

135

silent and pale from fright before collapsing to weep and beg forgiveness.

"It's clear you're not from around here. You're too old for me to fight, so just get out of here. Otherwise, I'll mop the ground with you!"

He finished with a shove, ignoring my provocation and rejoining the circle of his friends sitting on the pavement that formed a median in the street. They were having a good time with their snacks, their cigarettes, and their narghiles. I moved away, but no farther than one step. I had walked the whole night without finding my prey, and my skin was itching. There was no way I could leave, just like that, without one of them destroying my body with a beating that would send me to bed disjointed but with my head cleared.

A breeze stirred and carried the smell of a burning narcotic herb. Belatedly, I understood the secret of the young gang's forbearance, and why they chose not to punish my impudence. Their virility usually went off like gunpowder for the paltriest of reasons, and their aggressiveness only ramped up at the sight of tears, but now both were dozing, drugged, slack. What rotten luck, I told myself. Looking up and sighing into the sky, I saw small banners for some political party fluttering in the air atop the lampposts. Glinting yellow in the dark, the banners whispered what I had to do in order to enrage those people who had brushed me off like an insect. I threw back my head, and with all the force I could muster, I spat into the air. Before the gob even fell back to the ground, the bearded young man leapt up like a madman, outpacing his companions to wrap his hand around my throat. He drove his thick-soled tennis shoe into my guts . . .

What a genius I am! How did I come up with that brilliant idea? And how many signs there were! Yellow, white, orange, green, black, and blue, they differed from one street to another, one neighborhood to the next, sometimes even from apartment to apartment within the same building. I only had to rip one down and spit or step on it for a volcano to erupt upon me. Before long, I discovered that the reaction was not limited to political parties. All it took was an insult to any flag, any slogan—belonging to a soccer team, a Boy Scout troop, a civic organization, a school, a company, an animal humane society—and I would ignite the fuse of a nuclear explosion in the brains of its followers, members, supporters, and defenders. They would swoop down on me, without giving a damn about anything. Don't all people everywhere chant about shedding blood and laying down their lives for this or that cause? I guess that included teaching me a lesson by sending me sprawling on the pavement.

After a few weeks, I gave up on the parties based in the neighborhoods of Bourj Hammoud, Al-Nab'a, Sin el Fil, and all the other miserable districts that floated like islands upon a sea of destruction. The party loyalists had gotten to know me too well, and they began avoiding me after I acquired the reputation of "the madman." And if it happened that someone fell into my trap, others would quickly step in to protect me and put an end to the quarrel. Indeed, some of them even began treating me kindly. They would give me something to eat or drink and ask how I was doing. Yes, the damn parties had cut off my living, and I was forced to wander elsewhere to ply my trade.

Fortunately for me, the neighborhoods farther out were richer than the cave of Ali Baba, with many entrances, numerous tunnels, and plentiful surprises. Passing through on foot, they never failed to surprise me with the creatures, communities, nationalities, languages, and dialects they contained. Eventually, I had the bright idea—and it shone brighter than the sun—that I should specialize in foreigners and immigrants. Yes, this was a lost flock, with neither Lord nor Master. Among them was no one to question me or offer protection, and I would become the willing victim of whoever wanted it badly enough. They were the majority here, so it made sense that they had the greatest right to me. The result of the experiment confirmed the excellence of my choice, the soundness of my reasoning. For in their beatings I found another meaning, something new and different from the beatings I received from men who shared my skin, who clung so stubbornly to their sects, their parties, and their lairs, like flies wallowing in shit.

To get what I wanted in those neighborhoods, it was enough for me to make fun of their dialect, their language, or their nationality, or just to utter those magic words, "Go back to your own country!" The people there were the most cruel, the most wild, the most ferocious—perhaps because they suffered subjugation at the hands of the entire world. Then it occurred to me to prepare little "gifts" for the worst among them. I would leave things in my pockets or in my wallet, such as a stash of money, a watch, vouchers redeemable at the most exclusive stores. Taking these things would make them think they were not only getting their revenge on me, but also plundering me, just as we were plundering them ...

The beatings wore me out. There wasn't a single spot on my body that hadn't been damaged. I had to stop for a while to recover and regain my strength in the apartment before getting back out there. But I began feeling cramped at home, and the walls pressed in on me. I was thirsty for the bowels of the city again. Then a new idea came to me. I would go out and scatter my writings. Lyrical lines, excerpts of prose, words written out by hand or else typed. I chose small white envelopes and colorful slips of paper that would attract attention: yellow, pistachio, pink, blue, and so on. I prepared my slips with care, and then went out to drop them here and there. I stood nearby and watched as a passerby decided to bend down to pick one up. If I saw someone open the envelope and slowly read the words inside, I felt for a moment that I possessed his mind, that what I had written was now toying with him and making him believe he had received a sign sent by fate.

I was that fate. Packaged into just a few words: pithy, spontaneous, poetic, unusual, appropriate, impertinent, harsh, crazy, dirty, emotional, clever, stupid . . . anything, really. Whoever picked up the envelope would read the contents and be driven mad. He would begin searching out the meaning hidden behind its lines, the idea, the prophecy, the message that would solve the riddle and give his life purpose. A line was all it took. A fragment, or just a few words. The reader would turn over the page like a treasure he had stumbled upon, even if he had never picked up a novel in his entire life.

A man picked up one of my small envelopes and sat on the sidewalk across from me to open it and read what was inside. I stared intently. It was a piece of paper with some words in my handwriting. The man raised his eyes. He was crying. He folded the paper back up and pressed it to his heart, head bowed, before breaking down in bitter sobs.

Curiosity was eating me up. What was on that paper to touch his heart like that? I, who had written dozens of pages and a number of books, had never succeeded in touching anyone so deeply before. I approached and said apologetically that the small envelope he was holding had fallen out of my pocket. Without looking at me, the man extended his hand to give it back. Other people were just as curious. Pedestrians gathered in a circle around him. They began asking questions about why he wept. He explained that his family had drowned in the sea in the attempt to emigrate to a safe country. His wife and two children had died. He had escaped, but they had not. Escaped? I whispered to myself. No, they are the ones who escaped. It is he who has died.

In my mind's eye, I could see the coast guard as they cast their lines and nets into the sea, their hearts sinking. They pulled small bodies out of the water, bent and folded like soggy paper. The bodies they dragged onto the sand had been manhandled and torn by the waves. The coast guard could not understand why the sea was delivering such unnatural issue, born with hearts frozen by cold and fear. Why had these drowned souls found no one to make room for them, to permit them even the smallest portion of this thing called life? These drowned strangers, even if they died, had never actually counted among the ranks of the living. They had bodies that seemed alive, yet living souls never opened up and blossomed within them. No soul can enter that world of theirs; it is too miserable and black. Only the sea remains. It silently builds graveyards for the thousands who are not taken into account, and who take no account of themselves ... Room to bury hundreds of thousands, and the space stretching broader and deeper as the leaky boats increase. Candidates elected for death, staring impassively at the destinies carved in marble before them. So they throw their bodies into the dark waters of tin and tar. They reach for the wave crests and embrace the danger as tightly as they would a life preserver.

"Take me!" shouted the exhausted man to the waves. He cared nothing for death and stood at the edge of the world, one step from the final abyss. "Suck me in, and do whatever you want. The land has spit me out, heaven refuses me, and I have nothing left but you, stretching out your arms for my miserable death! I was desperate, so I sold all I had and took a loan that brought a glimmer of hope. I rolled the dice of my life and of the lives of my wife and my two sons, and I did not look back. There was nothing left for me there, no trace of our lives, no field to plant. I gathered our papers into a bag, handed them over to that smiling man with the bronzed face. 'Don't be afraid,' he told me, 'I'll bring you all to dry land, and when you arrive, the clock of life will begin ticking again. Seconds, minutes, hours, and days in a long, vast, unending train. On the far shore, you'll pile up real days, days of flesh and blood and bone, days of nourishment, sleep, warmth, and the feeling of security. Don't be afraid! Give me everything you have, and put yourselves in the captain's hands ... ' My wife tied my sons together tightly. 'Either we all arrive together, or not at all,' she said, her lips split by the salt and tears filling her vacant eyes. 'No, untie them,' I told her. 'Perhaps one of the two will have different luck than we've seen. We've long been

141

enemies with luck, and they'll need some to survive, even if they are saved . . . ' The cold wind burned us. The cold waters slapped against us. The boat was rocking us back and forth on the confused sea as the waves grew higher. Everyone was screaming, 'Dear God, dear God!' Within minutes the angry sky swooped down upon us. 'Where are you fleeing to?' it said. 'Don't you see? After all this affliction, do you not yet realize?' The sky took my wife by the hand and pulled her up. She was cold and heavy, still tied to our two small children. So the sky took them all by brute force since she did not want to be separated from them.

"That's the whole story. Their souls rose together, and their bodies remained below, floating on the surface of the water. I alone was saved. The coast guard picked me out of the sea, threw a blanket over me, and set me down on a large metal locker. They asked my name, who I was, where I had come from, and whether I had come alone. I couldn't speak but just stared with vacant eyes. My information form remained blank. They wrote down that I was in shock and had lost the ability to speak from the trauma. They did not record that my soul too had been lost and drowned. It is still out there, floating upon the water . . . "

The man finished talking. With the sleeve of his jacket, he wiped the smear of snot, sweat, and tears off his face. It was too much for me, and I could not get away fast enough. A desire for my balcony suddenly overwhelmed me, and without any further delay, I decided to abandon that place of grief and return home before anything turned me from my path.

When I arrived, the balcony was waiting. The jasmine and carnation had grown and were covered in dust. I filled the watering can and went back to clean and water them. I used a feather duster on my chair and the table. Then I sat down, leaned back my head, and set my feet on the balcony. The power was out, so the neighborhood was dark. Everything was utterly still. I looked at the shade of the black demon: the tower was now in its final stage. In a matter of weeks it would be finished. No more than weeks. As it grew taller, my own building contracted. I could hear it thinking, "Whence this misfortune? Why me?" My building shrank like that man's family, and like him, I would not escape. I remembered the small envelope. Where had I put it? There it was. I drew it out of my pants pocket, opened it, and read what I had written, just a few words:

"Of water and salt."

———

When I entered my room, I found someone standing in front of the window, staring out, still and silent as a corpse. My entrance did not startle him, nor did he turn from the window to face me. I sat on the edge of the bed, worn out from my session with Andrew and wanting to sink into the stillness to give my ringing ears some relief from the noise of all his talking.

Daoud remained silent, frozen in place. All he did was raise his right hand to the back of his neck, squeezing and massaging the point where the skull connects to the spine. I imitated him, placing my thumb under the lower rim of my skull. I pressed down and took a deep breath. I held my breath for a few seconds, releasing it with a sigh. A delicious

143

numbness spread through my limbs. With my feet still resting on the floor, I lay back and sank into a deep sleep. I dreamed about my father, swimming through a sea of animal intestines, clean and white as plastic pipes. "Look how pure it is!" he cried as he plunged in. "Smells like lemon!" Then Thurayya appeared. Her mouth was painted red, like some misshapen clown. She was crying, and when she saw me, she turned and whispered, "I only want Dior!"

Dior was the only brand of lipstick she found acceptable. If anyone ever praised her beauty, she would pucker her red lips and say, "Dior of Paris!" When I was very young, before Mary came to us, I would hide in a corner of Thurayya's room in order to watch her, without her knowing I was there. Sitting at the dressing table where she kept her makeup, she would first comb her hair and put on her pearl necklace and her ring. Then she would open a wine-colored jar with a fine white powder inside and use a small pink velvet pad to brush it lightly over her face, neck, and décolletage. When she was finished, she would pass a mascara pencil across her closed eyelids and apply the red lipstick that I remembered.

When Thurayya finished making herself up, she would stand up, strip off her robe, and remain standing there in a silk chemise—either black or skin-toned—that hugged her thighs and revealed her legs past the knees. She would go to the wardrobe where her many dresses hung in a row, pick one out to put on, and then return to the mirror to spray her *Femme* perfume before taking one last look at herself and leaving the room to start her day. Thurayya never neglected her appearance. In all circumstances, she kept herself ready, as though about to go out, receive a guest, or attend some function. I wished she would hold me to her breast so I might smell her, play with her hair, and feel her touch. I wished she would seat me on her lap and wrap her bare arms around me, that she would place her hand on my head, upon my heart, on my secret spot. I sometimes surprised myself, when I lay between Neda's arms, halfway between sleeping and waking, by recalling that image of Thurayya, a woman alone in her room . . .

Daoud gave me a jab, saying, "Get up! I want to talk to you." I sat up on the bed, still groggy from sleep.

"People are constantly trying to persuade me that I did not kill my wife, and that she committed suicide. But I know better than they the deed I committed . . . Listen, I've heard Miss Zahra knocking on my door today. I don't want to talk to that cunning bitch. That's why I'm hiding in your room."

"Andrew told me the police were coming to question us. Let them do it. I didn't see anything."

"Yes, you did! You saw us, and I saw you."

"Really? Okay, everything except the very moment of the hanging."

"Maryam's time had come. It was all over for her."

"Yes, Daoud, I know."

"Who's Daoud?"

"You!"

"Where'd you get that idea? My name is Majid."

"Really? Sorry, I thought you were called Daoud . . . Can I call you Daoud anyway? It would be difficult for me to remember a new name now."

"Fine. Majid, Daoud . . . It doesn't matter."

145

"You said it was your wife who died? I thought your wife was a mute . . . the one you're always shouting at and who never says a word in return?"

Daoud considered me, lost in thought. Then he came and sat on the bed beside me.

"Silence is what killed my wife. My own silence, which spread over her head like a black cloud. I was like a storm that threatened to explode and sweep everything away. I maintained an utter, absolute silence. I didn't even let her hear the sound of my breathing. I refused to address her. I no longer saw her, even when she was right in front of me. She started melting away until finally she was gone. They say she killed herself. Bullshit! I'm the one who killed her. I stopped eating in the house, so she abstained. I spent nights out, so she stayed up and didn't sleep. That's what happened: she dissolved just like a lump of salt. No different from Maryam, whom I hadn't wanted to suffer the way my wife did. Maryam begged and pleaded with me for weeks. Poor woman. Death ate up her children and her husband. And my silence consumed my poor wife. When she died, all my words for her came out like water from a burst pipe. I couldn't stop! Was it regret? No, don't ask me that. Nothing can justify what I did. I actually took joy in my tyranny. The more she weakened, the more I harassed her. The victim, too, creates its executioner, Mr. N. There can be no executioner without a victim. But then, after her death, my wife became my executioner. She shrank, she faded, she withered away, as I expanded and became stronger. They say she swallowed pills and slipped into a coma, dying before she ever woke up. But no. She just melted away. Her light went out, and she vanished. As for the pills, I'm not sure. No doubt they gave people a reason not to come after me. Even in her death, she was afraid of me. Then my strength bounced back against me, for who was there to exercise it upon? What could I do with it on my own? I became an executioner without a victim. So I became my own victim. Then I became nothing, just as you see me now.

"They put me in this wing because I'm rich. The country's whole iron supply passed through me. I rose from nothing, and my family were farmers from Akkar. I obtained a high school diploma by sheer effort but didn't go to college. When I went into business, I began by selling nails. I sold old ones and bought new ones. Then, at some point, the prices suddenly shot up at a crazy rate. I started selling the stock I had built up at a tenfold profit. Yes, I'm the master of iron. Iron is me. Here: feel my hand and you'll see how cold and metallic I am. Poor Maryam was made of straw. Thin and light as straw. When I put the rope around her neck, it was moist, not at all what I was expecting. She was so emaciated, I thought her neck would be dry and brittle as bone. But no, her skin was damp, as though she had just dried it after a shower. Damp, tender, and light, like a doll when you lift it up and wave its feet through the air . . . My wife was of salt. Grains of salt, ready to dissolve. Salt always has a kind of coercion. There's something in its flavor that tastes like distress . . . Miss Zahra said I was bothering you with my shouting. Did she tell you how I replied? 'Tell him to go jump in the sea!' That was the night Maryam tapped at my door and invited me to dinner. Time after time, she sat me at her table and cooked up amazing dishes in her head. She insisted that I eat from her empty dishes and sip from cups filled with water. For a while, Maryam made me forget my wife and my crime. Then she opened up to me about her secret plan and asked me to see her through it. It's okay, Maryam! I'll help you on your way! And she'd help me forget . . . "

Daoud stopped talking when we heard a knock next door, followed by the sound of Miss Zahra opening the door and calling. Daoud jumped up and hid behind the bed, on the side facing the bathroom. He pulled the blankets over his head.

"Don't tell her I'm here! I don't want to see her. Miss Zahra is made of rubber, and I loathe rubber."

"Perhaps the police have come," I told him. "You have to go to the interrogation. Don't worry. I'll tell them I heard you talking in your room, and that you didn't leave it the whole night."

Daoud's face lit up with a smile. "Really? What a friend!" Then he got up and headed toward the door, which he opened and went through. I heard him greet Miss Zahra. Their voices receded down the hall as they made their way to the director's office.

————

I nearly forgot Luqman. But I started meeting dozens like him every night. I tried to forget the angel who occupied my thoughts for a while, for I realized I could never reach her now that the monster had made her his own. My angels were of another kind now, with colorful skin, rough hands, and worn-out bodies. Black, yellow, and red, untouched or tattooed with bruises and scars, wearing skimpy clothing and covered in pictures, drawings, and obscure words I couldn't understand.

Like Jonah in the whale, I had dropped into the belly of the city and begun wandering through its entrails, deeper and deeper, to the lowest of the low. Down where even the darkness was hidden, where rats found refuge and insects made their nests; where lepers, amputees, and the heartsick hid themselves away. I would retreat to my apartment for a few days when I needed to recover my strength, and then I would resume my descent to the bottom. I would be beaten until I lost consciousness, only to wake up each time somewhere new: sometimes on a street corner, sometimes a building foyer, or else near the garbage cans or in a gutter, in vagrants' rooms and the dens of drunkards. And one time—magically—in the bosom of a woman.

Shaygha had a body like a prepubescent child. Nothing about it was big or adult-sized except her wide eyes. The pupils moved about in a way that made you dizzy to follow, as though you were floating around a planet with no gravity. Shaygha took me in when she stumbled across me in the street, far from her country of Nepal. She picked me up despite how much smaller she was. Even though I had lost a substantial amount of weight as a result of my beatings and my wanderings, I was still heavy for her, and she dragged me bodily to her room with her small, skinny arms. She cleaned away the mud, sweat, spit, piss, and blood that covered me. She peeled off my foul-smelling clothes and washed, dried, and ironed them. In this way, I awoke to find she had restored my human appearance.

Soon after waking, when I felt strong enough to do it, I stood up, expressed my gratitude, and got ready to go. But she didn't want me to leave. She held my arm and shook her head no. She pulled me away from the door and sat me down. Then she sat on my lap and embraced me, burying her head against my chest. I let myself be carried away by her, for you cannot say no to a small woman like this. We found ourselves united in the coop: she the hen, I the cock. The space, barely large enough for us both, was filled with a bed, a small dresser, and, tucked in the corner along with a plastic chair, an unassuming table, upon which had been placed a purple cloth and a vase with plastic flowers. Above the raised threshold that separated the narrow kitchen and bathroom from the main room, a transparent plastic curtain had been hung—Shaygha's idea, no doubt, to contain the cooking smells and to keep the light that came through the kitchen window from escaping.

She would stretch out over me and lower herself down on delicate, skinny limbs. Then we'd doze off like two intertwined insects. She made me food from Nepal and bought me clothes from China, talking to me in the basic Arabic words that she had managed to learn. I liked that I didn't understand much about her. I liked that she was a woman of few words, made no sudden movements, and displayed only moderate emotions, showing neither great sadness nor excessive joy. Then she told me I had to remain hidden, since "Mr. Joe," the owner of the bar where she worked, didn't like to see her with men he hadn't introduced to her. I didn't comprehend the situation at first, but then I realized that she had a pimp. She had arrived in Lebanon with the intention of being a housekeeper, and when fortune hadn't been kind with the employer it matched her with, she ran away and became a prostitute.

I don't know why I decided Shaygha would be my woman, and I her man. I surrendered to her like a father giving himself over to some game his daughter has invented. In the same way, I entered the story that Shaygha wove in her imagination about me. I guess she liked finding someone who was weaker than her. Or she liked that I was weak, a victim, while at the same time came from the class of people who sought her services. The truth is I loved having sex with her, someone who did not know anything about my long abstinence from women, or anything about who I was. Someone who never asked questions, just as I did not.

She would go out at night after completing all her duties toward me—or what she supposed were her duties as my woman. She would shower, put on perfume, get dressed up, and strap on the silver high heels that seemed almost as long as her legs—all after extracting from me a promise not to follow her out into the dirty streets that were unsuitable for me, to wait in my bed like a sensible child until she returned, or to read the old newspapers that she brought home for me from work.

Apparently, Mr. Joe was a reader. He would buy the daily paper, *Ad-Diyar*, and leave it in the nightclub he owned, a gathering place for women of diverse nationalities fleeing their fates: Ethiopians, other Africans, Palestinians, Syrians, Iraqis. And one of them, Shaygha, was from Nepal, which gave her coworkers a reason to look down upon her. They would make her do the things they wouldn't dare ask from the others, but Shaygha did whatever was asked: she made coffee, she washed the dishes, she cleared the tables, and so on. All she wanted was not to have too many clients, and not to spend too long in the back. For the back of this modest club led out to a narrow, dead-end side alley that hid a world of tiny rooms, not unlike a row of cardboard boxes. Some were completely empty, while others contained just a chair or were furnished with a bed, according to the request of the client and his financial means.

Unlike her coworkers, Shaygha preferred the empty rooms, where the clients did not ask for much and did not take long. The sturdier women would take the ones with chairs, while those with soft, white skin would be escorted to the beds. Shaygha was in greatest demand for oral sex, perhaps because the customers saw her as the smallest, most abased woman in the club. Also, because she was good at the kind of sex that satisfied them quickly and didn't cost too much. She would uncover her barely grown breasts and kneel down. The client would give her his penis, which she would work with her small hands and compact mouth until ejaculation. Some were embarrassed and closed their eyes, half-apologetic. Others were cocky and aggressive. They grabbed her hair, spat in her face, and hissed foul language. Once, one of them began beating her, striking her head against the wall. When she screamed, Mr. Joe came with his men and taught the man a lesson he would remember to the end of his days, no matter how long he lived.

Shaygha would return at dawn, exhausted. It was as though she had been gone for years and returned an old woman. Her eyes would be turned into black, unmined coal. Her sleek, coal-black hair would be glued to her small skull.

Her makeup would be running down skin wet with vinegar and water. When she came through the door, she would not look at me but would head straight for the bathroom, where she would remain until she had peeled away that worn-out skin and emerged restored and renewed. Then Shaygha would recover her smile, her childishness, her voice, and her gaze. She would touch me, and I would touch her. She would speak to me, and I to her. The day had drawn near, and we would retreat into ourselves and sink into our den.

As though in paradise, I lived with Shaygha for two months. The bliss was double because I had abandoned all hope entirely before receiving this gift that caressed my soul and gave me a new skin, just like a snake. I forgot Luqman. I forgot the heart of the city and its streets. I forgot the damn skyscraper and my poor apartment I had abandoned. I forgot Thurayya's cruelty, my father's egotism, Sa'id's rise, my abandoned writing, and the wickedness of Miss Zahra. No . . . No, at that time I had not yet moved to the hotel or gotten to know Zahra; I was still living in my apartment, as far as I can recall. Mary had left for her village. Thurayya was still alive: Alzheimer's had impaired her mind, and they had moved her to an institution. Sa'id had traveled to be with his wife, his villa, and his acquaintances, a prelude to moving abroad later on . . . Yes, Shaygha was my compensation for all that: my mother, my father, my brother, and my writing—which I was resisting, and which resisted me.

Miss Zahra entered, and I surprised her by being ready—completely ready, no less. I had arranged the papers, pencils, and other things on my table, made my bed so neat and flat that it showed no wrinkle or flaw, and put away my clothes and various other things inside the wardrobe. I had cleared the place of any chaos that might annoy a visitor or catch someone's eye. Then I had combed my hair and sat down on the chair, which I had placed with its back to the table, facing the door. I was wearing the same suit with the jacket that resisted being buttoned at the belly on some other occasion. Given the recent events, I was expecting Miss Zahra to come, and I wanted to make it an official visit, to force the conversation to take an official tone. I looked at the clock. Exactly 10:25 p.m. I felt a burning desire to know the fate of Daoud and what had become of him after his interrogation, now that the police cars had left the hotel and carried him off into the nearby streets.

After greeting me, Miss Zahra looked slowly around the room. I received her with a smile, though I did not get up. She approached apprehensively, inquiring how I was and whether I had eaten any dinner. I wasn't hungry, I assured her. Then I asked her what she was doing so late at night. She apologized for the inconvenience and the late hour. She was about to go but stopped short when she noticed I was wearing a suit.

"Mr. N, shall I help you change into your pajamas?"

She asked the question with the excessive courtesy typical for someone at the end of an exhausting day, when the blue circles ring their eyes, their energy droops, and their voice can scarcely be heard. Mr. N shook his head no, adding that he was wearing the suit especially for her, and that he had been waiting for her. Miss Zahra cocked her head, surprised and confused by his words. The left side of her upper lip began twitching.

(*Ah! Here I am reverting to the third-person pronoun. What makes it so hard to write "I"? Just one letter, and I would become the center around which things are divided up and arranged. My brother, Sa'id, has his "I," which surprised me for so long. An enormous, gigantic, terrifying "I" that showed up and overshadowed everything around him. His "I" flies on awful wings of colorful feathers that blind your sight. Resounding, rumbling, chaotic. But as soon as the wind blows, they scatter. Thurayya's "I" was solid, firm, heavy, severe. There was no ambiguity about it. Hard as ice. No, even harder! Thurayya drained my body of all its "I." She pressed it down and squeezed until she turned it into nothing.*)

Miss Zahra coughed lightly, an invitation for me to continue. She appeared distracted and confused, she who typically needed the rooms to be radiant, and who left them triumphant, as though she had declared war in her heart on all the residents of this wing. For she considered them prisoners of a certain standing, and while she showed them respect and decency in her interactions, that didn't mean that she was in their service. And that is precisely what began exasperating Mr. N—(*Fine: I'll erase that and try again.*) And that is precisely what began exasperating me, despite my attraction to her, an attraction of the kind that walks the line and might at any moment turn into hatred.

"Please, take a seat. You look tired. No doubt you've had a long and exhausting day."

Miss Zahra suddenly melted, and another woman took her place. She softened like a candle when the fire gets close, and she took the form of a woman who was only waiting for a warm word to revive her after having been broken and lost, a white flag raised in surrender. I poured her a glass of cold water. She said thanks and accepted it. Then she sat on the edge of the bed nearby, and I said in a gentle voice, "What happened to Daoud? I mean, Majid?"

"They've brought him to prison to await trial."

"On what charge?"

"The charge of murder, of course."

"Whose?"

"Maryam's, of course."

"But he didn't kill her."

"Of course he did! It's clear that he's a criminal. That's what the police concluded."

"Maryam committed suicide. Just like his wife committed suicide before, and he blamed himself for her death."

"No! No, the camera showed all the details of the nightmare that Maryam lived."

"Camera?"

"Yes, the one attached above the entrance to the garden."

"Didn't the camera also reveal that Maryam didn't resist, but that she embraced Daoud gratefully before going willingly to her death?"

Miss Zahra leapt from the bed as though pushed from behind. Her eyes widened, pupils dilating, and her ears stretched back. "And how do you know that, Mr. N?" she said, speaking in a strange tone and with a forced rhythm. "No one has seen the video besides the police and us."

"Actually, I saw it too, watched it live."

"Impossible!" cried the first Miss Zahra, driving away that other Miss Zahra. "Did you have a hand in this?" she asked, taking a step back. "Did you help him? How? My God!" Her voice was choked as she pressed her hands over her mouth. Tears ran down her cheeks. "Poor Maryam! Poor, unhappy Maryam! What did you two deranged men do to her?"

I grabbed both Miss Zahra's wrists. She was on the verge of a nervous breakdown. Gripping her hands, I drove my eyes into her like nails. "We didn't do anything to her," I whispered. "The war in her country is what did it. The war is what ended her life even before we first laid eyes on her. The ghoul ate her family and destroyed her city, but it left her alive to prolong her torment. Daoud said she had reached her limit, and Daoud wasn't lying. She really had reached her limit. She would invite us to dinner and beg and plead for us to help reunite her body with her soul. The soul of Al-Dante remained back there, Miss Zahra, back where her husband and her children were killed, and it was calling for her body to rejoin it. Daoud is innocent! He didn't hang her. She hanged herself with his help. If you'd heard her recite Dante's passage about the River Styx, you would understand, and you would have helped her too."

I began reciting:

> We set off across the water, leaving the shore behind.
> Sluggish, that ancient boat embarked,
> Weighted as never before.
> As we crossed that lifeless slough
> The mud rose up, and from within came a voice:
> "Who are you, you who have come here before your time?"
> "I am one who weeps."
> "May you weep and wail forevermore . . . "

I finished my recitation with a flourish. My voice rose as high as the ceiling and would not come back down to earth. Suddenly, I was a Shakespearean character, a Greek tragedian calling to the chorus and the audience. I was Wahid Jalal in *Order in the Court*; I was Marlon Brando in *Julius Caesar*; I was Youssef Wahbi, augustly calling out, "Free the soul of Al-Dante! Let her fly free through the sky of her city, Aleppo! Grant the innocence of my client, Daoud Majid Daouuuud!"

When I released Miss Zahra's wrists, her hands were about to explode from the blood swelling her veins. Fear was etched on her face: true fear, the kind that changes the color of your skin, shortens your panting breath, draws the sweat from your body like water pouring from a clay pitcher, freezes the blood in your veins, and bends your bones until you fold like a blade of grass. A third Miss Zahra appeared before me, in such agony and terror that she was about to fall to the ground. Throughout all my years of living there—so many I could no longer count them—I had never seen her in such a state: melting, dissolving, shaking, and nearly breaking apart and shattering, mirror-like, into a thousand pieces.

Miss Zahra began massaging her left wrist as she slowly edged backward. Scarcely believing she had reached the door, she put a hand behind her back to fumble with the knob. "It's getting late," she said, forcing her lips to open in the semblance of a smile. "Have a good . . . Well, I'll see you tomorrow."

As it happened, tomorrow arrived, but I did not see it. I slept a long time, far off, where I met a great number of people. I got lost, returned, and settled in a magnificent house. I began to explore its rooms, its floors, its gardens, its mountains, and

I wandered with a woman among its various wings. Then Neda appeared, pale and regretful, half-naked under an open overcoat. She was wearing pink and black underwear, and she placed a finger over her lips as she whispered, "Sshh!" It occurred to me that she was working as a model, or as a salesperson, and someone was forcing her to wear Victoria's Secret as she tried to make me understand something. Next I saw my father, standing at the window with his back somewhat hunched. He was lifting one leg as though to jump, but this time he was frozen inside a painting and did not move. I came close to the painting and used a white towel to wipe away the window frame and the outside details that had been drawn there. The colors started running on all four sides and began to cover the man. I was terrified at what was happening to the painting and cried out: "Father! Father! Jump! Come on, jump!" At that point, I leapt from a bed soaked with my own sweat.

I waited another hour, until it was exactly 10:25. When Miss Zahra did not appear, I decided to go and find her. I was hungry and annoyed. I pulled the door handle violently, but the door didn't budge. I tried again. It remained stuck. After a few more tries, I began kicking it and shouting, "Let me out of here! Miss Zahra! The door is stuck! The handle won't turn!"

After a few minutes, I heard footsteps in the hallway coming toward my room. A hoarse voice announced itself, keys were inserted in the lock, and a young, broad-shouldered, blond man appeared. "I'm Hazim," he said. "Sorry for the delay. I'll be back in a few minutes with your breakfast."

I stopped him with a yell. "Where's Miss Zahra?"

"Miss Zahra has been transferred to a different floor."

"Do you people think you can lock me in?"

"Those are the orders."

"I want an interview with Andrew. Now! This instant!"

"Fine. I'll let him know. Don't worry." Then he closed the door again and locked it.

When something unexpectedly crashes into you, you look around to make sure it isn't all a dream. Then you make sure the situation actually relates to you and isn't just a coincidence. You stare at things, reassemble the details, and sniff the air. In the end, when you are forced to admit that, yes, it's you, and the event actually did happen, you're left in a daze, and then the shock settles in.

Had Miss Zahra informed anyone about our conversation last night? Did she tell the police that I was Daoud's accomplice in the crime of Maryam's suicide? But how could the suicide be a crime, and how could the video recording prove that? On the other hand, given that they have placed Daoud in prison, how could it not show Daoud pushing Al-Dante to her death? And what about me? Would they arrest me, guilty as an onlooker who did not offer help to someone in need? There's an offense in the penal code called "Failure to Provide Assistance to a Person in Danger," and I, yes I, had committed it, at least according to the most straightforward interpretation.

Suddenly, Lazarus came to mind. I wondered what became of him after he was raised from the dead. Was he happy to come back to life? Just as Maryam was happy to leave it? I didn't find myself inclined to answer that question in the affirmative. For he is the only person who pierced the veil, the only one who realized what was on the other side of life, yet he didn't favor us with any comment or explanation. To tell the truth,

Lazarus may have made a report when he returned. He must have written something, left something behind somewhere. It's inconceivable for someone to live through that experience and say nothing about it. But no doubt someone else tore it up, wiped it away, and blotted out those words, which, were they discovered, would shake the very foundations of heaven and earth.

They have placed poor Daoud in the grave, and who will come to raise him from the dead?

———

Shaygha came home from work early, which was unusual. She shot through the door like a rocket and threw the paper bags she was carrying onto the table. It was dinner, judging by the smells of grilled meat, garlic, and pickled vegetables that wafted through the room. I jumped up to embrace her, and she clung to my neck before wrapping her arms around my waist. Her face lit up with happiness, like a child who has just been released on summer vacation and runs through the park as fast as her legs will carry her. She spoke so fast that she tripped over her words.

"Mr. Joe was informed about a police raid this evening, so the girls were sent away while the club stayed open. There's no trace of us or the services we perform, so the police won't find anything wrong when they arrive. Mr. Joe will graciously invite them in and offer them something to drink. Then they'll take themselves off, and we'll get the all clear. Mr. Joe is generous. He feeds the large and the small. He gets away every time, and we escape with him."

Shaygha let go of me and went into the bathroom to wash her hands. She came back to the table to lay out the dinner she'd brought, but I stopped her with a word.

"No, we won't eat here tonight. Dinner's on me."

She looked me over, confused. "Why?" she asked, her voice unsteady. "Have you decided to leave?"

I laughed as I took her face in my hands and shook it left and right. "No, you crazy fool! Just the opposite."

I went to the bed and took out a big bag I'd hidden underneath. From it I drew a red dress, black shoes, and a small purse. I slowly placed it all on the bed. Then I made her sit beside me and asked her permission to proceed. I took off her shoes, then her clothes. I loosened her hair and let it fall onto her shoulders. I got something to wipe off her makeup and the polish on her fingernails and toenails, which I cut very short. Without offering the least resistance, she remained frozen on the bed.

Next I took her hand and led her to the bathroom, where I sat her on the seat in the shower. I turned on the water and slowly began washing her, as though I had a lifetime to wash off all her stains. Through it all, she remained silent, submissive, her eyes closed, as though the water might pass through her skin to wash her heart, her soul, and each of her organs. I finished rinsing off the soap. Then I dried her with a big towel and carried her back to the bedroom. I dressed her in her underwear and the new dress. Last, the shoes. I brushed her hair and pulled it back tight, braiding it into a single plait that hung to the middle of her back. I finished by spraying her with a light, gardenia-scented perfume.

162

Shaygha sat down. Like one of those lenticular cards that show different images when you turn them, she was a woman whose identity wavered between child and lady. Innocence shone on her skin, only to transform into the alluring brown gleam that she carried from her distant country. Her dress had a simple cut that hugged her body and her small, rock-like breasts, as well as the curve of her legs. I didn't feel any sense of arousal toward her, nor was I struck by the desire I usually felt whenever I touched her. I had separated her from me—and from herself—by what I had done to her, so that I might be able, just this once, to see her from a sufficient distance. Just like that, on her own. Independent of me, and in an ideal light. In that condition, Shaygha possessed some of Thurayya's remoteness, some of Neda's indifference, some of Mary's purity. I did it all to confirm my decision, which I made entirely on my own, to make her part of my life.

As if in a dream, Shaygha raised enthralled, indebted eyes to me. Then they registered shock and concern. In that moment of overwhelming joy, it had not occurred to her to ask how I had known she would return early. And how had I purchased those expensive gifts, after she had been the one who spent all the money to clothe and feed me? Her features froze in sudden alarm. She broke out in a flushed sweat at the thought that I might have appropriated the fruits of her labors, all the money she had been saving up over the years. She leapt up, turned the mattress over, and thrust her hand inside to pull her treasure out of its hiding place in a hole on the bottom. When she found it there, wrapped in newspaper inside a plastic bag, she burst into a flood of tears. Overwhelmed by joy and gratitude, she began kissing my hands and begging forgiveness for having doubted my honesty, even for a second. All those emotions were a lot for her small body. I lifted her up and embraced her. Then, overcome by a blinding desire, I entered her, feeling how soft and wet she was. With a convulsing spasm, she arched her back before collapsing on the bed. She asked for a moment to compose herself in the bathroom before we went out.

I opened her purse and put all her money inside. I didn't inform her of my resolution to remove her from her life. I didn't inform her that I had been planning everything for more than a week. I had decided upon that day and was waiting for her to come home from work to run away with her, and it was pure chance that she had returned before the usual hour. I had purchased suitable clothes for her and had secretly made arrangements with a taxi driver to bring us to the restaurant next to my building. I had already picked out some of her things and packed them in the trunk of his car. She didn't have much: work clothes that were not appropriate to wear during the day; daytime clothes, which were largely just for sleeping; and her life's earnings, which she feared she had just lost. Likewise, I didn't inform her that I was undertaking something so bold as to "kidnap" her. I knew that would terrify her, and she would refuse, saying, "No one escapes from Mr. Joe. No one!" as she always used to repeat. "Yes, they do!" I silently insisted. "You will escape. I will make up for everything. I will protect you, despite him and despite yourself, because you returned my soul to me."

Yes, in her meagerness and her weakness, Shaygha had returned my soul to me. She had restored something of my manhood and my self-worth. Shaygha, the little Nepalese sorceress, had fed me the magical bean pods that straightened my spine and revived my strength. My heart jolted into rhythm. My head got right. Indeed, it occurred to me that I might even reconcile with my writing—if only for her, so she could be proud of me in front of others and know that she did not have a homeless failure for her spouse. I wanted to surprise her with my home, my social status, my ability to protect her and care for her. That's all I wanted, and for once my wish came true, when that bastard Mr. Joe made things easy by sending her home early.

I took out my phone and sent a brief text to the taxi driver: "Wait for me at the corner in thirty minutes. Don't be late!"

———

When I got out of the car, I felt I was in another country: one I was visiting for the first time, or perhaps a place I was returning to after many years. Even though it had been only two months since I had abandoned my apartment, I forgot who and what was in my own neighborhood. A strange combination of familiarity and newness gripped me—as did Shaygha's hand, which clung to one arm like a tote bag, while my other hand pulled her small suitcase. Shaygha asked which part of the city we were in, and what was there. "We've arrived!" I said, avoiding the question.

We entered Al Dente Restaurant in the Albergo Hotel. I was a local and a regular customer, and the maître d' with protruding eyes, Saleem, hurried up to receive me. "Mr. N, it's been so long!" he said. "Thank God for your safe return!"

Then he turned to Shaygha, her arm passed through mine, and he greeted her with a courteous bow of his head, being uncertain about which language to use in addressing her. No doubt he thought I had taken some trip, and here I was, coming home bearing the kind of spoils that travel on two feet. He put the small suitcase I was carrying in the corner behind the door and said, "A table for two?" I nodded with the unaccustomed feeling of someone returning to his family home after a long absence and finding it just as it had been, with nothing changed: the lights, the smells, the green chairs, the orange wooden doors, the large bronze chandelier hanging in the center of the room. The scene was perfect, without the least thing to offend a sense of taste or harm the mood. A cozy place that invited you to let yourself go and sink in.

I took Shaygha's hand and untwined it from where it had burrowed under my arm. I guided her around the table and sat her down opposite me, whispering, "It's okay. You're safe here." She was trembling again, from the shock of seeing such things for the first time. These things went beyond all expectations, and she was probably afraid I couldn't pay the bill in such a place. To tell the truth, I was focused not so much upon her as upon myself in that moment, when I was returning to my natural surroundings, my native element, and sitting at my usual table in my usual restaurant, served by my personal waiter. And beside me, my woman.

I suddenly sensed that the months of wandering and roaming had exhausted me, and that I wanted the quiet stability of home. Yes, I had climbed mountains and descended into valleys; I had dwelt in caves and encountered beasts. I had fought and lost. Now I wanted to return to my home and my woman to tell the tale, sitting in a comfortable chair in front of the fire as a log crackles upon the hearth. I don't know where that feeling came from. Great travelers circle the globe to explore and discover, and then a moment comes when they lay down their nomadic burden and abandon their peregrinations. Sitting there across from Shaygha, savoring the calm and looking at everything around me, I felt I had reached precisely such a point.

The restaurant was uncommonly empty, apart from a few guests who had finished dinner and were talking quietly together over a digestif or a cup of coffee. Some others were sitting at the bar and having a drink as they waited for someone. The manager of the Albergo Hotel greeted me from across the room. He was sitting with what looked like a group of work colleagues. Maître d' Saleem soon brought my glass of Chivas Regal on the rocks, and I ran through my order: antipasti, first course, main course, and dessert. I sank back in the chair, feeling I had just sketched the borders of my empire, by land and by sea, with my Nepalese serving girl sitting at my feet to fan me with feathers and listen for any murmur I might make.

After finishing our first glass, my features began to relax. A look was stealing into Shaygha's eyes, that of a slave toward her master. She contracted and shrank, sitting on the edge of her seat and eating confusedly as she realized how out of place she was, and that she didn't belong with me. I ordered us each a second glass. I reached out my arm, took her hand, and kissed her palm as a way of saying no to all those thoughts.

I'm still me, with my vagrant heart and soul. She's still her, the good little witch who raised me from the mire.

"Shaygha," I said, "from this moment you are my woman. We'll live in my apartment, not far from here. From now on, you won't think about your past or ever go back to it."

She leaned her head to one side and smiled at me, her eyes overflowing with love and gratitude. "My dear," she said, wiping her mouth with a napkin and pushing away her plate.

"Shaygha," I repeated, "you aren't understanding me. All your things are in the small suitcase, and we won't ever go back to Bourj Hammoud. All your trials and tribulations are over, I swear it! You saved me when I was lying in the dirt, and now I'm saving you."

The smile faded from Shaygha's face, replaced by pale terror. She pushed her chair away from the table and stood up. "Enough!" she said. "I'm going back now." She shot like an arrow for the door. I gave Saleem a sign to put the bill on my tab and found Shaygha outside, looking for a taxi. I grabbed her arm and begged her to calm down, promising I would bring her back before dawn. All I asked was for her to visit my apartment, since we were so close.

Shaygha climbed the four flights. On the way, she didn't look around at anything, and I could tell she was furious. I struggled to keep up, panting and carrying her suitcase. We entered the dark apartment. I turned on the lights in the salon and opened the windows. Shaygha was sad. She looked at nothing, with the exception of the big sofa, where she sat down and put her head between her small hands. I sat on the floor at her feet, not saying a word and waiting for the right moment to speak. There I was, transformed from master into slave in the blink of an eye, gripped by the fear that she would leave me, and I would revert to what I had been.

"It's clear you don't know Mr. Joe," she said.

"In any case, I won't let you leave," I said, as I locked the door and put the key in my pocket. "He doesn't frighten me. Don't be afraid! He doesn't own you."

"Yes, he does," protested Shaygha. "None of us owns ourself. Don't you understand? Look at yourself. You have all this, and you came to live with me in a pit! Now you want to save me? You've stolen me from Mr. Joe. You're a liar and a thief, that's all you are!"

"I'll buy you back from him," I replied, crying. "I'll pay whatever he wants. I'll settle everything with him tomorrow. Relax."

"Things aren't that simple, N. Who will support my family after I stop? Who? Tomorrow, when Mr. Joe discovers I'm gone, he'll go crazy. You've sentenced us to death."

I didn't believe her at the time. I took her in my arms and said, "You're in a state of shock. Tomorrow, you'll calm down, and everything will turn out okay. Mr. Joe can go to hell! His whole family can go to hell! It's he who ought to fear me. I'm Mr. N! And if he doesn't, I'll tell the police about him . . . Fine, I won't tell on him. I'll leave him alone, and he'll leave me alone. How will he find me anyway, when we've left without a trace?"

I left her there to cool off and went out to my balcony. The gardenia and the carnation had breathed their last. A thick layer of dust covered everything. The tower stood nearby with an ominous calm. The heavy night mounted over my head like cliffs of black grease. I closed the balcony door, went to my room, and fell asleep, while traces of the whisky rose in my head as vapor, visions, and strange apparitions.

———

The human ability to adapt—to things positive and negative, to plenty and scarcity, to life and death—is terrifying.

I watched Shaygha transform day by day. She contracted within the apartment; then she expanded to fill it. She feared her pimp would find her; then she relaxed into her new situation and her new identity. She felt anxiety for her family; then she grasped at a future still not ripe enough to promise anything certain. She fell asleep as one person and woke up as another. She was getting used to me in my new guise, and I felt her skin expanding, her limbs lengthening, her face settling into gladness. I saw her unwinding into something more tender, softer, like dough when it relaxes.

Over the course of about two weeks, Shaygha eased into the idea of her disappearance. She allowed my persuasions to convince her, so long as she didn't leave the apartment, not for any reason. A wretch does not need long to become convinced of their salvation; they'll believe any story you sell them . . . I sold Shaygha the most beautiful stories, and she bought them all. She wasn't stupid, and she did not need proof. I was the proof. It was my story that she believed, with my lineage, my station, and my financial situation. She began believing in my passion and my desire to have a relationship with her.

After several more days, she gave me a list of things to get her from a shop at the Cola Roundabout that imported things that foreign women bought. I proposed going down to Daoura Circle, which was closer, but Shaygha made me swear not to go back there. So what if I did? Who did she think would recognize me, now that I was a human being again and had recovered my former appearance? I promised her, but I didn't keep my word. I couldn't bear the crowding at Cola Roundabout, and Bourj Hammoud was calling to me after my long absence.

I put on my black sunglasses and got into a taxi that took me to Daoura Circle. From there, I entered Armenia Street at its far eastern end, and soon I found the store I was looking for, with all its signs in languages that only foreign customers understood.

The Sri Lankan employee hurried up to me and asked, surprised, what I needed. I handed him Shaygha's piece of paper, written in her own language. I thought he would hand it back, but instead, he inspected it closely and then began passing up and down the aisles, dropping bags, packages, and different kinds of vegetables into a basket he hung from his arm. I watched the street through the glass storefront. Luqman's shop was not far away. I could pass by it and then catch a taxi in the next street back to Achrafieh. Suddenly, my heart was beating faster, and my knees felt weak. It occurred to me that I was a fool for believing that Luqman hadn't recognized me before, and that he had abandoned the idea of killing me after I had tried to kill him years before.

I turned back to the Sri Lankan and asked him to hurry. "I have to go. I have an important meeting." He added two more items to the basket and declared loudly that he had finished the entire list, that nothing was missing. After packing everything into some bags, he asked if he could go with me to my car, then was very surprised to learn that I didn't have one. I paid the bill with the Lebanese employee at the register—who scarcely turned to look at me—and went outside to look for a taxi. I decided I wouldn't pass by Luqman's shop at all, even though I knew he wasn't usually there in the morning. I'd take the first taxi and go straight home.

Suddenly, I was intensely thirsty. I crossed the narrow street to the juice shop across the way and ordered a large carrot juice. Taking shelter inside the shop, I set down my bags and waited as my drink was being prepared. When it came, I drank it in one go. I still felt thirsty, so I bought a cold glass of premade lemonade, which I picked because I couldn't wait. I drank it desperately, but the persistent thirst still did not go away. Next I bought a bottle of water, which I also drank in one gulp. Finally, my thirst subsided, which helped clear my mind to figure out what to do with myself—and make the decision to go where I had decided not to go.

I picked up the bags again and hugged them to my chest to give my arms a break from the weight. At the corner, I stopped and looked down the side street before crossing. It was quiet and empty; nothing seemed out of the ordinary. There was only a lady of a certain age who had gone out in her nightgown. She was sweeping away the water she had poured in front of her door, after having first watered the plants and flowers that were arranged to prevent cars from parking there. I took the right-hand side of the street, which was opposite Luqman's shop, proceeding with a moderate speed that would not attract attention. When I got close, I slowed a little to steal a glance inside, making a pretense of adjusting the bags on my chest to keep them from falling.

And I saw him. He was standing in the back of the shop, facing the Egyptian employee. I knew him from his broad shoulders and the way he towered over the Egyptian. Even though the place was below street level and dimly lit where those two were standing, there was still enough light to leave no room for doubt. It was Luqman. I could pick him out of thousands, and from a mile away. Joy pricked the bottom of my stomach as I felt the blood surging through my veins. From now on, I know exactly where you are, and you know nothing about me. I am your creator, your god. You have no god but me.

Tensing my legs to keep from breaking into a run that would give me away, I managed to maintain my pace. Then it occurred to me to go past Mr. Joe's bar to get a sense of the atmosphere there, even though I knew it would be closed at that hour. I couldn't resist. One last bout of madness, and then I would relinquish all such adventures forever, I swore to myself. I quickened my step and went down an alley. I came out only to plunge into another, until in the end I concluded I was lost. Fine. I had tried and gotten lost. No loss, no regrets, and I wouldn't be able to say I hadn't tried.

I stopped someone and asked the way back to Armenia Street. He showed me the direction to escape the spiraling alleyways and reach the famous statue of Saint Rita. From there, I had to proceed to the statue of the Armenians, and then to wind my way through the alleys on the opposite side to a final one that opened onto Armenia Street, near the Akil Shop.

I followed the instructions to a tee, but before I reached the first statue, I saw that I had stumbled across Mr. Joe's bar. I stopped at the end of the street and looked carefully. The metal grate was half-raised, and sudsy water was gushing out into the street. What if I just passed by without looking in? It was impossible for Mr. Joe himself to be present; he never left his establishment before daybreak and would not yet be back. I took a deep breath and moved forward. When I came up to the bar, I slowed down to avoid the muddy puddles forming in front of his door. But a final gush from the rubber drain hose sprayed dirty water over my pants and shoes.

"Forgive me, sir!" shrieked an Ethiopian woman. "Forgive me! I didn't see you coming!" She bent down to wipe my pants with her wet hands.

I stole a glance inside. The place was empty. She was the only one there, and the chairs, like inverted insects, were set upon the tables, which had been gathered together in the middle. She invited me to come inside and have a seat so she could clean me off better. I complied and followed her inside. She set one of the chairs on the floor and had me sit down. Then she wet a white towel and began wiping off the dirt. I smiled at her and patted her shoulder, saying, "Don't worry. It will soon dry."

Her grateful eyes looked up from an ugly, twisted face. I asked if she knew Shaygha, a woman who worked there. Surprised at my question, she said she didn't associate with the girls and just did her work, which was to clean every morning, before heading off to do a similar job elsewhere. "Are you looking for a housekeeper or a maid?" she asked.

I said no and, thanking her, got up to leave. It was clear she couldn't give me any information.

Suddenly, she put her hand to her head, closed her eyes, and rubbed her forehead.

"Shaygha . . . Shaygha . . . " she repeated softly. "Wasn't she the Nepalese girl who ran away with her Lebanese friend? I heard Mr. Joe talking about it on the telephone last week when I came to collect my pay. Do you happen to know her? Mr. Joe promised a large reward for anyone who could tell him where she is."

The tone of the Ethiopian woman had changed, and she began giving me a suspicious look that stopped the blood in my veins. "I'm a regular customer," I said, "but it's been a while since I've been here. That's why I asked about her. Maybe she ran away home to her family," I added.

The woman shook her head. "How could she travel when Mr. Joe has her passport?" she said. Rubbing her first two fingers with her thumb, she added that she could keep me notified if I paid her a bit of money.

I put my hand in my pocket for my wallet. I took out a twenty-dollar bill, which the woman snatched from me, saying, "Mr. Joe swore he'd kill her as soon as he found her. He said he'd slit the throat of whoever stole her from him, after first cutting off the man's dick and feeding it to him." She laughed, showing her black teeth. This was the first Ethiopian I'd seen who didn't have teeth that gleamed white as snow.

I gathered myself up and hurried away, half-running, while her piercing, metallic voice followed behind, floating the whole length of the street. "You didn't say your name, mister . . . Don't you want me to tell Shaygha you asked about her?"

The door was still locked from the previous evening, and that damned Hazim hadn't returned as promised. They left me like that until the early morning hours of the following day, and I dozed in my chair, still wearing my clothes, hungry and uncertain. Details from my past came bubbling up. I saw scenes of myself in my old apartment before the specter of the tower destroyed its peace and quiet. I heard the voice of Thurayya telling me to get dressed quickly because my First Communion was about to begin, and it would be very bad to keep Jesus waiting to come into my heart.

I was nine at that time, and Sa'id was sixteen and a half. I asked him to go with me, but Thurayya scoffed at my request, saying she needed him at home, and I didn't need him—or anyone—to attend. Sa'id just looked at me and smiled, even though he was perfectly able either to persuade Thurayya or to dig in his heels, as he did whenever something seemed good for him to do. Where was my father, you ask? He had left through the window. So Thurayya decided I needed no companion, that I could go on my own like an adult.

Early that morning, I took a shower, combed my hair, and put on my white suit. It was actually Sa'id's suit, the one he had worn for the same occasion. Alterations had been made, but no matter how hard they tried, the tailors failed in their task, a fact that became clear the moment Thurayya saw me and declared that nothing would ever fit a body like mine.

When I left our building, I originally intended not to go to my Catholic school, where the ceremony was to be held, but instead to a movie theater not far away that was showing a kids' movie at ten o'clock. I would spend two hours there and then return home, pretending to have taken the Messiah into my heart. But I got scared that the school administrators would notice my absence and tell the monks on me, and I would get in trouble. So I walked down the sidewalk, hanging my head and thinking about what I would say when asked why my family wasn't there. I came up with an appropriate reply: "They'll be coming later," or else, "They're here, just sitting in the back."

We stood in a long line between the chairs, the boys in their white suits on the right, and the girls looking like brides in white dresses on the left. We started walking, two by two, toward the altar, where the priest would give us Christ's body in a white Eucharist wafer dipped in red wine. After that, we would return to our seats in the front row, hands clasped and eyes lowered, suffused with humble awe.

At my side at the end of the line stood Celine in her thick glasses and her short black hair. Beautiful Rita, meanwhile, stood in the front with her chestnut hair, beside beautiful Ibrahim, the two of them resembling gossamer angels who might rise into the air at any moment. That's how the order went from start to finish: most beautiful to least, which meant I was second-to-last, with no one behind me except Fadi, big and fat as a drum.

After the mass was over, the families rushed forward to congratulate their children. They stood together for the professional photographer who had been hired to take pictures to commemorate the occasion, and then went off to the buffet that had been prepared in honor of the ceremony. I was afraid the photographer would see me, so I edged away whenever

I saw him prowling about. Given that my fears are usually realized, he eventually did catch me standing in the corner. Determined not to lose the fee of an additional photograph on account of some naughty boy slipping away, he grabbed my hand and paraded me in front of the assembled families, asking whose son I was. There was not a father or mother he didn't ask, and they all denied me. Thus, it was discovered that I was there as an orphan, with no family or support.

In the end, I bit his hand and ran away, cursing him, cursing my father, cursing Thurayya, cursing Sa'id, and cursing the entire universe. I roamed the streets, furiously kicking everything in my path before breaking down in sobs. When I got home, I screamed in Thurayya's face—the first time I'd ever done anything like that. "Why did my father have to die instead of you?" I said. We were forbidden to say he had committed suicide, or so much as utter that word in her presence. All she did was raise her hand and slap me as hard as she could. Then she punished me further by confining me to my room; I was allowed out only to go to school.

Today, when I think about what made her send me to First Communion alone, I can find no excuse for her. And whenever I come across the photo of my brother at his First Communion, smiling that smile that seemed to embody the purity of his heart—eyes raised to the sky just as the photographer no doubt had asked him to do—and alongside that photograph another of him standing between his parents; whenever I see those photographs, the same bitterness wells up inside me that made me run away from the school, swearing, crying, and cursing the Messiah who needed all those elaborate preparations in order to enter my heart . . .

The lock in the door clicked open, and I leapt up from my seat, crying, "Miss Zahra!" But it was the wild blond guy, Hazim, who appeared, carrying a breakfast tray and apologizing preemptively for his absence the previous day on account of extra duties Dr. Andrew had assigned him. Doctor? Bravo! Miss Zahra disappears, I become a prisoner in my hotel, and Mr. Andrew becomes a doctor!

"I want to see him immediately," I said. "Did you convey my request yesterday? I won't stay in this hotel after today. Not one day longer!"

"Yes, of course, I let him know. He promised to come as soon as you've finished your breakfast."

I wasn't hungry. Rather, I was hungry, but it wasn't real hunger. I felt empty, like I needed something to fill me up, no matter what it was. Empty and disjoined, about to curl up like a snail. My bones were melting, my muscles turning to jelly. My transformation into a mollusk was suddenly possible; indeed, it was inevitable. I could no longer stand on my feet and keep ahold of myself.

I picked up a small pita and tore it in two, dipping half into the yogurt and oil. I took a bite. I shoved a couple olives into my mouth, two mint leaves, and half a small cucumber, and began moving my jaws up and down. I nearly spit it all out as it mashed together and almost squeezed out of my mouth, but I was able to keep my stomach down, and together we somehow passed the trial. I ate the other half of the pita with the same determination, finishing it off with a few gulps of tea. I added extra sugar to give me the energy I needed to confront this despicable conspiracy that was being plotted against me.

I felt the warmth passing into my limbs and my veins suffused with energy. It was only a matter of seconds before Andrew appeared, in a dark gray suit I had not seen before. He had shaved and was moving briskly.

"I haven't been to the office yet," he surprised me by saying. He proceeded to set his black leather bag on the table and give Hazim a sign to step out and leave us alone. Then he pulled the chair back from the table and settled onto it.

As soon as Hazim closed the door behind him, I addressed him in a tone that meant business. "Mr. Andrew, my time here is done. I want you to draw up my bill, because I've decided to leave."

Andrew stared at the floor in silence. After a few seconds, he spoke, without raising his eyes to look at me. "Do you really want to leave us after all these years? I know you are annoyed because we locked you in, but what Miss Zahra said left me very concerned. I persuaded her not to tell anyone about your conversation together, otherwise the police would have come back, and you'd have to take it up with them. That, as you know, would not have turned out well at all for you. In any case, perhaps we need to resume your former treatment. I consulted your brother, Sa'id, on the matter, and he thinks—"

I jumped to my feet. "Sa'id's not the boss of me! I'm not a child who needs permission to wipe my nose! This discussion is over. I'm leaving the hotel tonight, and there's no going back on my decision."

"But where will you go? Mr. N, didn't your brother, your legal guardian, tell you that he sold your old apartment and has been using the proceeds to pay for your stay and your treatment here? You have to know that I cannot permit you to leave unless Sa'id agrees and signs off on this request of yours."

A faint dizziness came over me, and I felt the earth sway beneath my feet. Closing my eyes, I leaned against the table and took a deep breath. Andrew came over to me and took hold of my arm. He sat me back down on the bed and held my wrist to take my pulse. I was in a state of shock, like someone receiving tragic news that he hasn't fully processed yet; or like someone who fears something but doesn't dare to think about it yet; or like someone who is aware of something terrible in his subconscious, even though he has entirely suppressed it from his memory.

Andrew opened his black bag and took out a blood pressure gauge. Wrapping the cuff around my arm, he pumped it up until it squeezed tight. "One seventy over one hundred," he said with a frown as the pressure eased. He gave me a small pink pill with a glass of water. "Don't worry. It's just Amlor. Take it, and you'll feel better immediately." He took out his phone, pressed a button, and spoke in a low voice. "I'm in Mr. N's room. I want you here right away." When he turned back, he was smiling. "We'll give you back Miss Zahra. Well, happy now?"

I felt a deep sadness float down like a fine veil that landed on my head before descending over my whole body. It was as though I had woken up in some endless flat expanse with the taste of fire and regret in my mouth. I was a child of nine, and my father had carried me in while I slept. He had gone away and left me there alone before I awoke. I lost all sense of direction, and I realized that evening would soon arrive. I understood there was no way out, and my father had abandoned me forever, never to return. Tears flowed down my cheeks, large and heavy. A tear would swell up with my sadness and fall, only to be followed by another, all regular and orderly. I was crying without crying, since I didn't know the reason for my tears, but my misery was bigger than I was able to ignore or contain. If only Mary were here with me now to fold me in upon her ample bosom with the smell of laurel, hiding me away. If only Shaygha were sleeping naked across my torso, her slender legs wrapped around me like a giant insect. If only a hand would drop from the sky onto the secret spot on my back and still the waterfalls of my soul, thundering down so violently over the stones of my life!

Miss Zahra entered. She looked pale and afraid, but when she saw me crying, she approached Andrew, who whispered some clipped, muffled phrases. I was able to catch only a few words: "The old treatment . . . forty milligrams, each morning and night, chlorpromazine . . . I think he realizes we aren't running a hotel . . . " He wrote something for her on a piece of white paper and then left the room.

———

I closed the taxi door. "Abdel Wahab El Inglizi Street!" I cried, only to realize I was speaking much louder than was appropriate for the short distance separating me from the driver. But it was necessary, given the noise outside. The commotion subsided a little, and suddenly I realized I had forgotten all my bags in Mr. Joe's bar. For several moments, I was torn over whether to stop the car and go back to get my things, but there was someone inside me, scolding me and shouting, "Careful! Don't go back there! And don't stay in the area to buy anything else!" Fine. I'd tell Shaygha that I hadn't found the shop in the Cola district, but had just gotten lost and came back when I got tired.

The driver looked at me. "So, sir, you live in Achrafieh?" he said, darkly. I regretted having taken a chance on sitting next to him in the front seat, instead of in the back as I usually did. "Yes," I replied, saying nothing more in the hope he would take the hint that I had no desire to enter into conversation of any kind. I leaned my head against the window and turned my eyes to a group of young women crossing the street, shrieking loudly to each other.

The driver went on talking. "They come as housekeepers, and then they run away and become whores. That profession pays better, sure, but this area is teeming with them. The cops know they don't have papers, but they don't arrest anybody. Why? They've taken on a kind of brotherly regard for them. One girl told me she wasn't afraid to wander around without papers because the whole thing amounted to no more than two hundred dollars if she got caught . . . Do you think their presence here and their cheap prices will prevent another war? How else do you expect so many nations and so many foreigners to gather in this dwarf country, scarcely large enough for its own people, without tearing each other apart? Five thousand lira buys you a quick orgasm, and if you want something more . . . "

I opened the door even before asking him to stop the car and dug ten thousand lira out of my pocket just to get him to shut up. His words seeped into my ears like poison and made me sick to my stomach. I planned to walk as far as the bridge over the river and stop another car there. Taxi drivers in this country were a plague. They carried contagions and passed them on to their passengers without even realizing the harm they caused. They were the bane of the country. They entered our lives without so much as asking permission, and then they settled in to make themselves at home, pushing our buttons and riling up the evil instincts buried inside.

Traffic was nearly at a standstill, and the sun's rays were already being sharpened on its fiery whetstone. Disgusting smells were about to ripen completely and run riot through minds and moods. The entire scene was liable to melt together, blending colors, skin tones, and voices. Seeing it was 10:25, I quickened my pace. I'd pick up something for lunch on my way, I thought, since Shaygha wouldn't have time to prepare the Nepalese feast she had promised.

When I reached the bridge, I plugged my nose as I met the smell of everything that had transformed Beirut River into a gutter of shit and filth and slaughterhouse scraps. Before I crossed into the neighborhood of Mar Mikhael on the other side of Armenia Street and bade farewell to this accursed little planet, I promised myself I wouldn't tread this spool of humanity ever again. I even thought, as I walked, that I should think about going abroad and settling down somewhere—in Europe, for instance, maybe France or England. I should get back to teaching creative writing—or any teaching at all. I could talk to Sa'id about selling the apartment and the land we owned and buy a house somewhere—calm and apart—or else acquire some plot of land and live, my wife and I, off what we could grow or raise. My imagination quickly carried me off to that farm, and I saw Shaygha raising chicken and sheep, making milk, yogurt, and cheese, and growing tomatoes, lettuce, green beans, and cucumbers. I saw myself sitting at my desk, typing out my books on a laptop as I watched her, coming and going in the distance, exhausting herself all day as I did nothing besides write and think.

I felt a sudden dizziness and the beginnings of nausea taking root in the pit of my stomach, and I stopped, mastering the urge to vomit. The idea bothered me very much that I would sink so low as that, right there in the street in view of everyone, and I swallowed my feelings of constriction. I flagged down a passing taxi and asked to be taken quickly to my apartment in Abdel Wahab El Inglizi Street.

This time I rode in the back. I was overjoyed to find it was an actual taxi and not a shared-service taxi. When I got in, the driver closed the windows and turned on the air conditioning. He didn't say anything after asking which part of the street I was heading for. Near the Albergo Hotel, I told him. He nodded his assent and turned his eyes back to the road, scarcely acknowledging my presence after that. Maybe it's my appearance, I thought, or else his youth and the necessity of earning a living in this profession, that inspires his reserve. Or maybe it's the address, which for so long made me feel a sense of distinction, especially when you bring together "Abdel Wahab" and "El Inglizi." It imparted a sense of peculiarity and foreignness, something you don't often get from the names of other streets.

I don't remember how old I was when I asked my father about this person who gave his name to our street. Though it wasn't actually our street's name since we lived in a small, dead-end side street leading off Abdel Wahab El Inglizi. My father told me that Abdel Wahab had been a Syrian nationalist, executed along with some other people by Jamal Pasha, aka "The Bloodthirsty," on May 6, 1916. "He wasn't English, then?" I asked indignantly. "No," my father said. "That was just a family nickname going back to his great-great-grandfather, who was said to be irritable and would blow up quickly, just like English gunpowder." I won't hide the disappointment I felt at the time about this Abdel Wahab, how he wasn't English after all, wasn't even Lebanese, and on top of all that, had been executed! In those days, I was inclined toward strong heroes. I hated losers and weak people, just like Thurayya did. Deep down, I was convinced that was the reason she hated my father, and I believed that if he were strong and firm, and if he treated only Thurayya, she would have loved him. Then she also would have loved me, his progeny, just as she loved Sa'id, her tough and brilliant progeny.

We arrived, and I gratefully gave the driver all the cash I had left in my pocket to cover the fare. I felt a deep sense of relief at the thought of being in my apartment very soon, close to my woman, possessing the freedom to remain right there or to leave for anywhere I wanted to go. I went up the stairs, in a hurry to reach my apartment on the fifth floor, and knocked on the old wooden door with two panes of glass set behind iron tracery. It was polite to knock, in order to let Shaygha know I was back. I was also feeling lazy and didn't want to dig the key out of my pocket.

Shaygha did not come to open the door for me, even though I knocked and waited three times. I felt slightly concerned, afraid she might have left. My fear abated when it occurred to me that perhaps she was taking a shower, and I quickly searched my pockets for the key. That's when I realized that my small leather wallet was not in its usual place in my back pocket. "I'll have to look for it later," I thought as I pulled out my key and put it in the lock. But then an image of the wallet popped into my mind, from the time I was paying for things at the store. It was followed by another image of my taking out twenty dollars to pay the Ethiopian woman at the bar. God! I had accidentally left it behind when I rushed out!

I entered the bedroom and found three people standing there, waiting for me. The first was Mr. Joe. I recognized him by his short stature and the black leather cap that covered his bald head. He looked like a cartoon character, with his small feet, his shining black shoes, and his smooth, thin mustache set above sharp, cruel lips. How could so much force and so much cruelty, with all the dread and terror it inspired, be concentrated within a small man like this, who didn't at all look the part? Perhaps because power is not a muscle, just a strong persuasive authority, nothing more. You see yourself as powerful and capable, and others automatically adopt your view of yourself. Just let those two goons step away from Mr. Joe, and he would discover he was not brave enough to face me for a minute. He couldn't stand up to a beating from me for a second. He would collapse before me, no question, because my power lies in my frightening capacity for endurance and suffering. I have been loaded up with deprivation as a burden I have borne. I have been weighed down with hatred, cruelty, isolation, and death, and I have taken it all. I exceed the Messiah Himself in my ability to endure cruelty and humiliation. What is the cross compared to what I have suffered? Beatings are nothing, believe me, because the most violent pain exists on another plane.

Mr. Joe came over to me with his eyes lowered. He stood close, examining his fingers as he turned his hands over. Then he drew from his pocket a bracelet with small, pointy studs, through which he inserted his four fingers before curling his hand into a fist. Before I could react at all, the two goons grabbed my arms in order to hold me in place. Mr. Joe remained calm and made a sign to one of them, who left the room while the other stayed behind to hold me. "Where is Shaygha?" I wanted to ask, but I was afraid of doing anything that might provoke them, so I kept quiet. He wasn't going to hurt her, that was for sure. They would lecture her a bit to teach her a lesson, and then they would send her back to her work. The bastard wouldn't harm the goose that lays the golden egg, even if he would punish me in front of her in order to scare her enough to stay away from me, and for me to keep away from her. Was he thinking of killing me? No. No, I didn't think so.

Shaygha's groan reached me from the other room. It sounded like she was waking up from a deep sleep. Then the goon must have slapped her, for the groan changed into the screech of a cat being tortured. I shot Mr. Joe a glance, appealing to him, but the corners of his mouth curled up in a smile and he shook his head as though to say, "Just wait. You haven't seen anything yet." Fear struck me—the kind I don't like, the kind I can't stand, the kind I hate. It plunged into my belly like a dagger, and the more I thought about Shaygha or pictured her in the hands of this beast, the blade went deeper. Yes, they would hurt her. They would hurt me. They would cut off everything that connected us so that she would no longer be able to stand the sight of me, or I the sight of her. The hatred one victim feels for another would fill our hearts and attach her to the executioner.

When I was still a child and could not endure much pain, I would seek Mary's lap whenever I felt afraid. She would overwhelm me, and I would feel her ample body folding around me and protecting me. When I got my first facial hair, I became too ashamed to go running to her, so I would lock myself in my room, neither coming out nor letting anyone in until my storm had passed and I became calm again. When the country settled into civil war, my fear changed and worsened. I could barely manage it until Neda suggested a solution she had once read in some magazine: "Imagine that the person frightening you is a child, and your fear will drain away." Just like Thurayya, Neda was addicted to reading women's magazines. She would send me out to buy them from the kiosks at all hours, day and night, come rain or come bombardment—Neda, whom I loved, whom I relied upon, and to whom I had delivered my soul, only for her to leave me suddenly because she was no longer able to bear me. "To bear you," she had said. Yes, she chose her words precisely, insisting that her problem with me was a problem of weight, not a problem of energy or her capacity to endure. That killed me. It was just some stupid phrase she uttered, but it was all over for me. To this day, I do not understand how an educated and cultured woman like her could have used such a phrase, purposefully and by design, especially a woman addicted to foreign magazines, each issue of which contained prescriptions for understanding love and emotional relationships, and gave advice on "how to keep your man."

Neda's magazines advised readers to imagine terrible and terrifying figures as children. Next, they advised readers to picture them naked. For my own part, I added the detail of them sitting on "the throne." And so, whenever I passed through a militia checkpoint, I would sit the gunmen down on a toilet, and they would seem ridiculous to me. As everyone knows, laughter is the best antidote to fear, so I imagined tyrants, soldiers, bosses, slanderers, liars, and criminals with their pants bunched up around their ankles, in the very moment that their constipated bowels strained to push out a stone-hard turd. I would build up the details of the picture, and every time I thought I had finished drawing it, I would think of something else to embellish the image. I did that with everyone who made me afraid, who hurt me, who humiliated me and savaged me. The number of those people was too great to be counted: at home, in the neighborhood, at school, in the university, in the community, and out in society, with everyone. Thurayya alone was the only person I did not dare put in that position. If I built up the courage and the idea slunk along at night into my subconscious, I would wake up in terror, as though I had imagined God Himself sitting where it is not at all proper to put him.

Shaygha appeared, slung over the shoulder of the goon who had just gone out, her head dangling and the side of her face pressed against the man's back. It was obvious from the slackness of her limbs that she had been drugged, and even now she was tottering across a delicate rope that separated consciousness from unconsciousness. The goon heaved her up, raising into view her blurry gaze and a face that was bloody and bruised. I felt a burning inside. I felt regret. I felt impotence and defeat. I tried to get away from the man holding me so that I could embrace her, but the bastard pulled my elbows back until the ribs nearly popped out of place one by one.

The goon lowered Shaygha from his shoulder and tried to stand her on her own two feet. She could not stand straight, and instead, her spine folded, pushing her torso forward. The man put his forearms under Shaygha's armpits to hold her up. Her neck bent, and her head rested back against his shoulder, as her feet remained suspended above the ground. A tear came from nowhere and slipped out the corner of my eye when I saw how small she looked. Never had she seemed so tiny! One of her shoes was dangling from her foot, while the other had fallen off nearby. I felt a strong sense of compulsion, and more than once I nearly bent over to pick it up and put it on her naked foot, except that the goon holding me wasn't about to let go.

Mr. Joe stepped forward, his face right up against mine. In a low voice, scarcely moving his sharp lips, he snarled, "Did you really think you could mess around with me, steal one of my girls, and just disappear? If you had tried to negotiate for her and I refused, perhaps I would have understood. But for you to snatch her away, just like that, means you don't take me seriously, you're making fun of me. Tell me, are you making fun of me?"

I nervously shook my head. Mr. Joe turned away and stepped over to Shaygha. When he took her face in his hands and peeled a lock of her hair off her swollen features, she opened her eyes. Her pupils completed a full circuit without focusing on anything in particular; then they rolled back again to show the whites. Mr. Joe slowly wiped away the line of blood running from the corner of her mouth and down her neck. Then he pushed his large thumb between her lips. He began moving it in and out, looking at me the whole time. His other hand began playing with her nipples before reaching down to grab her pussy. Shaygha suddenly gasped, like someone breaking the surface of the water in the very last moment before drowning. Then she purred, as a kitten might do as it rubs against its owner's leg. The filthy man stroked her some more, holding my gaze as he aroused her. For a moment, it appeared as though he had forgotten why he had come.

Afraid to anger him, I said in a shaky voice, "How much do you want to set her free?"

He continued staring at me as he set about adding, multiplying, subtracting, and dividing, taking care to make no mistake in the calculation. "How much do you think she's worth?" he said, as he crossed the room and sat down on the only sofa in the room.

"I don't know. It's up to you to set the price."

"You never told me: what do you do for work?"

"I'm not working at the moment, but before, I was a writer."

"You were a journalist? For which paper?"

"No, no, I mean a novelist. And a university professor."

"Ah, a storyteller, then! What do you say about me telling you a story that will make your hair stand on end. You write it down for me, and I'll sign it."

Mr. Joe turned around, laughing for the two goons, who burst out laughing in turn to imagine their boss as a writer. "You'll have to sign it, 'The Sphinx'!" suggested one.

"No!" cried the other. "'Skullcrusher' is stronger."

Mr. Joe wiped the merriment off his face and was frowning again. The goons broke off their jokes and fell silent.

"Her value might not be within your means to pay, so I'll leave it to you to propose a number."

Mr. Joe's words were ambiguous, as though laying a trap. Then I realized he was stalling before making a decision. He had never found himself in this kind of situation before, I was sure of it. None of his girls had ever escaped his grasp and fled with a customer. Yes, that was certainly what was going on. Mr. Joe was buying time as he looked for an appropriate price for giving up Shaygha and saving face. Then I realized that I was bargaining for a human being, and haggling with the buyer over the price! God! And they say that the time of slavery has passed, never to return. No! We've never had the freedom people claim we possess. For as long as we are the slaves of ourselves, the slaves of our families, the slaves of our feelings, the slaves of our impulses, the slaves of our society, the slaves of base and unjust life, the slaves of masters and the masters of slaves, we will subjugate and be subjugated because of skin color, because of geography, because of money, because of gender, because of status, because of weight, because of climate, because of shit, because of . . . we will enslave whosoever may be, howsoever we may, always and for all eternity.

Luqman suddenly appeared and slapped me on the nape of my neck. He stood behind me and whispered, "Enough of this prattling! Her life is now in your hands. Offer a price for her, and don't go overboard. Start at five thousand, and we'll take it from there."

"Five thousand dollars!" I stammered.

Mr. Joe was inspecting the details of the room around him, frowning, guessing that I must be able to do much better than that. I thought about doubling the price, but Luqman whispered a rebuke at my back: "Be firm! Don't raise the price one cent! Remind him that she is Nepalese, not Filipina, if you must."

Luqman persuaded me. I held firm and did not suggest the number I had intended. By then, I found myself maneuvering cleverly, sure of myself, and I added, "If you want, we can go straight to the bank. I'll give you the money, and we'll forget everything that happened. I promise, you'll never hear from us or see us again."

Mr. Joe nodded. Then he made a sign to the goon holding me to let me go and come close. He stepped forward, and Mr. Joe whispered a brief order in his ear. The goon went out for several seconds before coming back, holding something behind his back that I couldn't make out. The second goon smiled. He looked as rough and mean as the first. He sat Shaygha on the bed. Her body went limp and she lay back. The goon approached and put into my mouth a small wooden ball he had taken out of his pocket before winding a handkerchief across my mouth and tying it behind my head. I turned my eyes to look for Luqman but couldn't see him. I tried to call him up again in my mind in case he would recommend what I should do now, having followed his advice, but he did not come forward. I knew that I, as usual, was alone to face whatever was to come, something that appeared for the first time to be too heavy for me to bear.

Working together, the two goons forced me to kneel. They took my hands and spread them on the tiles before pressing my head to the floor. I was no longer able to see anything. I was in the position of someone half-blind, prostrate for prayer. Mr. Joe approached and spat out, "Five thousand, you fucker? Even if you said a hundred thousand, you would still have gotten what's coming to you!"

Then he swept down with a sharp blow on my right hand. I heard a pop as the bones of my forearm snapped. There was a second blow, even more violent, on my left hand.

I bellowed. My voice burst out like a foreign object, as though it were a sharp stake driven up my anus and all the way out through my teeth. The pain was beyond expression, beyond my ability to comprehend; it surpassed my capacity to endure. All the nerves in my brain failed, and I blacked out momentarily. But like someone who realizes he is in a bad dream and tries to wake up, I took hold of the delicate rope of consciousness, guiding myself by it and moving forward with difficulty until I was able to raise my head. Through the window leading to the balcony, I beheld Shaygha, her arched body swinging back and forth between the arms of the two goons who each held a hand and foot. She was so light, her body was so small, and they swung her like a limp doll. They swung her faster and faster, and then they threw her from the fifth-floor balcony onto the asphalt of the street below.

Shaygha flew up into the air before my very eyes, and then she disappeared from my field of vision. The sound of her hitting the ground was like a wooden door slamming. Yes, the door was slammed shut, once and for all, on her life, on her disappointments, on the years of her suffering, and on her constant striving for a better life. I didn't stay awake for long. As my vision went black, I saw her again, this time with two enormous wings that spread and carried her above the buildings, high above the clouds.

Madness is a low balcony looking out at the sunset.

I am sitting there, watching time pass without passing, a stretch of putrid time, ailing time, with pitted limbs. Insects crawl on me, pressing their legs and their faces into my bare skin. I shake them off in disgust and see them disappear without falling to the floor or flying away. There is a big black one on my belly that doesn't wander across my skin like the others, but crouches there, motionless, as though it's planning something. Indeed, it is certainly planning something. I look around. I am in a white room. I can't make out all the details because I am scarcely able to turn my head. I feel a desire to move, but my eyes are the only things that work properly. The rest of my body feels as though it were nailed fast to a wooden plank. Am I in a grave? Will our beloved Lazarus come soon to wake me?

A woman in white wakes me up with the touch of her cold fingertips. I tell her that a big black insect has gotten into my bed, and I'm afraid it might lay its eggs there.

"You've made this creature up," she reassures me. "You imagined it. You invented the whole thing in order not to notice the immense pain you are in."

"But the real pain is here." I look up, indicating my forehead.

"Give me a minute, and I'll change the sedative. Do you remember your name, or not yet?"

I stare at her blankly, trying to understand what she means.

"Fine. Do you at least remember the reason you're here?"

I turn away so she won't keep talking. She moves away, and I hear her disturbing the tranquility of things in the room. "Don't worry," she adds. "You're going to be fine. You just need some time to get better and recover the ability to move your limbs. The doctor will come soon to explain everything to you."

Her mouth opens and closes with some effort, as though her jaws have been secured with a rubber band. The words stretch out in her mouth, and their forms dissolve before the meaning appears. Or else I'm just not hearing too well since I have no desire to be where I am or to communicate with anyone. I have cut all lines, turned off the lights, and made my body still as I float on the black ocean, rising and falling with the waves. No, there aren't any waves. No motion. No desires. I am an inanimate shape, a thing, made of straw, of cotton, of sponge. Yes, I am made of some brittle material, shot through with hollow spaces filled with air. I float in nothingness. My being is centered in a single point at the front of my head that bulges and throbs like a time bomb counting down its final seconds.

The nurse goes out, and a doctor in white comes in, accompanied by two white young men. He introduces himself and the other two, saying, "I'm Dr. Ghassan, and these are Dr. Sami and Dr. Shafik. Praise God for your recovery! Apart from the broken bones that you suffered, which will take some time to heal, we can reassure you that all your vital functions are fine."

All my vital functions are fine? Amazing! My muscles wake up each day ready to set about their work with vim and vigor, performing their functions with smooth regularity. The heart pounds, strong and steady. The liver is in a state of peak readiness. The lungs are ensconced in their usual place. The stomach stands at the ready, awaiting orders. The brain polishes its connections and prepares the trumpet . . .

Is it true I'm still fine?! They tortured me, broke my arms, shattered my bones, tore out my heart and threw it from the fifth floor right before my very eyes—and I somehow didn't die? They did all that, while I suffered, endured, and fought. And in the end, I lived? Ah . . . It truly is remarkable, baffling, my ability to endure pain. I'm not really one of those people who love life or cling to it, for what good will it do me now that my claws have been pulled out, my weapons dulled, and I'm thrown into the den of murderers?

"What concerns us is your partial memory loss, on account, we believe, of the frightful shock you received, and the way your friend was murdered right in front of you. The mind sometimes refuses to remember atrocities that are too great for it to bear, and it proclaims its inability to function like some sputtering machine that needs time and rest before it regains its health . . . "

No, you man in white, I have not yet lost my memory. It is my memory that has lost me on account of my compulsion to sleep after what your assistant, the nurse, told me. You allow me not to know my name or what happened to me, and you interact with me on that basis. You do not realize that the malady lies in my fatal recalling of every detail and my brain's refusal to take in the full picture. So here I am, not grasping realities except through successive glimpses of the horizon, momentary flashes that reveal disparate, disjointed things, before putting them back together again. I know perfectly well that my four limbs were tortured, that I was crucified upon them, but I'm not certain if the blows were applied to my skull or not. If I were beaten there, how is it that I remember the beating? Wouldn't I have lost consciousness?

The doctor poses several questions, but I do not turn to face him. I do not hear you, doctor. And if I heard, I would not understand. If I understood, I would not reply. You know my story, no doubt, so why do you ask me to repeat it? You certainly know it. Otherwise, how would I have been brought here? Would you have been able to receive me, if you hadn't been made aware of who I am? Did the neighbors notify Sa'id, just like they notified the police, who brought me to you? And will he come to my bedside to be present for my final agony?

Of course he will come. I'm his only brother. I'm his little brother. I no longer have anyone in this whole damn world besides him. He's my brother, and I'm his. He will come, and when he sees me, he will mourn for me. The tears will flow from his eyes. He will refuse to leave me ever again and will remain by my side until I'm well. He will reach his hand inside his breast pocket and take out two plane tickets. Because he is not going to leave me after this. He will keep me company so he can watch over my safety and my health. Sa'id will be the mother I never had, not even for one day. He will be the father who resigned from his post and left me an orphan. He will admit that he persecuted me, that he broke me, that he walked all over me and thought of no one but himself. He will acknowledge that Thurayya was partially responsible, because she instilled in him a love for self and for appearances, but that he is fully responsible, because he accepted her behavior and took advantage of it to develop the egotism and self-love that was inside him. I will pardon and forgive him because he confessed his mistakes, because he grieved them, and because he is my brother, whom I loved, whom I was proud of, whom I was scared for.

And if we open up to one another and reconcile, I'll share with him everything that happened to me, all the things he doesn't know about, and I'll conclude my long discourse by saying: A beating hurts the body, brother, nothing more. It lands on the surface, on the skin, but it doesn't pass underneath or take a firm hold. A beating is a visit to the body, conducted by someone just passing by. He crashes into it, produces a few tremors, and then departs. But torture is something else. It penetrates the skin and nests within the cells of the spirit. It remains there with you for as long as you live. A beating can break your limbs, your nose, your jaw. But torture breaks your soul, it skins your pride, it wipes the ground with your honor. Torture strips away your defining features as a person and throws you in a pit with animals and cadavers. You never get free from torture, brother. And I never got free of you.

"Sa'id? Yes, he called more than once and was on his way to visit you, but something came up and he had to change his plans. He requested my personal number so he could call anytime to check on you . . . Why are you crying? Are you in pain?"

"Sa'id? I don't know anyone by that name," I say, as the nurse wipes my face with a damp lemon-scented cloth. "And I don't want to know anything about him. I don't have any parents or family. No mother, no father, no brother, no girlfriend. I'm a creature born by chance, a bulging tumor, a poisonous plant, a dark crack . . . "

A fit of coughing came over me as some saliva went down the wrong pipe. The white visitors thronged around me, concerned and anxious. If only I could have choked in that moment when I was surrounded by such emotion and solicitude! If only my spirit could have departed and circled up to the ceiling, looking down on my body, as all of you bent over me in compassion. Don't they say that when the soul departs the body, it is so light that it floats up until it bumps against the ceiling and, as soon as a window opens, the spirit passes out into the sky?

———

Death is a window looking out upon open sky.

My father played all his cards at once—the balcony card, the window card, the endurance card—and dived forward, swimming through the air. His soul did not float up to the ceiling of our apartment, but rather it left him even before he smashed into the ground. Perhaps even now it is hanging in the air. My father plunged to his death after having eluded it so many times. He took that last step and disappeared. In order to die, we don't need anything more than a step. Death is a threshold, and it takes but one step to cross over. My father now dwells beyond that threshold, and here I am, approaching him now. If only you would reach out your hand, Father, and pull me firmly toward you. You don't need any

204

great strength for it. Indeed, you don't need any strength at all, for I am already leaning toward you, not resisting or holding back. Take my hand, Father. It's all over for me. I'm done. Finished. Spent. I'm an empty bag, Father, with shape and form but nothing inside, swept by the wind high over scenes of life, where I have no place to go and no business being.

"Father!"

"Yes, N? Don't yell!"

"Sa'id has taken all the balloons! He is blowing them up and popping them!"

"It's okay. I'll buy you others."

"But I don't want others! These are my balloons! Let him pop his own balloons and leave me alone!"

Thurayya entered the room, and Sa'id looked over at me and smiled. I fell silent, and my father fell silent, while Thurayya approached to take her child by the hand and lead him out of the room. She was afraid for him because of me, even though he was twice my size and twice as old. Tears stained my cheeks, and my father didn't know what to do. Then he smiled and came over to console me. I dodged him and went into the corner of the room where I could secretly kill Sa'id and his mother with my bare hands. My father left the room slowly, as though he did not want me to notice him leaving, and I took my revenge on him too by calling him a coward. What kind of man was he to fear his wife and a child? Why wasn't I lucky enough to have a tough father who would rebuke Thurayya, punish Sa'id, and give me back my rights, which were constantly trampled in that house? I was furious, and I pressed my fingers into my palms so hard that the nails dug into the skin.

When the war broke out, and Sa'id became bigger and more unruly, I no longer hated my father. Instead, I began to be afraid for him. I heard terrifying news about kidnappings, killings, and amputations, and I did not trust that I would see my father coming home safe and sound each night before I went to bed and drifted off to sleep. It crushed me that Thurayya never worried about him, and that Sa'id scarcely thought about him at all. I found myself anxious for him on behalf of all three of us. Perhaps this triple concern of mine would protect and save him. Despite the war and its calamities, my father did not change his habits. He continued dedicating his Saturdays to the poor, but he started performing more of his medical work in the clinics, since moving around from one neighborhood to another had become risky, given a rash of kidnappings and murders on the basis of identity. This lasted until that day finally came, the day I had feared, when my father did not come home in the evening. Nor during the night. I did not see him until the first light of dawn, steeped in blood, his face pale, nearly collapsing unconscious where he stood.

Thurayya had sent Sa'id and me off to bed, saying, "Your father will return. Don't be afraid." It was the first time she had addressed me as Sa'id's equal, which made me realize that the situation was grave, and that my father might already count among the number of the dead. "I'll make a few calls," she added. "Go to sleep now."

Sa'id went first, and I followed him to his room, where he stretched out on his bed. "Do you think he's been kidnapped?" I asked.

Sa'id shot me an annoyed glance. "Oh, shut up! You and your stupid questions."

He turned off the light, and it was only a few minutes before I noticed his breathing take on the regularity of sleep. I looked at the clock. It was exactly 10:25.

I left his room and entered my own. Sleep came late and treated me badly. Stretched out on my bed, I tried to put out of my mind all the black thoughts that kept stealing in. Much later, sleep overpowered me and dropped me into a world of turbulent, striving nightmares. I hardly escaped one before I entered another. My missing father was the hero in all of them, while I kept trying to reach him, trying and failing. I don't know what it was that suddenly made me open my eyes, but when I did, I saw him sitting on the chair beside my bed, staring at me without a sound. I sat bolt upright, flooded with anxiety, not knowing whether I saw something real or was still swimming in the delirium of my dreams. Placing his hand over my mouth to keep me quiet, he whispered, "Don't be afraid! It's me. I've come back. I'm alright."

No. Ever since that day, when he suddenly appeared before me in a shirt stained with blood, with dazed eyes and a face drained of all color, my father was not alright. At the time, he did not utter another word, but stood up, stripped off his clothes, and dropped them at his feet. Then he eased into my bed and encircled me in his arms. He gave off a strange smell, different from the one he usually had when coming home—the one Thurayya never stopped complaining about—a mixture of sterilizers, anesthetics, detergents, and medicines for inflammation and ulcers. There was another smell that I hadn't encountered before, sharp and pungent, a little like the smell of rusted metal. I almost asked what it was before I realized that it was certainly the smell of the blood that covered his clothes. For the first time, I was smelling blood. "Whose blood is this, Father?" I wanted to ask, but I was too afraid. The important thing is that it isn't your blood, Father, and that you are here at my side. You didn't go to Thurayya or to Sa'id, but to me.

My father drifted off to sleep and snored a little at first. I timed the movement of my breaths with his until they were perfectly in rhythm, and that put me to sleep. He murmured frequently in his sleep, waking me each time. Yet each time I would fall back to sleep, overwhelmed by my drowsiness. His mutterings become more and more vehement and included fragments of speech. Then there were some words, the clearest being a strange name that my father repeated three times.

When I woke in the morning, my father was gone. No doubt he had gone to inform Thurayya of his return, or else to take a shower and get that disgusting smell off him. I closed my eyes and tried to recall the name he had uttered the previous night, which I had never heard before, but had no luck.

For days, my father remained a prisoner in the house. He neither went out nor received any visitors or patients. He didn't answer the phone. He locked himself in his office and came out only when Sa'id or I returned. He would sit with us in the evening, but he didn't address us, and he didn't respond if we spoke. We would nearly have sworn that he didn't even see us. Thurayya watched him out of the corner of her eye, and since she saw him looking grave and absent, she feigned indifference, pretending that she did not see him either. It was as though she were taking the matter personally, as something directed specifically at her and not connected with his coming home late that one night, drenched in blood.

Then Saturday came, and starting from very early in the morning, a number of his patients gathered in front of the door to our building, along with their children. Little by little, their number grew, until our narrow street and the stairs leading up to our fifth-floor apartment were occupied, reaching almost all the way to our dining table. By eleven o'clock in the morning, my father was still locked in his office, responding neither to our appeals to come out to them, nor to Thurayya's threats to call the police to drive them all out.

I stood in a corner of the balcony behind the flowerpots, stealing glances at the crowds massing underneath our apartment. With their coal-black faces, their tear-streaked cheeks, their dirty, worn-out clothes, and an anxiety that silenced the many children standing small and frozen among their parents, they could have been illustrations for stories about misery and wretchedness. Why don't you go out to them like usual, Father? Why do you leave them alone like this, clustered together and waiting? Aren't you afraid your wife will go out to curse them and drive them away? The doorbell rang. I heard Thurayya shout to Mary, "Don't open it, no matter who it is!"

"It's Mr. Kevork," Mary replied, leading the visitor through the salon and from there to my father's office.

Among the few residents of our building, only our Armenian neighbor Kevork had acquired my father's favor and won his company. My father liked his mixed origins, his charming accent, and his passion for reading history, something my father didn't have time for. I attributed my father's harmony with him to his being a widower. His wife, Fahineh, had passed away from a chronic illness, which is what first brought my father, the doctor, into Kevork's life. His two sons had emigrated to the United States to pursue their education and had decided to remain there. After my father came home in the evening, he and the Armenian would sometimes meet in his office to discuss the state of the world as they played chess or smoked a pipe. Kevork was the one who introduced my father to the ritual of pipe smoking by buying him the necessary gear, including the gift of a rosewood pipe. Then he began training my father on how to inhale and exhale, until the two of them shared the same habit.

Kevork suddenly appeared through the office window next to the balcony railing. "The doctor is sick," he called down in a loud voice. "He cannot receive any patients. Come back another time!" Those gathered below raised their faces to him as he spoke, and then, without a sound, the crowd dissipated. They didn't even wish him a speedy recovery, I thought to myself. They were too sick to wish a speedy recovery even for themselves.

I went over to the corner of the balcony closest to my father's office. Kevork had left the window open, and I anxiously took a seat, not knowing if our Armenian neighbor had been lying to my father's patients so they would clear out, or if my father truly was sick and too weak to help them. How was my father sick without realizing that he was sick? Wasn't he the doctor?

My thoughts were interrupted by the sound of a sob. Another sob, louder, was followed by a steady flow of tears. Then came the consoling voice of Kevork. "Cry, my dear friend, cry," he was saying. "The tears will cleanse the wound."

———

My father said:

"What I saw, Kevork, made me wish that they hadn't left me alive, but had finished me off just as they had done with hundreds of women, children, and old men. More than one thousand five hundred victims in two days! They were savage animals run wild, shooting and killing anyone at all. People were brought out of their homes, gathered together with their faces against the wall, and then they opened fire . . .

"Nurse Widad and I were in the room we had added to the clinic and dedicated to wounded and sick children. There were around fifteen children, the oldest being no more than ten. Some of them had been injured in a bombardment, while others had a fever, diphtheria, or were suffering from malnourishment. We did not know what to do or where to hide. At some point, I decided I should go out, waving a white sheet, in order to talk with the combatants. I would tell them that we were there in the children's wing, and that they had to lead us out to safety. But Widad was overcome by terror. She grabbed my white robe and started screaming like a madwoman: 'Don't go out, doctor! They'll slaughter us all if you do!' The sight of the children, fear distorting their faces, made me reconsider, and I stayed back in order to reassure them that nothing bad would happen. I had not yet seen what was going on outside, and I thought it was just a matter of scattered clashes between the militias. But it was one slaughter after another. From Karantina to Damour, and on to Dawalik . . . The cataract of blood was now pouring upon us, never to end. They were slaughtering people on one side and carrying them off on the other. People were being sorted according to religion—one of yours for one of ours. An eye for an eye, and a tooth for a tooth, and it kept getting worse . . .

"I'm a doctor, Kevork, a doctor! I cannot be with one side or the other. The flowing blood, the injuries, the pain: one fighter is the same as the next, and they are just like anyone who is injured or a victim. I see only damaged bodies. A wounded person, for me, is stripped of any identity: they have no nationality, no religion, no affiliation. A tortured body ought to be treated, cared for, saved. Many people tried to stop me from going to Karantina in those days. 'Only foreigners and strangers live there,' they'd say to me. 'Foreigners?' I'd reply. 'Strangers?' They were poor refugees from Palestine, Syria, and here in Lebanon, needing help and care. I used to go there to provide treatment once a month, and then I started going every week after the start of the war, when it was no longer possible to reach my clinic located on the front lines. Sometimes it was impossible to get home after roadblocks were set up and shells started flying, and I'd remain trapped at the clinic. Those nights, I'd call and tell Thurayya not to wait up for me because there were so many injured people, and I might be a while. She would just hang up the phone without comment, either to blame or criticize.

"The clinic was in a two-story building at the end of the camp, and we were in a one-story room that had been built on one side. The sound of gunshots and explosions, one after another, was getting closer. Then screams and wailing. The children were shaking like little animals and would scream in fright with every boom. Nurse Widad was crying out, begging the children to be quiet so they wouldn't attract any attention. But I knew they would search the buildings to drive out anyone hiding inside. I called to Widad and told her to inject the children with a sedative that would put them right to sleep, something I used to prescribe when a patient's pain became too much. She stared at me, wide-eyed and almost deranged. Then she began nodding her head violently. 'Yes, yes!' she cried, before heading to the medicine cabinet to take out needles and bottles of medicine. Widad injected all the children with the same needle, refilling it more than once. I didn't watch, and I didn't give her any instructions about how to do it safely. The children received their shots obediently. Then they lay down on their beds and, in a matter of minutes, drifted off to sleep.

"Don't ask me why I did that, Kevork. I've been posing the same question to myself without arriving at any clear answer. Was it because I thought those beasts, when they came in and saw the little ones sleeping, would feel pity in their hearts and wouldn't kill them? Or did I want to spare the poor children the sight of the ghouls who would eat them alive? Or was I simply afraid they would draw attention to us, and I wanted to quiet them down by any means possible? Or was it because I could no longer bear my impotence, their howling, and their fear? I don't know. In any case, we gave them sleep—and to Nurse Widad as well, for I saw her inject herself as well with the tranquilizer, saying, 'Forgive me, doctor! I cannot bear another massacre.' Poor woman! She was one of the refugees from Palestine in 1948.

"I pulled up a chair and sat in the corner of the long room, facing the door. The hours weighed heavily upon me. I thought about my parents, and about Thurayya. Would they renounce me after my death because I abandoned them to stand alongside foreigners and strangers? Suddenly, I sensed a growing calm, even as the air turned cold. In a matter of minutes, the day had slipped away into darkness. Even the sound of bullets receded. A short patter here, a sudden burst there . . . Then nothing. The silence gave way to screams, orders, pleas, gunshots, and then silence once again. Then, without warning, an explosion knocked over my chair, and shattered glass rained down upon me. Dear God, don't let it be the clinic! I thought. With all those elderly sick people gathered inside . . .

"The door crashed open. A militiaman had kicked it down with his army boots. He stood by the door, pointing a powerful flashlight and a machine gun into the interior. I had scarcely made out his spectral form against the smoke that filled the indigo air outside before I leapt to my feet, raising my hands high and screaming, 'Doctor! I'm a doctor! Don't shoot!'

"I don't believe it was my pleas that stopped him from killing me, but rather the sight of the children, stretched out upon their beds and sleeping. They had not moved or reacted at all to the explosion. 'What is this?' he shouted at me, appalled, before calling out, 'Luqman! Come quick!'"

Luqman! Yes, that was the name that my father repeated three times on the night he decided to enter my bed, smeared in blood. The first Luqman. That's how I ought to call the person whose name I heard as a child when my father recounted what happened to him that night in January of 1976. For many long years, that story lay hidden inside me. The name of the killer secretly took root within me and then returned as a character in a story from the years after the war ended. That one—meaning the second Luqman—was the protagonist of my novel. I thought he was my creation, not realizing he had emerged from the twilight of memory and the unconscious. As for the third Luqman: he's the one I met recently, retired from the fight, in an internet café in Bourj Hammoud . . .

———

The psychologist looked at me. She raised her eyebrows, drawn a reddish-brown, and said, "Now we have three Luqmans?"

"Yes . . . I mean, no!"

"Yes or no?"

"Yes and no. All of them represent the same person, and if they separated and became distinct from each another, it's only because they are children of different times, such that each of them exists as a possibility for the others. Even you could be Luqman . . . "

"I?" she replied, laughing at the joke I made. Then she pursed her lips in a whistle. Was it out of admiration or astonishment? Who knows! But she returned to her small notebook, writing down her observations and inviting me to go on. I learned later that she would make a note that I was suffering from dual personalities, or even triple, as well as the inability to distinguish between reality and imagination, which led me to confuse people and characters, and to suffer from the delusion that some of them were present with me.

I wanted her to understand that this is literature, that you have one foot in reality and one in the imagination, moving forward across a slender rope stretched tight between the boundaries of consciousness and unconsciousness, between absence and realization. What she truly needed to know was that my reality was catching up with my imagination, and that wherever I turned, I was meeting a Luqman. I looked at her again, my eyes caught by the orangish-red hair tucked behind her ears, and her face spotted with freckles. This ginger. Are you the one who will decide my fate after my limbs recover and regain their ability to move?

How long have I been here, patiently waiting to get my four limbs back? Weeks, I reckon, since they came only yesterday to take the casts off my arms, replacing them with bandages reinforced with lightweight metal splints, which are so much easier to wear. They said my legs need at least a week more. That is why my psychologist comes to me, instead of me going to her. She sits on the chair, calls me Mr. N, and poses questions about my childhood, my early manhood, and my relationships, as though, in this way, she would solve my riddles and untie all the knots inside me.

At first, I refused to answer her. I would close my eyes, pretending to sleep. Then I actually would drift off, and when I woke up, she would be gone. But after a few times, she began waiting for me to wake up. She knew it was impossible for me to fall asleep every time, and I would eventually get bored with pretending. At a certain point, I understood it was in my best interests to cooperate with her because this beautiful ginger would be the one to decide whether I was mentally competent and did not pose a danger to myself or others. She was also the one who would persuade my brother on that question, and he was the one who would decide whether to send me home or to a sanatorium.

My older brother is my legal guardian. A difference of seven years and seven months grants him that distinction. He's the one who left me here like this—broken down, limbs crushed, mind disturbed—without troubling himself to visit me or call. Coward! How will he reply when I demand that he leave, and that he hand over my share of the inheritance and the memory of our father, who left us through the window, and whose spirit is floating in the air? I will tell him I have deleted Thurayya's name from my ID card, and in its place have put Mary. Yes, Mary, who was my adoptive mother. Mary, Maryam the Virgin. And Sa'id, who was always hunched over his own navel, so proud of himself, always seeing himself through Thurayya's eyes, is no longer my brother but has transformed into a big black insect that is at this moment crawling across my belly and making me itch . . .

"Get it off me!" I screamed. "Get it off, before it makes a nest and lays its eggs and starts eating my organs!"

The psychologist tossed aside her notebook and stood up to reach a button that would call a nurse and notify the doctor. The nurse came running, pulling the cover off a sedative needle that she plunged into my forearm. Within a matter of seconds, I was quiet again. I indicated the small notebook with my eyes. The psychologist picked it up and gave me a glance to ask if that was what I really wanted. I stared at her ginger hair. It was ablaze from the slanting rays of the sun that played upon it.

"Your hair is on fire, miss," I said, struggling to move my tongue. "Is that its natural color, or do you dye it?"

She smiled, reaching up to touch her hair before sitting back down in the chair as a way to announce the resumption of our session.

"I used to tell Neda—you know who Neda is, right?" Of course, answered the doctor by inclining her head. "I would warn her in advance. I'm going to lie to you now, Neda, and you have to separate the truth from the lies in what I'm about to say. Neda couldn't figure it out, even when I exaggerated and said nonsensical and illogical things. In the end, she would get annoyed and protest: 'You're not only a writer, you're also an actor, and you're very good at it.' I did the same thing with Mary, but Mary would laugh her heart out. She would run over and give me a big hug, saying, 'There's no one smarter than you, my dear boy!' Mary would laugh, and Neda would get sad. Then Neda came to say she was no longer able to bear me. How could she have loved me then for all those years without seeing how much weight she had taken off my back? Tons! And how, despite my immeasurable lightness when we were lovers, how did she slip me off her shoulders and put me into a bag to throw on the café table and then just leave?

"Do you know Chagall, doctor?" The doctor shook her head, and it was clear she didn't know who I was talking about. I fell silent a moment to recall why I mentioned him. Ah, it was to make her feel my superiority, and to remind me that, no matter what my condition or illness, I remained me, and she remained her. I continued: "He has paintings that looked like us, Neda and me, at that time. One in particular, called *The Promenade*, where the man is holding the hand of his lover, who wears a pink dress and floats through the air like a balloon."

I shot the doctor a furtive glance and then closed my eyes. She was using her cell phone to look up what I had mentioned. Well done! I praised myself. Out loud I added, "In our painting, I'm the flying lover, and Neda is the man holding my hand as I swim weightlessly. And to tell the truth, there are only a few times in my life that I've been so light and weightless, floating like a body in space, the way I was with Neda—before she quit me and I quit life."

"Didn't you have romantic relationships after her?"

"Many years passed before I trusted women and gave away my heart again. Then I met Shaygha . . . "

"Excellent! You remember Shaygha then."

Have I previously said that I've forgotten Shaygha, or was I only pretending to forget? Things are getting more and more confusing for me. I'm forgetting things I've said, and remembering things I haven't. If only I were able to take notes on those sessions! But my fingers remain swollen and still hurt a little. Even if I could get them to move, they'd be clumsy, inefficient.

"Well, what about Shaygha? Do you remember what happened to her, Mr. N?"

"Shaygha from Nepal? Of course, doctor. She flew up and soared through the air like a dove. She stood on the edge of the balcony and jumped."

"No, that was your father."

"No, my father stepped through a window, and his spirit remains floating in the air."

The doctor sighed. She appeared frustrated. She thought I had forgotten what happened to Shaygha, and she was afraid to tell me, so as not to give me the shock of her death. Her murder. The beasts picked her up by her arms and legs and threw her into the air. As though she were a doll, some inanimate thing. Good, enchanting Shaygha, who raised me out of the depths, cleaned off my filth, fed me, and showed me compassion.

"You never finished telling me the story of your father. Did he escape the massacre that day?"

"Do you think even the survivors ever really escape that sort of thing?"

"I'm sorry. Was he killed that day?"

"Mostly."

"What do you mean?"

"I mean he became like a dead man."

"Tell me."

"Fine," I said. Then I fell silent for some seconds before opening my mouth as wide as it would go and letting out a scream. A shriek, really. I screamed and struck my head against the edge of the bed with all the strength I possessed. "What's happening?" she asked, trying to calm me. But with every word she uttered, I just kept screaming. I could no longer bear it. I no longer wanted her in the room with me. A nervous fit, and she would leave. She could not hold her ground. She would summon the nurse again, and the nurse would take her away because it was not possible for her to give me another injection.

The ginger clinical psychologist left the room, and I took a deep breath to regain my composure. I will close my eyes and focus on my breathing until my heart rate slows. The sedative is still active in my system, so it hadn't been at all easy to bring about the nervous fit. I don't know which drugs I'm currently on, but my favorite is the one I call the "weeping willow," because it makes me feel so light, as though my whole brain is floating in water.

Whenever it occurs to me to wonder about the absolute best scientific inventions, I conclude without the least hesitation: sedatives, in all their forms, and everything that eases or erases pain. Without pain, there is no fear of death, just peace and harmony. Pain is our punishment for original sin: we do not know who committed it, but it is we who bear the charge. Pain is our hell, our second skin. It is the salt of this earth, and if it loses its saltiness, how can it be made salty again? When we were cast down from paradise and made into humans, unending pain was written for us. What were we before that? Angels, most likely. Or perhaps animals that did not worry about their tomorrow. Have any of you seen a cat stretching itself in the sun?

My father said it was a matter of Nurse Widad giving the children a tranquilizer so they would sleep. I did not hear exactly how he phrased it as I crouched there in the corner of the balcony under the window, leaning my head against the stone column of the balustrade. If I had stood up and leaned over the edge, I possibly could have seen my father sitting in his usual place, telling Kevork what had happened. Did he tell the nurse, "Give them a sleeping pill"? Or did he say, "Give them an injection"? As I think about it now, the injection seems more logical, first because of its rapid action, and second because Widad injected herself too. "Forgive me, doctor. I cannot bear another slaughter." My father did not understand at the time what she meant by those words of hers. No, he must have understood, for he remembered that she was Palestinian, one of the refugees of 1948. Most likely, he half knew, even though the rest escaped him, for Widad had been a second mother to her young patients from the camp. She would rock them and caress them, worry about them, show compassion, and help them. Therefore, it never occurred to him that she . . .

The militiaman kicked down the door, pointing a flashlight and his machine gun inside. "What's this?" he shouted, stunned, when he discovered children sleeping in their beds. "It's the end of the world out there, and they're sleeping? Luqman!" he called at the top of his voice. "Come quick!" When the light hit my father's face, he leapt to his feet, screaming, "Doctor! I'm a doctor! Don't shoot!"

The so-called Luqman entered and began prodding the children with the butt of his gun, but they did not wake up. He went around to them, one after another. Then he struck Nurse Widad, who did not respond. He looked at my father with eyes full of rebuke before shouting, "What have you done to them!?" My father was upset, and he began stammering. He was trembling and stuttering and his mouth was so dry it felt like his tongue had been pasted to his throat. Luqman approached and bashed him across the face with his gun. A small volcano of blood erupted from the corner of his right eyebrow. Luqman hit him again, and my father fell to the ground.

"If you don't confess now, I'll send you to join them!"

"I didn't do anything! I told the nurse to give them a sedative to make them sleep. I could no longer bear the sight of their terror."

"To make them sleep? Really? Make them sleep, indeed, an eternal one at that."

"No!" screamed my frantic father. He ran for the beds to take the pulse of his young patients. He refused to believe they had all departed this life. When he confirmed their passing, one child after the other, he turned to Widad, from whose half-open mouth trailed a thin line of froth. He recalled her face as she told him, "Forgive me, doctor. I cannot bear another slaughter." In her fear for them, she had killed them! She had raced on ahead and finished them off. "God! Now it's my turn! Why don't you finish me off?" said my father in a whisper before collapsing to his knees, tears streaming from his eyes.

Luqman turned to his fellow militiaman and said something. The other nodded in agreement and left the room. Before following him out, Luqman bowed his head, like a knight honoring the courage of his adversary, and said, "We thank you, doctor, for you've done us a great service. Killing children is always tough work, no matter what the situation. It demands great strength and fortitude—like yours!"

———

The sky seemed very dark, and not even the gleam of a few scattered stars could lessen the inky blackness. Indeed, I suddenly realized that what I saw, standing there behind my barred window and looking out at the night in that slumbering moment, was nothing more than an illusion. Those final gleams of extinguished stars, absorbed by darkness, enfolded by frost over the ages, were like the illusion of the memories that momentarily flicker in my mind before the windings of my dark brain absorb them, like some vast abyss shrouded in mist.

Pictures of faces come back to me, but they are nothing more than billboards that my brain glides past, moving at a fixed speed down the middle of a road with no turns or bumps, no rises or falls. The chlorpromazine removes every obstacle that my brain might trip over; it removes every hindrance to my thoughts, and they slip through seas of oil. Yes, the chlorpromazine is a blessing that has descended upon me, the friend who lifts from my shoulders the heaviest of burdens. It is the strong adhesive that holds together the two halves of my brain, removing the confusion, the distorted events, and all manner of deliriums that have fallen into the crack between them. More, the chlorpromazine has begun interacting with another medication to make me feel grateful and quick to express my indebtedness. Behind every action I see good intentions, a desire to serve me, and an attempt to improve the state of my health, both mental and physical. I no longer feel annoyed, for example, that they lock me in. Instead, I see the locked door as a protective measure to keep me safe from any enemies—God forbid—be they external or internal, coming by night or by day. They have fenced me off from myself, equipping my soul with a strong, flexible screen that no feelings or agitations can penetrate.

Thurayya buzzes through my head, for example, and I see her as a fly trying desperately to pierce the screen. She crashes against it and bounces back. My father stands at the window and then steps into the void. He falls onto the pavement, and his soul remains suspended in the air. I turn from him to Mary's hands, as she kneads dough to make me a pie, then to the balloons that Sa'id is popping, which disappear into plastic scraps of color and spit. I open the Victoria's Secret bag; shredded fragments of my books fly out, and I read my words. I open my mouth to receive the Eucharist. The other children laugh at me, and the priest places white cotton balls inside my mouth, stuffing them into me as though I am an empty cloth doll. Neda floats up. I too rise in the air and call out for her to see me flying, to see how light I am. Delighted, I fill dozens of pages with a beautiful pen. Its ink runs out after a while, and I see stacks of white pages that I have filled with my black letters. I could be deaf as I see all that, for no sound comes from all the movement I observe through the window of my mind, which glides forward, precise in its movement, rushing ahead without stumbling on anything it passes by...

I am in this state of bliss and comfort thanks to the wholesomeness of chlorpromazine and its friends. I only regret that a hatred of writing has returned to me. I feel an aversion, a disgust for everything that has to do with letters, ink, and ideas. I've begun to sit sometimes for hours in front of my white page, luxuriating in the void within my mind, and feeling my brain fill with a clear, sticky liquid that is as sluggish as a swamp.

It's true that Miss Zahra has renewed all her attempts to persuade me to pick up writing again. She has resumed her visits to my room, her concern for my affairs, and her encouragement to take my medicine, which they began giving me again when they transferred me to this hotel after my months in the hospital, where I had stayed while my shattered limbs recovered... Take it easy, Mr. N. You're mixing up conflicting time frames. They're blending together in your head, like liquids of different colors that flow together to make a palette of chaos and confusion.

After the hospital, where you remained for months, the ginger psychologist decided, together with Sa'id, to transfer you to this institution. Yes, it's an institution. You have remained here a long time. And because you were not able to understand its function, you saw the place as a hotel, and you decided you wanted to stay here in order to escape that damned tower that had smothered your beloved apartment. But things didn't happen in such regular order, and here you are now, finally realizing that.

A fog often settles upon me, and under it, I'm no longer able to distinguish my position within events, or the position of events within me, or their positions relative to each other. It's as if the fog sticks to my mind and doesn't leave, while inside it, I'm groping my way toward nothingness. When I was a child, my father took me to the nearby mountains to spend a few days in the summer. Thurayya would constantly grumble about such outings—she was a city girl, one who loved only the city—and she gave in only when she thought about the health of one of the boys, not both. I was enchanted by the view of the fog when it descended to touch the earth, hiding all the rises and falls around us. As I imagined it, the sky had descended in order to raise us up, and we were swimming through space, close to the birds and the clouds, spreading our wings, light and free of every burden. Sa'id would grumble, because the fog prevented him from going out, and Thurayya would mutter, feeling that a paving stone had been lowered onto her chest, but my father and I were secretly delighted that everything was wiped away, leaving us suddenly so light. And then, when the fog lifted and drifted off, the colors jumbled together, and the view took on a flash, a freshness, a radiance it did not have before.

Good. At this point, the fog has lifted from my mind, and I'll record the events on a sheet of paper to hang over the table so as never again to forget their connections or their order. This is what it will take to hold onto my life and keep it together, in case it becomes big enough for me to settle back into.

The spot on my back ... Mary ... the war ... my father's suicide ... a nervous breakdown ... early treatments ... writing ... my first novels ... teaching creative writing ... Neda ... stopping my medication ... devoting myself to writing ... a Victoria's Secret bag ... a second breakdown ... ceasing to write ... my wanderings through the belly of the city ... meeting Luqman ... Shaygha ... the hospital ... the institution ... Miss Zahra ... my return to writing ... stopping my medication ... the death of Thurayya ... Maryam's suicide at the hands of Daoud ... Sa'id selling the apartment ... chlorpromazine ...

I hang the page directly under the window. I don't like where it is, so I move it, sticking it above the table, in the middle of the white wall. Is that what my life can be boiled down to, a long train of words? Each word is a compartment full of characters and events, followed by a coupling that joins it to another compartment filled with other characters and other events. I wander from one to the next but do not come across myself. Where am I in all of this? Or from all of this? Maybe because they aren't organized in my head—the train compartments, I mean—or at least, not lined up in their proper order.

Yes, that is the only difference between me and everyone else. My head is a train of many cars, each of them going in a different direction. All I need to do is put them back in line so they might travel in the correct direction. Is this my entire life that I have put on the wall? How old have I become now? Something past fifty, I know. I'm at the stage where people begin to calculate how many years they have left. Are they on the team that will depart in their sixties, in their seventies, or their eighties? Such people, from the time they begin to calculate how much life remains, are among those who will certainly leave, just as before that moment, they were settled residents. A lifespan isn't reckoned up in the first half, but in the final third, when a person thinks they still have a firm grip on existence. Take me, for instance. How much is left for me? Will the proceeds from selling the apartment be enough to cover the days that remain? What if Sa'id dies before me? That's only logical, indeed it's likely, since he is older by seven and a half years.

My big brother, Sa'id, was not truly older than me for a single day, for it was I who had to try to understand him, comprehend him, support him, help him, and pity him, while it was for him to race me, compete against me, and walk all over me. "That's how Thurayya raised him," my father once whispered in dismay, before he went through the window and remained suspended there, not departing. And this is how you raised me? I scream at him in tears. No one raises anyone, Father. It is life that sets a person apart, that compensates, that punishes, that kills. Is that how your mother, Eugénie, bore you, with such a meager ability to endure, such that you would abandon me, your little one, after you witnessed the death of those other little ones? You aren't the one who killed them, Father, so why did you punish me—me!—with your death? Why didn't you think of me—me!—your fatherless little one?

They moved me to the mental institution immediately after I left the hospital, accompanied by the ginger psychologist's report. It included details about my lips moving to address individuals who weren't present, my mixing of fantasy and reality, my inability to distinguish between the two, and the assent of Sa'id, who was not able to undertake the care of a sick brother. Andrew read the report when he received me, communicating to me that he would take the place of the doctor to look over me and complete my care. I can't say why that suggestion made me feel so giddy I could have laughed out loud, even though I held myself back. It was odd how they thought I was addressing imaginary people, when those were actually the characters in my novels, whose existence I could establish in that they had been printed and were still found in bookstores. Don't they know that what we dream becomes reality, fully real, from God all the way down to Satan, and that whatever we give a name to immediately rises up before us, and takes on flesh and blood? Don't they know that the stories we tell are the ghosts that secretly reside within us, the demons hiding in the closets of our souls, the brothers of all our misfortunes and disappointments in this life? They even accused me of inventing the third Luqman, not believing that I met him by chance in the internet café, nor that he was an extension of the second Luqman, who was the son of the first Luqman and the embodiment of his potentialities upon this earth. Then some people came who informed the doctors of my long solitary confinement in my apartment, followed by my brave exploits in rough neighborhoods, my masochistic

229

addiction to beatings, my homelessness and my sleeping in the streets, which ended up with my meeting Shaygha . . .

I didn't need anyone to persuade me to stay, for I had decided to live here for a time, in what resembled a fancy hotel. The place seemed calm and clean. Miss Zahra was very accommodating, while Andrew liked my brother, Sa'id, and was satisfied by his financial position. What's more, I didn't want to return to my apartment where my father made his leap, where Shaygha was thrown from the balcony, and where the enormous tower stood defiant. When I arrived, they locked me in, but eventually they stopped locking the door when it became clear that I wasn't about to leave, not for all the temptations of the world. Where would I go, after I had begun feeling a lack of security, just as others feel the heat or cold? It seemed that this feeling of mine had been planted under my skin ever since I was born, pressing against my pores, threatening to burst through at any moment—that was the spot of deprivation that used to weigh upon me until at times it broke my back.

After years of living here, I learned that Sa'id had sold our home after Dr. Andrew confirmed for him that my condition was not improving. He could not risk letting me out in my condition, sending me out where there was no one to take care of me. I came to understand Sa'id's reasons after Miss Zahra explained them to me, for she helped me understand that he was afraid for me, and he wanted me to enjoy the very highest level of care. That's why he sold the apartment, insisting that I remain on the floor for wealthy patients, "the one that's like a five-star hotel, not the one that's like a public toilet." To tell the truth, I found Miss Zahra's comparison to be spot on, since the voices of those who occupied the lower floors sometimes reached me when night came on and the traffic outside quieted down. I would hear them howling like wolves, or like wounded animals in cages. None of it bothered me except when hysterical laughter rose up the outer walls to grab the bars of my window, trying to get in. That's when I would retreat to my bed in terror and bury my head under the comforter. I sometimes asked Miss Zahra about those people, but she told me to forget it. So I didn't think about them, for I am here in another world, even if we are all inside the same building.

Now they've started locking me in my room again. Why should I leave, anyway? Mealtimes are set at the best possible hours. The schedule for my medication is fixed. There are appointed times for showering and for walking in the hall to get the blood flowing in my legs, now that I no longer like going out to the garden after the passing of Daoud and Maryam. I dream about them sometimes. Once I saw Daoud hanging Maryam from the tree branch. She looked like a small doll, the kind used to decorate Christmas trees. Another time, I was walking in the garden, and I got hungry, so I picked an apple to eat. Inside there was a big worm that somehow made me think of Daoud . . . I don't go into the garden but am content with the long hallway. It has a window at the end where I can look out at my sisters, the three trees, since I miss them when the wind blows through their branches and they call out to me.

Why should I leave? How lucky I am to live as the king of this private ward! That's what Miss Zahra tells me repeatedly, and what she wants me to repeat after her so that I'm filled with gratitude. And when she points out my blessed condition with such insistence, I'm gripped by anxiety that this blessing of mine might one day come to an end, and they will demote me to the floor of the wolves. Miss Zahra hints at that whenever I put up a fight about something. Then I repent and comply, thanking my Lord that I'm in the wing of the tame, not in the cages of the wild. Yes, and it happened that Andrew visited me—Dr. Andrew, I should say, for he is the doctor supervising me and the director of the institution at the same time. He came to reassure himself about me, as he put it. He was in a hurry, and I didn't find an opening to raise the question of how much money there was, and whether it was enough to cover the cost of my staying there for however many years I had left. I was also afraid to pose that question to him, fearing a negative answer, so I kept it to myself, promising myself I would ask Sa'id when he looked in on me.

Ever since Thurayya's death and my breakdown, Sa'id hasn't visited, even though I've been told many times that he reassures himself about me and follows my progress from a distance. He is my big brother, older than me by seven years and seven months. He is the legal guardian for me, for my money, and for my life. He alone knows how many years I have left, for my life is tied to the time I stay in this wing. Sa'id, my big brother, cannot be relied upon. Even though he succeeded and became rich, his eye has remained upon paltry me and the little that I possess. Sa'id, my brother, who is never satisfied because Thurayya convinced him that he deserves more than everyone else. My mother taught him that. Fine. But why didn't my father teach him something too, such as love for his little brother? Sa'id put on his contests to compete with me and defeat me, even as I kept my distance. He struggled with me, vied against me, raced me, and triumphed over me all by himself, without my joining in the game. That's how the powerful are: on their guard and in a constant state of battle. That's how they constantly win and crush. We've been in this state, my brother and I, ever since we were born. I pull back, and he advances. I decline, and he ascends. I shrink, even as he grows larger. I don't want to fight with you, Sa'id. You're my brother, and here I am, ever since birth, being dragged along behind you. How do you not realize that? How do you not get tired or feel any sympathy? You're my brother, the son of my father, so where does it come from, all this spite you have against me? These claws? All those fangs?

Sadness washes over me. I feel it rising from my lower limbs, way down, from a distant place hidden within me, as though it were the memory of a taste that is still close, underneath my tongue. I perceive it with my mind more than I feel it with my senses. And what is it that comes immediately after sadness? Because now I've entered that, and I don't know what to call it.

I study the black sky, which has become an even deeper black. A dying star flickers out, having just emitted its final blaze. In less than a second, its life comes to an end. A tenth of a second, and it is no more. There is nothing left but sleep.

My heart is a cold star, and the night is long.

––––

"My eyes sleep, but my heart sleeps not," for watchful hearts can never relax, but stand always at the threshold waiting for their owners to return. Such is life: absence and waiting and hearts rent by longing and desire. My heart is a hungry wolf, howling to the open sky. But there is no one who hears, no one who answers ...

"I'm here! I hear you, N! You are not so alone as you like to pretend. Open your eyes and see me. I'm right on top of you! My head on your head, my trunk over yours, each limb matched to yours."

I shivered with fear when I heard that voice. Leaping out of bed, I walked toward the door, arms outstretched and groping for the light switch. I heard the sound of my heavy, tense breathing. The sweat poured out of me as though leaking from a clay jar whose seams had failed. I felt the warmth of wood, the cool of plastic. Suddenly, a hand grabbed mine and dragged it back before I found the switch.

"Let's stay in the dark. You don't need light to see me. Or have you forgotten your dear Luqman?"

Saying that, he took me by the arm and sat me on the chair beside the table, while he sat before me on the edge of the bed. Some excruciating moments of silence passed, long as a lifetime. As my eyes adjusted to the dark, they could make out a ghostly form. He was leaning forward, forearms resting on thighs. A car passed in the street, and its headlights reflected on the ceiling before descending to reveal Luqman's features, just as I remembered them. Yes, it's you: my curse, my ghost, my demon.

I gathered up my courage and said, "Why are you here at this time of night? How did you even get inside the institution? Aren't the doors barred and my own room locked?"

Luqman slowly raised his head. His lips curled back to reveal a great mass of yellow teeth. "Do you think locks can stop me? It's as though you don't know me, don't know what I'm capable of. Or maybe you've simply lost it, Mr. N?"

I stood up and threatened to scream if he didn't leave at once. He stood up in turn and came close. Grabbing the lapels of my pajamas, he pushed me back down. "If you raise your voice, I'll choke you with my bare hands. You understand?"

I nodded. He released his grip, smoothed my lapels, and patted my shoulders, adding, "Don't be afraid. I won't bother you for long. Just a few days and I'll move on, while I wait for the police to stop looking for me. There's someone out there slandering me. Can you imagine! They said my internet café was nothing more than a front for selling drugs to students and minors. The police put out a warrant for my arrest, and I fled before they come to get me in the morning. I thought for a long time about who I could go to, where I might hide. Then I remembered you and thought it must be you who's telling these lies. But when I asked around, I discovered what had become of you and where you ended up, and I realized you had to be innocent."

At that, Luqman burst out laughing.

"You turned out to be crazy, eh? And I was thinking I knew you from somewhere in my past. If I had known the full story, I wouldn't have laid a finger on you, believe me. I have no problem with crazy people, brother! How is it that you remained here with me in a country like this, without any customs or laws? Take me, for example. Ever since the war, I've only been trying to get out alive, and every time I get close to breaking free, something happens that sets me back by light-years . . . Anyway, you must be some kind of aristocrat for them to put you in a fancy room like this. Tell me,

Mr. N, who covers the cost and pays your expenses? Do you have family? Parents?"

I didn't reply. I wouldn't let him mock me. Was there nothing I could do to get him out? I thought. Fine. But tomorrow, when they open the door on me and discover what he's up to, they'll send him straight to hell. To hell, Luqman, to hell!

Luqman suddenly stood up. He looked me over, frowning, as though he heard what was passing through my head. Then he turned and took a book from the small shelf over my bed.

"What do you do with these books? Are they here for decoration?"

He held the books farther away so he could read the titles. His eyes opened wide.

"Whoa, this is your picture here! Did you write these? I don't believe it!"

He came over and eagerly pulled me up out of the chair. Wrapping his massive arms around me, he lifted me off the floor and shook me from side to side. I submitted to the embrace and his sudden celebration of me.

"You are the first poet I've met in my life! God knows how many kinds of people I've come across: doctors, university professors, lawyers, engineers, thieves and snipers, rich and poor, farmers and small business owners, office workers, and so on. But a poet—"

"I'm not a poet," I interrupted, scarcely able to speak on account of the pressure constricting my rib cage.

He fell silent for a moment. He set me down, perplexed at my objection. "What do you mean? Aren't you the one who wrote these books?"

"Yes, but I don't write poetry."

"Poetry, prose . . . It's all the same, my great literati!"

He finished the sentence with a laugh. Then he began undoing the buttons of his shirt. He took off his belt, followed by shoes, socks, and pants. I looked at him, confused, as he dropped his clothes in a pile at his feet before walking naked to the bathroom. He closed the door behind him and called, "I'd be grateful if you'd lend me a T-shirt and some underwear . . . Don't get up! I've found everything I need on the small shelf in here."

I heard the water splashing in the shower. I suddenly felt exhausted and decided I'd lie down to wait for him to come out of the bathroom. Maybe I could find some pretext to persuade him to leave. If not, Miss Zahra would scream when she saw him. Most likely she would run to get Hazim and the nurses from the floor below. Andrew would go insane out of fear for his operation. One tragedy was enough, and the first scandal had led to the death of Maryam and the imprisonment of Daoud . . . It occurred to me to ask Miss Zahra how the trial of that unfortunate man had ended up. I had told her many times that I was ready to testify to his innocence, for it was poor Maryam who had begged him to help her to end her life. But each time, Miss Zahra would get angry and scold me, telling me to forget all about it.

". . . But the matter at hand, Your Honor, isn't Daoud. My client has not committed any crime, even if Maryam's death wasn't a suicide. As it happens, it was not. It was the deliverance of a corpse that had passed away under the rubble caused by barrel bombs dropped from the sky over her country. The bombs destroyed her family and her home, her husband and her children, and everything that meant anything to her in this world. Members of the jury, would you convict my client in this situation, when he is innocent? He did nothing more than help a corpse that was sick with thirst, that just wanted some soil to cover her at last. Nevertheless, a black mark remains on my client's record, and that's the suicide of his wife, even though he, the stupid man, claims to have killed her. Here, there is no option but to resort to the testimony of the psychologists who examined him and confirmed that, after the passing of his wife, he was no longer the same, but had entered a dark tunnel in which his nerves collapsed upon him . . .

"And the matter at hand, Your Honor and members of the jury, is that each of us tests our capacity to endure and suffer. Each of us takes it as far as we can, and we record a number for ourselves, a measurement of our affliction as we pass through this life. Yes, everything has a scale and units of measurement, up and down, from most to least. Just as there are measurements for length, pressure, time, mass, earthquakes, and oscillations, there are measurements for pain and the capacity to endure. I, for example, have pushed my capacity in this area to the limit. Naked, I entered the ring and faced wild beasts and ghouls, like Thurayya, Sa'id, and even my father. I was abandoned, I spat blood, I resisted, I wrote, I lived, I kept silent, I was beaten, I was humiliated, I was tortured. I'm still here, standing before you on my own two feet, unprepared to take any more . . .

"And the matter at hand, Your Honor, is those students who would enroll in my class. I could see the emptiness that echoed between their ears like a drum. I didn't know how to deal with them, these students who came to me so that I might inform them that creativity is within the grasp of everyone, and that writing is a recipe that they could perfect in their kitchens by following the directions carefully. Neda—my colleague, at first, and then my girlfriend—would rebuke me for what she termed my cruelty. I'd object and tell her that I didn't think I was being cruel, but rather merciful, because my creative writing courses helped determine the measure of their talent and prevented them from perpetrating more mediocre, 'eminently serviceable' books that harmed our souls and our trees ... Then Neda started going on about the need to 'democratize' the arts and put them into the grasp of everyone. I got angry at her ignorance, she got angry at my obstinacy, and for two whole days when we crossed paths at the university, we didn't speak and she wouldn't even greet me. Inside, I was laughing at her naïveté, wondering how she could possibly put up with me and how I could possibly love her, until I realized that love is far too stupid a thing to demand answers or reasons ...

"And the matter at hand, my dear sirs, is that damned tower, which is squatting down upon my chest. It poisoned my soul and drove me from my balcony, my home, and my beautiful neighborhood. It rose up, higher and higher, until it reached heaven, which itself has grown more distant and remains so far away, no longer hearing the complaints and prayers that we send up ...

"And the matter at hand is the antipathy sparked within me by words. It is my feeling of disgust at the abundance of what has been written, and how little use there is in what is read. It is my burning embarrassment at all that impudence, that arrogance, that presumption, until disgust has become a feeling I live with constantly. Revulsion is a disease that no medication or treatment can overcome. I have not found any means of shielding myself from all those assaults apart from silence, turning away, withdrawal, contraction, shrinking, and cutting off my fingers and my hands if they reach for the paper or try to say anything within this chaos, this Sodom and Gomorrah of ideas, this Babel of words . . .

"And the matter at hand—"

"The matter at hand is that you need to stop talking in your sleep, Mr. N, and that you wake up! It's already past nine thirty. I've come to check on you twice already, but you were still sound asleep. Well, did we stay up late last night?"

Miss Zahra was sliding back into her use of the plural pronoun, which meant she was feeling more comfortable and was no longer afraid of me, now that the chlorpromazine had stabilized my nerves and was keeping my bouts of madness under control. She passed through the room like a tornado, setting down the breakfast tray, opening the window, picking things up, organizing the table, putting out a new glass of water, emptying the wastebasket . . . I watched her with half-closed eyes, afraid of getting up, trying to avoid her coming over in order to make the bed, lest she discover Luqman hiding underneath it, or else go into the bathroom and find him there.

"Come along! Get up and have your breakfast. I'll be right back with your medicine," she said. She went out and closed the door behind her.

I threw off the covers and slowly got up. "Luqman?" I hissed. When there was no reply, I got down on my knees and put my head against the floor tiles to look under the bed. He wasn't there. I stood up and looked around. I went to the bathroom, where he must have hidden when Miss Zahra came in. But the bathroom was empty too, apart from the reflection of a face in the mirror, no doubt my own. I stopped, my brow furrowed in confusion at what could have happened. Did I fall asleep while he was taking a shower, and then did he leave early after getting a little sleep? Or could I have dreamed the whole thing? Was he nothing more than a vision I saw in my sleep, one so real that I confused the dream for reality?

I washed my face with cold water and put a wet hand on the back of my neck. I shivered so much that I momentarily forgot all my other afflictions. Then I went to the table and sat down to eat my breakfast, thinking about my nighttime conversation with Luqman, his escape from arrest, and the threat he made against me. No, he had not been here, no matter how certain I was about his presence. He cannot possibly pass invisibly through the walls. When Miss Zahra comes back, I will tell her my dreams before I forget. That is what Dr. Andrew advised me to do whenever I have one. I'm supposed to write it down on paper or else tell it to Miss Zahra. I have no patience for writing, so I'll just tell it to her, and she'll let him know. Every time I see him now, he asks me to tell him about my dreams, and for a long time, my answer has been that I've stopped dreaming altogether.

———

There's half a headache rattling around in this skull of mine— but only half, because the other half of my head is barely there. It's the effect of the chlorpromazine, which is making me half-insomniac and half-somnolent, and interferes with

241

my movement and my balance. Yesterday, my hand suddenly began trembling, and I dropped what I was carrying. I no longer remember exactly what it was, but it was something heavy, because it made a loud thud when it crashed onto the floor. I told Miss Zahra about it, and that I was feeling involuntary muscle spasms in my face. She reassured me, saying it was a typical side effect of the chlorpromazine. Okay, then. You can't get something for nothing, and in exchange for the disengagement and detachment that this medicine grants me, I am paying the price through a diminished performance in some of my faculties. The tremor, to be precise, is what confused me the most. It began after Luqman's visit. I'm not saying he caused it, but it did start after he came.

Miss Zahra informed Dr. Andrew about my recent symptoms, and she did not neglect to convey my dream to him. He came to ask about the details. "Well? Have the voices come back to your head? You say that you saw Luqman, and that he was in your room? Perhaps we need a stronger dose."

Before I could reply with a yes or no, he was writing nervously in his small white notebook. He tore out a page and gave it to Miss Zahra before adding, "You know that no one can get in here, and that all the doors are locked, right?"

"Yes, it's impossible for anyone to get in . . . "

"So?"

"So no one got in . . . except Luqman!"

Andrew has convinced me with his irrefutable arguments that what I saw was nothing more than my confused dreams. But even though his words persuaded me, I have begun to feel Luqman's presence with me. I sense him, and I hear the sound of his breathing nearby. I turn around suddenly to surprise him, and when his face does not appear, a chill wave sweeps over me from head to foot, making my joints creak and my body shiver. Sometimes I pretend to be asleep, stretched out on the bed with my eyes closed, exhaling and snoring in rhythm, in case that might make him feel secure enough to come out of his hole. But the game takes too long, and in my weariness I drift off, or else I get out of bed, my patience having run out.

I listen closely. I hear him living. He comes and goes at random times. Nevertheless, the doubt planted by Andrew persists, and I spend my time on the lookout, waiting. It makes me behave as though I were constantly under his watch, as though he were here, even if he is not. Later, I became certain of his presence and his ability. I perceived a thumping on the wall of my room that made me sure he could pass through whatever stands in his way. His voice came clear and distinct from the two neighboring rooms: the one across the hall where Maryam used to live, and the one adjacent, in which Daoud stayed. That suggested that my room and I were not safe for him, and he preferred to stay in rooms that he knew no one would enter so long as they remained unoccupied.

I once whispered to Miss Zahra between two sentences, "I hear voices in the neighboring rooms." She waved her large ring of keys in my face, of all different shapes and sizes, and said, "There's nothing to be afraid of, Mr. N. The rooms around you are locked and empty. No one goes in them without my knowledge and permission." That did not reassure me, and as a result, Andrew came to visit me again. He sat with me and grilled me for a long time, concluding with the necessity of adjusting my treatment, ramping it up, for he observed that his previous adjustment had not produced the effect he was hoping for.

"I don't understand why your condition is deteriorating, despite all the prescriptions I've given you. You have to improve, Mr. N, because raising the dose means an increase in the side effects. Do you understand?" I could hear the disapproval and annoyance in his voice.

I listened silently, even as I thought, "You say that Luqman doesn't exist, that he's just in my head. At the same time, even though I don't see him, I hear him moving around, and I can't help but be aware of his existence. Is not seeing something proof that it doesn't exist? What about the existence of God then?"

And then I saw him one evening. I was standing by the window watching the traffic in the street. It was all very ordinary, and nothing provoked my specific attention. Then there he was, right there, down below, leaning his back against a lamppost, enveloped in light, and raising his head toward me ... What was he waiting for? How was I to know what he wanted? And if I knew, would I give it to him? My heart beat faster, and I broke into a sweat. Despite the tension and fear, I remained nailed in place, staring at him, unable to move. As he was looking at me from afar, he slowly smiled and took a yellow book from under his arm. He raised it up and waved it ... Wait, it was my book! The very one in which he is the protagonist.

I ran to the shelf above my bed and began searching for my copy of the novel ... All my books were there except ... God! Luqman actually had been here! I had not been hallucinating or imagining things. He really did come into my room, mess around with my things, and take his book from my shelf. Then he left, and now he has come back. He enters and exists without anyone spotting him, and he is down there this instant, waving at me. Isn't he doing it to make me understand that he has come to realize that he is the same Luqman as the one in my novel, and that therefore I must acknowledge it too?

I returned to the window, my legs shaking and scarcely able to hold my weight. I stood off to one side, thinking maybe I could see him without him seeing me. When I leaned over to steal a glance, the electricity suddenly cut out, and I could see nothing but darkness. I glanced at my watch. It showed 10:25. That meant the power had gone out a full twenty-five minutes behind the daily schedule.

———

These two cadavers of flesh and bone and blue veins, lying here in my lap—are they my hands? And these creased, knotted chopsticks connected to my palms, are they really my fingers? Is this cold slab that rises and falls under my chin at a steady rate, is it my chest, behind which hides my heart? How is it that I am sitting inside my body without feeling it, and I cannot see any of the organs or distinguish the different parts?

I remain a hermit locked in my room. I see its objects gather around me, keeping my silence company for hours without getting bored or complaining. It's in my power to remain like this forever, not moving, not thinking, not feeling. Or else I could leave and go elsewhere, without any particular reason behind the change. I do it all with a remarkable ease and flexibility. It's only my bouts of trembling, which have intensified recently and shift between my different limbs, that make me lose control of myself. That, and also the absence of my body, which I do not see, and which no longer comes along when I move or try to do something. It just stands there, stubborn and headstrong as a mule.

After he went through the window, my father exited his body because it was no longer residing in this world. When the body is no longer a resident, the world erases itself. My father erased the world. Then he left his body, and his soul remained suspended, without anyone to pull it down. Who is it that plucks the souls of the fathers from the tree of life if not their sons? Neither Sa'id nor I did it, so my father's poor soul remains hanging in the air.

I stand in front of the square mirror, and I do not see a face. I move my hands, and I do not see my hands. Where could this person be, standing in the bathroom in front of the mirror above the sink, where no reflection is to be seen? And if the person standing there isn't me, where might I be? I reach my hand to the tap and turn it on. The water flows out and goes down the drain in the middle of the white basin. It is water flowing from a faucet that I turned on, but I see it as if through a pane of glass, as though everything were flashing by on a screen and not before my very eyes. I can't feel things no matter how much I touch them, turn them over, handle them. There is some diaphanous film separating me from everything, a fine coating of rubber that sticks to everything—rubber and intangible, so I do not see it covering my soul and my limbs, separating them from everything around me.

I think about raising the veil off my body. I strip off my clothes and stand naked. I begin tearing at my belly, my legs, and my arms as though I might rip it off me. And since my fingernails aren't much use, I run to the table, searching for anything that might be able to help. I find only some knives that I have saved from my food trays—plastic knives, now that metal ones are forbidden. I begin scratching and scraping as much as I can, in case the veil is invisible and beneath it I will find my actual skin, a skin that still feels, still senses, that still shivers in the cold . . .

"N!"

Luqman startled me with a yell before pulling me to him in a powerful embrace. "What are you doing to yourself, you crazy man?" he said in a whisper. His voice is different this time, and it's as though he is choking back hot tears that catches in his throat. "You're all bloody!" he said, stepping back and taking the knives out of my hand. "Come. I'll put you in the bath."

He led me by the arm and made me stand under the spray of the shower. The water poured over me and ran down the drain with a faint red tinge. He asked if the soap burned, and I shook my head, staring at him, submitting to his movements. I was afraid he would disappear if I so much as blinked.

"I've been waiting for you for days. Ever since I saw you down there, leaning against the lamppost. At first I was terrified, I ran to barricade the door with everything I could find. But do you know what? I'm not afraid of you anymore."

He brought me out from under the water and wrapped me in a large towel that he began pressing against me gently to avoid irritating my wounds. I smiled and told him not to

247

worry too much because they were superficial injuries that did not hurt, that what actually hurt was buried deep inside, where no hand could reach. My breath kept catching with involuntary sighs, the kind that come after a bout of crying when a warm embrace comforts you. Meanwhile, Luqman dressed me, combed my hair, and brought me out to the other room to make me lie down on the bed. He gently pulled the comforter over me.

"Do you love me?" I asked. No reply. After several moments of silence, I added, "Won't you stay here with me tonight?"

"Yes," he said, and he stretched out on the bed beside me, on top of the comforter, just as he was, in his jacket and shoes. He leaned his head back against the wall. Then he drew the novel from his pocket and began to read with deep concentration and attention. I cried as I watched him, literally drowning in gratitude and feeling guilty for having treated him with so much cruelty and so much meanness instead of searching for extenuating circumstances, or trying to understand his situation and the ugly cycle of war and its vicious effects upon people.

As though reading my thoughts, Luqman turned and said, "How is it that you're not afraid of me when you've treated me so badly, really loaded me down with every sort of filthy evil you could imagine? A prince of war who specializes in planting mines, who's best friends with a sniper and a torturer. And when the war was over, you turned me into a womanizer, an exploiter of women, making them spend their money on me! Admit it, N, you never gave me a chance."

"You people didn't give us a chance, either."

"We people?"

"Yes. You weren't alone, Luqman. There were so many of you."

"Don't lump me in with the others. Just let me go to Paris and meet up with my girlfriend, Shireen. When that happens, I'll change. You'll see."

"Even innocent Shireen, whom you claim is your girl-friend—you laugh at her too. Killers don't change, Luqman. You know that."

"But I'm your protagonist, the hero of your novel!"

"Yes, you're my protagonist."

"Tell me: Do you plan on killing me?"

Sleep weighed heavily on my eyes, and I left his question hanging in the air. How could the thought of killing occur to him, when he had not yet reached the end of the novel? I heard him turning the pages. If only he could realize that true fear is meeting a killer whom you kill, only for him to return, forcing you to kill him again . . .

Sleep dragged me under.

I saw books with wings flying through the air. Sentences fell from them into the water and glittered like ash. One dropped into my hands, and I read, "Madness is a low balcony looking out at the sunset." I found myself sitting among the pages of my first novel, written in my early twenties, at a time of war and the agony of power outages, when the roar of the generators drove me to madness. I turn that sentence of mine over in my hands, and suddenly it is a balcony. I am sitting upon it, trapped inside a scene that repeats endlessly. Behind me is a house haunted by mourning. Its cracked walls guard vacant rooms, and the wind whistles through its brittle doors. I know I'm not one of the people of the house, and

I'm only here because its owners have entrusted it to me. Why in the world would they entrust me with a ruin when they are dead and I have no weapons and no strength? I am standing guard over a heap, a wreck, over something that does not return.

I hear a step behind me. Paralyzed, I start trembling. The sound of two heavy feet shuffling over the tiles, dragging through the dust piled thick in front of them, etching a long gash in a field of loss. It is Lazarus! I hear him wandering inside the house of the forsaken, and I fear he might reach me and invite me to join him.

"Our beloved N is sleeping, and I have come to wake him," he will say to his sisters. A lump rises and gets stuck in my throat like a leech. It begins turning and boring. It plants itself, turns, and bores deeper. The two sisters of Lazarus are crying. They call to him, "Let him float in the mist!" If only I had a sister who would pity me, a sister who would wash my wounds with her tears and dry my feet with her hair. One who would pour expensive perfume over me and celebrate me. If only I had a sister to give me bread to eat and water to drink, and who would smooth my hair as I lay my head back upon the stone.

Lazarus approaches. "Don't come!" I scream at him. "Don't come, and don't look at me on the balcony! I'm not here. I don't want to return. I don't want to wake up. Let me stay buried here, in my head, where the earth contains me, where the dust envelops me."

———

"N, why did you kill me, N?"

He was right above me: his head on my head, his torso over mine, each limb paired, his eyes in my eyes, and his mouth to my mouth. Not more than a few centimeters separated us. He repeated the question:

"Why did you kill me, N, when I was your protagonist?"

I tried to get away. I sucked in my belly until it was touching my back. I contracted my organs. I dropped my chest, endeavoring to get out from under him, but he put his hands around my neck, and he gradually began squeezing until I could no longer breathe.

"Why did you kill me, N, when you have no one besides me?"

All the air had left my lungs. I gripped his hands and strained to pull them off my neck. Then . . . I don't know how I did it, but I found myself rising from the bed and backing toward the window. I stood there, catching my breath and massaging my neck. "I killed you because you are a killer!" I screamed. "Yes, you are a killer, and there was nothing to do but kill you!"

Luqman's face darkened. His eyes wavered. Then he leapt upon me like a feral cat pouncing on its prey. He began kicking me and scratching me with his fingernails. I tried to fend him off, my back pressed against the table.

"You're not real! You're an illusion! Just as I created you, I can now end you!"

I reached a hand behind me, grasping for anything that might help me against him, while my other arm pressed against his chest to push him as far back as I could. But he only became more ferocious. He was bashing my nose and the sides of my head the way a person might strike a drum when trying to punch through it. Meanwhile, I flailed with my arms and feet, windmilling them through the air, until my hand fell upon the pencils that were behind me, newly sharpened and lying in their place beside the paper. I closed my hand on as many as I could, raised them up, and with all the strength I possessed, I hit him. I hit him again. And again.

Luqman's eyes bulged out. He stopped struggling and his body arched back after the final blow landed in his solar plexus. I didn't really believe I'd done him any serious harm until the moment he staggered back. His color had drained away, and he was pressing his hands to his belly as he fell to his knees, a broken man. I peered more closely and saw that the bundle of wooden pencils had entered deep into his soft skin. Blood was spreading in a large stain across his belly, with a second near the top of his chest.

I got down close to him and helped him to the floor, leaning his back against the bed. Then I sat beside him. I was trembling from fatigue and the shock of what had happened. It occurred to me to go to the door and start pounding and screaming until people arrived and saved him, but he took hold of me, begging me not to tell anyone because they would hurt us both. He pleaded for me to remain there with him until we found some solution. All of a sudden, he was drawing my hand toward him so that I could pull the pencils out of his belly, which I did. They were warm to the touch, anointed with blood.

I felt an unexpected sadness wash over me like a fine rain. My tears broke free as the image of him alone as a child, an orphan, with no friends or family, flashed before my eyes.

I felt I had treated him cruelly and unjustly to have made him as I did, only to demand that he behave as though he were something else, as though he were me, trapped within the bowels of my own intertwining, knotted thoughts, and not himself, straightforward as a stallion in his physique and his passions.

The blood was still gushing out and now covered his entire belly. I went to the bathroom and brought back a towel, which I balled up and pressed against his wound. Miss Zahra jumped into my head, and I saw how annoyed she would be to find the room in such a chaotic mess. Then I thought how stupid it was to be concerned with such a trivial thing, considering the enormity of the crime I had just committed.

"Is it you, come back to kill me? How long will this go on, N?"

"Until you stop pursuing me."

"I've never come looking for you. It's you who come to me."

Yes, I'm the one who came to you, because you were still here, alive in the city I believed I had flooded under the rains. How are you still here when I killed you once with gas, and then with a flood? When I used to wander through the neighborhood of Bourj Hammoud, Luqman, I thought about its being the first area to be submerged by the flood coming out of the sea. A giant tsunami that would sweep away the rocks and people and voices and languages. A symphony of waves to rival the sky, advancing like united armies to destroy everything in their path: women, children, and elderly; livestock, horses, and dogs; trees, car frames, balconies, ugly curtains, and electrical poles and lines. Residents and foreigners, vendors, travelers, the disabled, the whores, the laborers, and the beggars. A divine, cosmic tsunami that would end the world in order to begin it again. No! To end it, without any mercy. A rough draft, full of mistakes, and then a cosmic eraser to make the page white again.

"Every time I get myself ready to die, N, you bring me back to life. Haven't you had enough of me yet?"

This time, Luqman, you'll certainly die. I will kill you this time for good and all, and you will die.

EPILOGUE

In his report to the police, Dr. Andrew related, in part:

Because she suffered a confusion of identity and other psychological afflictions, Mrs. N spent more than fifteen years in our institution, during which time not a single person came to visit her, despite her being a well-known writer of works that attracted great interest when they were published. She first came to us expressing a fear that murderous spirits were transforming her into a killer, and we received her and pursued her treatment, both psychological and medical, throughout all these years. (See attached report 1.)

When Miss Zahra opened the door to Mrs. N's room this morning, she found Mrs. N swimming in a pool of her own blood. She had stabbed herself with new Faber-Castell pencils under her right shoulder only to pull them out and plant them in her torso, directly in the solar plexus. This caused serious blood loss, which led to her passing shortly before dawn. (See forensic report, attached.)

Scattered around her, we found many papers, some of them stained with blood. It was clear that they belonged to a single manuscript of numbered pages bearing the title *Mister N*. Under her hand was a fresh sheet, and using a finger dipped in her own blood, she had written:

Finally. I've finally freed myself from him.

TRANSLATOR'S NOTE

Reading *Mister N* is a pleasure on multiple levels. That is even more true for translating it.

The novel demonstrates Najwa Barakat's characteristic descriptive power, applied both to her fictional characters and to the city of Beirut in approximately 2016. Even before the port explosion of August 2020 and Lebanon's subsequent economic collapse, we see a city fighting to survive. The garbage goes uncollected, the river runs with mud and waste, and once beautiful buildings are retrofitted with ugliness. Yet still the city grows, a home to migrants past and present who flee war, persecution, and starvation: Lebanon's poor, Armenians, Palestinians, domestic workers, sex workers from Africa and Asia, and now refugees from neighboring Syria at the height of its civil war.

Mr. N is driven out of the shelter of his comfortable apartment into the chaos of this bewildering city, and it provides the setting for the shock he experiences on a side street when Mr. N encounters Luqman, the murderous antihero of a grim novel he himself wrote fifteen years before. How a fictional character can appear in the flesh is as much a mystery to Mr. N as it is to the reader, and we follow Mr. N's memories, reflections, and investigations as he grasps for the truth. Suffering from psychosis and memory loss, this unreliable and inconsistent narrator begins to excavate painful stories long buried. Like Mr. N's mind, the narrative is disjointed and fragmentary. It circles back and contradicts itself as it slowly uncovers the mystery of Luqman—and of Mr. N.

As a literary translator, I delight in the process of composing English sentences that capture as much as I can of the meaning and artistry contained in Arabic ones. As a translator of Najwa Barakat, my goal is to preserve the rich texture of her sentences, the vivid descriptions of people and of cityscapes, the willingness to explore human pain and human cruelty.

As a general rule, translating verb tenses in Arabic narrative prose can be challenging. They contain less specificity than is required by English, and it is common in Arabic to use the present tense when narrating the past. The translator must adapt these passages to equally standard forms of narration in English, while trying to preserve Arabic's sense of immediacy, and without getting bogged down in coordinating frameworks. Verb tense in *Mister N* is particularly tricky to translate since the narrative jumps without warning between time frames. Episodes may be Mr. N's present reflections, a memory from the near past or the remote, or even prose written by Mr. N, often about himself, now in the first person, now in the third. This structure mirrors the instability of Mr. N's mind: his failure to comprehend his situation, his inability to remember critical details, his confusion about the sequence of past events. While translation always demands interpretation, the translator of *Mister N* must take care to avoid erasing these ambiguities in the text.

Among other things, this is a novel about the relationship of an author to their characters. What are a character's conscious or subconscious origins in the author's mind? What does an author feel about characters after they are committed to the page? What does an author owe them, and how might a character react to their portrayal? In what sense are characters real? While such questions naturally arise from a novel in which the main character grapples with the meaning of language and the terror of encountering a protagonist from his own early fiction, the final pages of the *Mister N* take us one step deeper by connecting the narrative and the characters even more closely to the author of them all, Najwa Barakat, who wrote the very novels ascribed to Mr. N before abandoning fiction for fifteen years. Once again, fiction steps out into the world.

On a personal note, I am doubly grateful for the opportunity to translate this novel because of my work on Barakat's *Oh, Salaam!* some ten years ago. My former Arabic teacher, Khaled Al-Masri, introduced me to that novel about Luqman, and his dissertation chapter about the depth of Barakat's exploration of gender and violence persuaded me to undertake the translation despite an initial reluctance to become more intimately acquainted with such brutal characters. The themes and style of Barakat's novels in the 1990s played an important role in the development of contemporary Arabic literature, and I look forward to collaborating with And Other Stories again in the very near future to make her modern classic, *The Bus*, available at last to English readers.

LUKE LEAFGREN, 2021
CAMBRIDGE, MASSACHUSETTS

Dear readers,

As well as relying on bookshop sales, And Other Stories relies on subscriptions from people like you for many of our books, whose stories other publishers often consider too risky to take on.

Our subscribers don't just make the books physically happen. They also help us approach booksellers, because we can demonstrate that our books already have readers and fans. And they give us the security to publish in line with our values, which are collaborative, imaginative and 'shamelessly literary'.

All of our subscribers:

- receive a first-edition copy of each of the books they subscribe to
- are thanked by name at the end of our subscriber-supported books
- receive little extras from us by way of thank you, for example: postcards created by our authors

BECOME A SUBSCRIBER, OR GIVE A SUBSCRIPTION TO A FRIEND

Visit andotherstories.org/subscriptions to help make our books happen. You can subscribe to books we're in the process of making. To purchase books we have already published, we urge you to support your local or favourite bookshop and order directly from them — the often unsung heroes of publishing.

OTHER WAYS TO GET INVOLVED

If you'd like to know about upcoming events and reading groups (our foreign-language reading groups help us choose books to publish, for example) you can:

- join our mailing list at: andotherstories.org
- follow us on Twitter: @andothertweets
- join us on Facebook: facebook.com/AndOtherStoriesBooks
- admire our books on Instagram: @andotherpics
- follow our blog: andotherstories.org/ampersand

THIS BOOK WAS MADE POSSIBLE THANKS TO THE SUPPORT OF

Aaron McEnery
Aaron Schneider
Abel Gonzalez
Abigail Charlesworth
Abigail Walton
Ada Gokay
Adam Lenson
Adrian Astur Alvarez
Adrian Kowalsky
Aifric Campbell
Aisha McLean
Ajay Sharma
Alan Felsenthal
Alan Hunter
Alan McMonagle
Alan Raine
Alastair Gillespie
Alastair Whitson
Albert Puente
Aleksi Rennes
Alex von Feldmann
Alex Fleming
Alex Lockwood
Alex Pearce
Alex Ramsey
Alexander Bunin
Alexander Williams
Alexandra Stewart
Alexandra Tammaro
Alexandra Tilden
Alexandra Webb
Alfred Tobler
Ali Ersahin
Ali Riley
Ali Smith
Ali Usman
Alice Morgan

Alice Radosh
Alice Smith
Alison Lock
Alison Winston
Aliya Rashid
Alyssa Rinaldi
Alyssa Tauber
Amado Floresca
Amaia Gabantxo
Amanda
Amanda Geenen
Amanda Read
Amber Da
Amine Hamadache
Amitav Hajra
Amy and Jamie
Amy Benson
Amy Bojang
Amy Finch
Amy Hatch
Amy Tabb
Ana Novak
Andrea Barlien
Andrea Brownstone
Andrea Oyarzabal
  Koppes
Andrea Reece
Andrew Kerr-Jarrett
Andrew Marston
Andrew McCallum
Andrew Ratomski
Andrew Place
Andrew Rego
Andy Corsham
Andy Marshall
Andy Turner
Aneesa Higgins

Angelica Ribichini
Anita Starosta
Anna Finneran
Anna French
Anna Hawthorne
Anna Milsom
Anna Zaranko
Anne Boileau Clarke
Anne Carus
Anne Craven
Anne Edyvean
Anne Frost
Anne Ryden
Anne Sticksel
Anne Stokes
Anne Withane
Annie McDermott
Anonymous
Anonymous
Anthony Alexander
Anthony Cotton
Anthony Quinn
Antonia Lloyd-Jones
Antonia Saske
Antony Osgood
Antony Pearce
Aoife Boyd
April Hernandez
Arabella Bosworth
Archie Davies
Aron Trauring
Arthur John Rowles
Asako Serizawa
Ashleigh Sutton
Audrey Mash
Audrey Small
Barbara Bettsworth

Barbara Mellor
Barbara Robinson
Barbara Spicer
Barry John Fletcher
Barry Norton
Bea Karol Burks
Becky Matthewson
Ben Buchwald
Ben Schofield
Ben Thornton
Ben Walter
Benjamin Judge
Benjamin Pester
Bernadette Smith
Beth Heim de Bera
Beverley Thomas
Bianca Duec
Bianca Jackson
Bianca Winter
Bill Fletcher
Birgitta Karlén
Björn Warren
Bjørnar Djupevik
  Hagen
Blazej Jedras
Brenda Anderson
Briallen Hopper
Brian Anderson
Brian Byrne
Brian Callaghan
Brian Smith
Bridget Prentice
Brooke Williams
Buck Johnston
Burkhard Fehsenfeld
Caitlin Halpern
Caitriona Lally
Callie Steven
Cameron Adams

Cameron Lindo
Camilla Imperiali
Campbell McEwan
Carl Emery
Carla Castanos
Carole Burns
Carole Parkhouse
Carolina Pineiro
Caroline Lodge
Caroline Perry
Caroline Smith
Caroline West
Catharine Braithwaite
Catherine Cleary
Catherine Lambert
Catherine
  Lautenbacher
Catherine Tolo
Catherine Campbell
Catherine Tandy
Catherine Williamson
Cathryn Siegal-
  Bergman
Cathy Sowell
Catie Kosinski
Catrine Bollerslev
Cecilia Rossi
Cecilia Uribe
Chantal Lyons
Chantal Wright
Charlene Huggins
Charles Dee Mitchell
Charles Fernyhough
Charles Kovach
Charles Rowe
Charlie Errock
Charlie Levin
Charlie Small
Charlie Webb

Charlotte Holtam
Charlotte Ryland
Charlotte Whittle
China Miéville
Chris Gostick
Chris Gribble
Chris Holmes
Chris Lintott
Chris McCann
Chris Potts
Chris Stergalas
Chris Stevenson
Chris Thornton
Christian Schuhmann
Christine Elliott
Christopher Allen
Christopher Smith
Christopher Stout
Claire Riley
Claire Williams
Clarice Borges
Claudia Mazzoncini
Cliona Quigley
Colin Denyer
Colin Hewlett
Colin Matthews
Collin Brooke
Cornelia Svedman
Courtney Lilly
Craig Kennedy
Cris Cucerzan
Cynthia De La Torre
Cyrus Massoudi
Daisy Savage
Dale Wisely
Daniel Coxon
Daniel Gillespie
Daniel Hahn
Daniel Hester-Smith

Daniel Jones
Daniel Oudshoorn
Daniel Sanford
Daniel Stewart
Daniel Syrovy
Daniel Venn
Daniela Steierberg
Darryll Rogers
Dave Lander
David Anderson
David Ball
David Cowan
David F Long
David Greenlaw
David Gunnarsson
David Hebblethwaite
David Higgins
David Johnson-Davies
David Leverington
David Miller
David Richardson
David Shriver
David Smith
David Thornton
Dawn Bass
Dean Taucher
Deb Unferth
Debbie Pinfold
Deborah Green
Deborah Herron
Deborah Wood
Declan Gardner
Declan O'Driscoll
Deirdre Nic Mhathuna
Delaina Haslam
Denis Larose
Denis Stillewagt &
  Anca Fronescu
Denton Djurasevich

Derek Sims
Derek Taylor-
  Vrsalovich
Dietrich Menzel
Dina Abdul-Wahab
Dinesh Prasad
Domenica Devine
Dominic Bailey
Dominic Nolan
Dominick Santa
  Cattarina
Dominique Hudson
Dorothy Bottrell
Dugald Mackie
Duncan Clubb
Duncan Macgregor
Duncan Marks
Dustin Hackfeld
Dustin Haviv
Dyanne Prinsen
E Rodgers
Earl James
Ebba Tornérhielm
Ed Smith
Ed Tronick
Ekaterina Beliakova
Elaine Juzl
Elaine Rodrigues
Eleanor Maier
Elena Esparza
Elif Aganoglu
Elina Zicmane
Elisabeth Cook
Elizabeth Braswell
Elizabeth Cochrane
Elizabeth Coombes
Elizabeth Draper
Elizabeth Franz
Elizabeth Leach

Elizabeth Seals
Elizabeth Wood
Ellen Beardsworth
Ellie Goddard
Ellie Small
Emily Walker
Emily Williams
Emma Bielecki
Emma Coulson
Emma Louise Grove
Emma Post
Emma Teale
Eric Anderson
Erica Mason
Erin Cameron Allen
Erin Louttit
Esmée de Heer
Ethan Madarieta
Ethan White
Eva Mitchell
Evelyn Eldridge
Ewan Tant
F Gary Knapp
Fawzia Kane
Fay Barrett
Faye Williams
Felicity Williams
Felix Valdivieso
Finbarr Farragher
Fiona Liddle
Fiona Quinn
Fran Sanderson
Frances Christodoulou
Frances Harvey
Frances Thiessen
Frances Winfield
Francesca Hemery
Francesca Rhydderch
Francis Mathias

Jean Liebenberg
Jeff Collins
Jeffrey Davies
Jen Calleja
Jen Hardwicke
Jenifer Logie
Jennifer Fosket
Jennifer Harvey
Jennifer Mills
Jennifer Watts
Jenny Huth
Jenny Newton
Jeremy Koenig
Jess Hazlewood
Jess Howard-Armitage
Jess Wilder
Jess Wood
Jesse Coleman
Jesse Hara
Jessica Kibler
Jessica Mello
Jessica Queree
Jessica Weetch
Jethro Soutar
Jo Keyes
Jo Pinder
Joanna Luloff
Joao Pedro Bragatti
  Winckler
JoDee Brandon
Jodie Adams
Joe Huggins
Joel Garza
Joel Swerdlow
Joelle Young
Johannes Menzel
Johannes Georg Zipp
John Bennett
John Berube

John Bogg
John Conway
John Down
John Gent
John Hodgson
John Kelly
John Reid
John Royley
John Shadduck
John Shaw
John Steigerwald
John Wallace
John Walsh
John Winkelman
John Wyatt
Jolene Smith
Jon Riches
Jon Talbot
Jonathan Blaney
Jonathan Fiedler
Jonathan Harris
Jonathan Huston
Jonathan Phillips
Jonathan Ruppin
Joni Chan
Jonny Kiehlmann
Jordana Carlin
Jorid Martinsen
Joseph Novak
Joseph Schreiber
Josh Calvo
Josh Sumner
Joshua Davis
Joshua McNamara
Joy Paul
Judith Gruet-Kaye
Judith Hannan
Judith Poxon
Judy Davies

Judy Lee-Fenton
Judy Rich
Julia Von Dem
  Knesebeck
Julia Rochester
Julia Sanches
Julia Sutton-Mattocks
Julian Hemming
Julian Molina
Julie Greenwalt
Julie Hutchinson
Juliet Birkbeck
Juliet Swann
Jupiter Jones
Juraj Janik
Justin Anderson
Justine Sherwood
JW Mersky
Kaarina Hollo
Kaelyn Davis
Kaja R Anker-Rasch
Karen Gilbert
Karin Mckercher
Katarzyna
  Bartoszynska
Kate Attwooll
Kate Beswick
Kate Carlton-Reditt
Kate Morgan
Kate Procter
Kate Shires
Katharina Liehr
Katharine Robbins
Katherine Brabon
Katherine Sotejeff-
  Wilson
Kathryn Burruss
Kathryn Edwards
Kathryn Williams

Kathy Wright
Katia Wengraf
Katie Brown
Katie Freeman
Katie Grant
Katie Smart
Katy Robinson
Kayleigh Dray
Keith Walker
Ken Geniza
Kenneth Blythe
Kent McKernan
Kerry Parke
Kieran Rollin
Kieron James
Kim McGowan
Kirsten Hey
Kirsty Simpkins
KL Ee
Klara Rešetič
Kris Ann Trimis
Kristen Tcherneshoff
Kristin Djuve
Krystale Tremblay-
  Moll
Krystine Phelps
Kylie Cook
Kyra Wilder
Lacy Wolfe
Lana Selby
Lara Vergnaud
Larry Wikoff
Laura Newman
Laura Pugh
Laura Rangeley
Laura Zlatos
Lauren Schluneger
Laurence Laluyaux
Lee Harbour

Leeanne Parker
Leelynn Brady
Leona Iosifidou
Leonora Randall
Liliana Lobato
Lily Blacksell
Lily Robert-Foley
Linda Milam
Lindsay Attree
Lindsay Brammer
Lindsey Ford
Linnea Brown
Lisa Agostini
Lisa Dillman
Lisa Hess
Lisa Leahigh
Lisa Simpson
Lisa Tomlinson
Liz Clifford
Liz Ketch
Liz Starbuck Greer
Liz Wilding
Lorna Bleach
Lottie Smith
Louise Evans
Louise Greenberg
Louise Jolliffe
Louise Smith
Louise Whittaker
Luc Daley
Luc Verstraete
Lucie Taylor
Lucinda Smith
Lucy Banks
Lucy Leeson-Smith
Lucy Moffatt
Lucy Scott
Luke Healey
Lydia Trethewey

Lyndia Thomas
Lynn Fung
Lynn Martin
Lynn Ross
Maeve Lambe
Maggie Kerkman
Maggie Livesey
Maggie Redway
Malgorzata Rokicka
Mandy Wight
Manu Chastelain
Margaret Cushen
Margaret Jull Costa
Mari-Liis Calloway
Maria Ahnhem Farrar
Maria Lomunno
Maria Losada
Marie Cloutier
Marie Donnelly
Marie Harper
Marijana Rimac
Marina Castledine
Marina Jones
Mark Bridgman
Mark Reynolds
Mark Sargent
Mark Scott
Mark Sheets
Mark Sztyber
Mark Waters
Martha W Hood
Martin Brown
Martin Price
Mary Addonizio
Mary Angela Brevidoro
Mary Clarke
Mary Heiss
Mary Wang
Maryse Meijer

Mathias Ruthner
Mathieu Trudeau
Matt Davies
Matt Greene
Matt O'Connor
Matthew Adamson
Matthew Banash
Matthew Black
Matthew Cooke
Matthew Eatough
Matthew Francis
Matthew Gill
Matthew Lowe
Matthew Scott
Matthew Woodman
Matthias Rosenberg
Maura Cheeks
Max Cairnduff
Max Longman
Meaghan Delahunt
Meg Lovelock
Megan Wittling
Mel Pryor
Melissa Beck
Melissa Stogsdill
Melissa Wan
Melynda Nuss
Michael Aguilar
Michael Bichko
Michael Boog
Michael James
  Eastwood
Michael Floyd
Michael Gavin
Michael Kuhn
Michael Roess
Michael Schneiderman
Michaela Goff
Michelle Mercaldo

Michelle Perkins
Miguel Head
Mildred Nicotera
Miles Smith-Morris
Miranda Gold
Molly Foster
Morgan Lyons
Moriah Haefner
MP Boardman
Myles Nolan
N Tsolak
Nancy Foley
Nancy Jacobson
Nancy Kerkman
Nancy Oakes
Nancy Peters
Nanda Griffioen
Naomi Morauf
Nargis McCarthy
Natalie Ricks
Nathalie Teitler
Nathan McNamara
Nathan Rowley
Nathan Weida
Nicholas Brown
Nicholas Rutherford
Nick Chapman
Nick James
Nick Marshall
Nick Nelson & Rachel
  Eley
Nick Sidwell
Nick Twemlow
Nicola Cook
Nicola Hart
Nicola Mira
Nicola Sandiford
Nicola Scott
Nicole Matteini

Nicoletta Asciuto
Nigel Fishburn
Niki Sammut
Nina de la Mer
Nina Nickerson
Nina Todorova
Niven Kumar
Norman Carter
Odilia Corneth
Olga Zilberbourg
Olivia Scott
Olivia Turon
Pamela Ritchie
Pamela Tao
Pankaj Mishra
Pat Bevins
Patricia Aronsson
Patrick Hawley
Patrick McGuinness
Paul Cray
Paul Ewing
Paul Flaig
Paul Jones
Paul Munday
Paul Myatt
Paul Nightingale
Paul Scott
Paul Segal
Pavlos Stavropoulos
Penelope Hewett
  Brown
Peter Griffin
Peter Halliday
Peter Hayden
Peter McBain
Peter McCambridge
Peter Rowland
Peter Taplin
Peter Watson

Peter Wells
Petra Stapp
Phil Bartlett
Philip Herbert
Philip Nulty
Philip Warren
Philip Williams
Philipp Jarke
Phillipa Clements
Phoebe Millerwhite
Pia Figge
Piet Van Bockstal
Prakash Nayak
Rachael de Moravia
Rachael Williams
Rachel Andrews
Rachel Carter
Rachel Darnley-Smith
Rachel Van Riel
Rachel Watkins
Ralph Cowling
Ramona Pulsford
Ranbir Sidhu
Rebecca Braun
Rebecca Carter
Rebecca Ketcherside
Rebecca Moss
Rebecca O'Reilly
Rebecca Rosenthal
Rebecca Shaak
Rebecca Söregi
Renee Thomas
Rhiannon Armstrong
Rich Sutherland
Richard Clark
Richard Dew
Richard Ellis
Richard Gwyn
Richard Mann

Richard Mansell
Richard Priest
Richard Santos
Richard Shea
Richard Soundy
Richard White
Riley & Alyssa
  Manning
Rishi Dastidar
Rita Kaar
Rita O'Brien
Rob Kidd
Robert Arnott
Robert Gillett
Robert Hamilton
Robert Hannah
Robert Wolff
Robin McLean
Robin Taylor
Roger Newton
Roger Ramsden
Rory Williamson
Rosalind May
Rosalind Ramsay
Rosanna Foster
Rose Crichton
Rosie Ernst Trustram
Rosie Pinhorn
Roxanne O'Del Ablett
Royston Tester
Roz Simpson
Ruby Thiagarajan
Rupert Ziziros
Ruth Deyermond
Ryan Day
Ryan Oliver
Sally Arkinstall
Sally Baker
Sally Bramley

Sally Foreman
Sally Warner
Sam Gordon
Sam Southwood
Samantha Pavlov
Samuel Crosby
Sara Bea
Sara Cheraghlou
Sara Kittleson
Sara Sherwood
Sara Warshawski
Sarah Arboleda
Sarah Brewer
Sarah Lucas
Sarah Manvel
Sarah Pybus
Sarah Spitz
Sarah Stevns
Scott Astrada
Scott Chiddister
Scott Henkle
Scott Russell
Sean Kottke
Sean McGivern
Sean Myers
Sez Kiss
Shannon Knapp
Sharon Dogar
Sharon McCammon
Shaun Whiteside
Shauna Gilligan
Sian Hannah
Sienna Kang
Simon Pitney
Simon Robertson
Siriol Hugh-Jones
SK Grout
Sophia Wickham
Sophie Church

Sophie Rees
ST Dabbagh
Stacy Rodgers
Stefanie Schrank
Stefano Mula
Stephan Eggum
Stephanie Miller
Stephanie Smee
Stephen Cowley
Stephen Eisenhammer
Stephen Pearsall
Steve Chapman
Steve Clough
Steve Dearden
Steve James
Steve Tuffnell
Steven Norton
Stewart Eastham
Stu Sherman
Stuart Grey
Stuart Wilkinson
Su Bonfanti
Sunny Payson
Susan Jaken
Susan Winter
Suzanne Colangelo
  Lillis
Suzanne Kirkham
Sylvie Zannier-Betts
Tania Hershman
Tara Roman
Tasmin Maitland
Teresa Werner

Tess Cohen
Tess Lewis
Tessa Lang
The Mighty
  Douche Softball
  Team
Therese Oulton
Thom Cuell
Thom Keep
Thomas Alt
Thomas van den Bout
Thomas Campbell
Thomas Fritz
Thomas Mitchell
Thomas Smith
Tiffany Lehr
Tim Kelly
Tim Schneider
Tim Scott
Tina Rotherham-
  Winqvist
Toby Halsey
Toby Ryan
Tom Darby
Tom Doyle
Tom Franklin
Tom Gray
Tom Stafford
Tom Whatmore
Tory Jeffay
Tracy Heuring
Tracy Northup
Tracy Shapley

Trevor Wald
Ursula Dawson
Val & Tom Flechtner
Val Challen
Valerie O'Riordan
Vanessa Dodd
Vanessa Fernandez
  Greene
Vanessa Fuller
Vanessa Heggie
Vanessa Nolan
Vanessa Rush
Veronica Barnsley
Victor Meadowcroft
Victoria Eld
Victoria Goodbody
Victoria Huggins
Vijay Pattisapu
Vikki O'Neill
Wendy Langridge
Wendy Olson
Will Herbert
William Black
William Dennehy
William Franklin
William Mackenzie
William Schwartz
William Sitters
William Wood
Yana Ellis
Zachary Maricondia
Zareena Amiruddin
Zoë Brasier

CURRENT & UPCOMING BOOKS

Najwa Barakat was born in Lebanon in 1961. After receiving a degree in theater at the Fine Arts Institute in Beirut, she moved to Paris and studied cinema at the Conservatoire Libre du Cinema Français. She has hosted cultural programs produced by Radio France Internationale (RFI), the BBC, and Al Jazeera, and is the author of seven novels as well as the Arabic translator of Albert Camus's notebooks.

Luke Leafgren is an Assistant Dean of Harvard College. He has published five translations of Arabic novels and received the 2018 Saif Ghobash Banipal Prize for Arabic Literary Translation for his English edition of Muhsin Al-Ramli's *The President's Gardens*.